THE QUEEN OF EGYPT
SHORT FICTION

Novels by Susan Fromberg Schaeffer

Poetry

THE
QUEEN
OF
EGYPT,

SHORT FICTION

Susan Fromberg Schaeffer

E.P. Dutton
New York

5/1981
am. Lit.

For information contact: E.P. Dutton, 2 Park Avenue, New York,
N.Y. 10016

Library of Congress Catalog Card Number: 79-54205
ISBN: 0-525-18667-0

Published simultaneously in Canada by Clarke, Irwin & Company
Limited, Toronto and Vancouver

10 9 8 7 6 5 4 3 2 1

FIRST EDITION

For Timothy Seldes

Acknowledgments

Some of the stories in this volume first appeared in the following magazines, to whose editors grateful acknowledgment is made: "Advice" in *National Jewish Monthly*, "Destinies" in *Denver Quarterly*, "The Exact Nature of Plot" in *Little Magazine*, "His Daughter's House" in *Sands*, "The Taxi" in *Triquarterly*, "Why the Castle" in *Story Quarterly*, "The Yglesias of Ignatius Livingstone Island" in *Pembroke*.

Contents

I

TWO NOVELLAS

Destinies

It is impossible to know what the infant child makes of his new world, especially since, for the first three days, he cannot see it. It is perhaps as impossible to know what the new parents make of their newly minted child. For the mother it may be that he is the reward for having come through nine months of swelling and fear; for the father, he may be the sign and token that the marriage so innocently entered into will have to endure. And it is questionable if even the ugliest child who resembles his parents can in any way offend the twin protectors bending over the bassinet since almost everyone believes in his perpetual right to live, no matter what he may look like, and the gargoyle with his eyes sticky-shut appears to be holding that right in his small snail-like fists. It is certain that the child and the parents will never again stand in the same relation to one another once the child has begun to grow, and cry, and finally to walk, and, worst of all, talk.

"Remember what your mother told you about Irishmen,"
someone once said, interrupting a colleague's musings over the
fate of a friend. (The colleague had, in all carelessness, forgotten
the friend was Irish.) "They all drink and they beat their wives."
"Mine just told me to keep away from them," he replied, nodding
his head and inclining it as if hearing an echo. So the child
in the crib is also an Irish child, or a Jewish child, or an Episco-
palian one, and, moreover, he is German, or English, or Swedish,
or Russian. And no matter where you may find him, standing on
the pinnacle of Mount Olympus, free from the least shadow, it
may be that he is his shadow, the shadow of the two dark figures
that stood over him before his eyes opened and before he could realize they were standing between him and the window, the window and the light. In the tracks of time, where days stir up dust
like motorcars in Kansas, and in the flux of days, where familiarity
breeds familiarity, it is natural to assume the modern (or, depending on one's point of view, the ancient) fallacy that a person is
what he makes himself, that a person can create himself, that so
many days has he come from Walter and Helen Donovan, so far
has he come from the small child who obediently went with his
parents to church, who believed in whatever they said, who pos-
tulated the existence of a sliding panel in his roof to explain how
God could watch him while he slept. But perhaps in the mind
there is no space, only vertical extension, and the new experiences
are merely standing on the head of the original ones, as in an acro-
batic act, so that if the legs holding the pyramid buckle, the whole
tumbles to the ground to the horror and of course the joy (though
we do not like to admit this) of the interested spectators who now
find they were never spectators at all.

It is possible that scenes from childhood, like the blue and white
beads in the bracelet spelling out the new infant's name, are strung
together to form the vertebrae of a life. Yet it sometimes happens
that later, twenty years later, or thirty, one may not remember
anything which occurred before a certain arbitrary point in time.
For them, the past does not exist, for, as Saint Augustine demon-

strated, the past cannot exist unless it exists in the memory. Yet their pasts live in the memories of others, and a fishing expedition in the dark pools of time yields the most innocent things: a rattle, a scene from church, a Sunday afternoon at home, an American cheese sandwich from a lunch box, already slightly warm and stale from sitting through morning classes next to a red and gray thermos. Something is missing.

Scenes from childhood: the first of the four Donovan sons is learning to point. For two weeks he has been opening and closing his fist, rotating it and examining it, opening his hand wide, trying to tuck in his fingers. No one knows how it happens (or even why he wanted to learn to point) but one day when his mother picks him up he points at some flowers on the sill. "Flowers?" she asks him quizzically. He squeaks in delight. *She* is overcome with delight, and at noon calls her husband where he works on a tractor clearing land for new roads. Cars are multiplying and covering the country like ants. He is never out of work. "He points," Mr. Donovan announces to the other workers with pride; "only eight months old and he points." Mrs. Donovan carries her son Marcel (named, daringly, for Mrs. Donovan's matinee idol) around from object to object; they do not have too many, matching pictures of a dog and a cat on one side of the refrigerator, a display of potholders on another wall, a large picture of the Virgin Mary ascending to Heaven on the living room wall above the curio cabinet, a small picture of the infant Jesus in the roseate colors which also bless the commercial calendars Mrs. Donovan solemnly nails to the kitchen wall next to the phone each year.

It is a lovely and remarkable thing, this pointing. It is a guarantee the child will make it through this world, that his mother has not failed him in bearing him, that there is nothing defective about him. Without realizing it, Mrs. Donovan sighs a sigh of relief which allows her to sleep at night like a stone; without realizing it, Mr. Donovan begins to wonder what it will be like when they have two, and then three, children.

But the pointing continues. Mrs. Donovan is a simple woman

who never finished public school. Hers is a story that has been told so many times it is no story at all, and as threadbare as the motive behind it: a sick mother, a tubercular father, then no father at all. At the end of the last chapter, she could say she had enough money to bury her mother decently and to put a stone over her head of which no one need be ashamed. She did not get married because she was pregnant, as did most of her cousins. She married because a man was kind to her, and not terribly ugly, and worried when she cried, and took her to movies. She did not feel "given away" by her father-in-law during the ceremony. She was given to someone and was no longer alone in the world. Was there anything more to life? If there was, Mr. and Mrs. Donovan were happy to see it flicker and die every Friday night at the movies, the celluloid flames burning away the boredom of the week. When Mr. Donovan began to stay later at bars and drink with the boys, this too was expected, and no cause for alarm, for Mrs. Donovan had been Miss Reilly and all Irishmen drank. And she was a kind woman whose suitor had taken her to see "what he did," and she saw the amount of dust he breathed in sitting atop his tractor. She imagined, and that was the end of it, that the job made him thirsty.

Now she was the mother of a son; this was expected. But a son who could walk and point at eight months! This was remarkable. The noontime calls continued and the Donovans were very proud of Marcel. Yet the pointing began to worry Mrs. Donovan. "Radio," she would say, "radio," and then the next day, if Marcel pointed and she said "table," he would twist around to look at her, his little face contorted into a frown. Disapproval was written all over him like mud. She began to tire of naming the objects in the house: refrigerator, stove, radiator, flowers (they were plastic), Jesus (she felt sacrilegious), the cross (she felt frightened), steps, door, doorknob, circle, star. She began to feel she was doing something wrong to the child, or that there was something wrong with him himself. He had all the childhood toys: the stuffed bear, an old oilcloth book with bright pictures. He was supposed to play with them and enjoy himself. Instead, he walked around the house, hardly reaching her knees, tirelessly pointing. "Jesus," she said, "Jesus, cross, cross." The baby beamed ecstatically at the sound of the words, but Mrs. Donovan's brow was beginning to furrow. The issue was soon resolved, because at nine months old Marcel began to talk. "Jesus, cross, duck, hot, Mamma," he said them all with equal pleasure. Embarrassed, Mrs. Donovan moved the huge picture of the crucifixion into the bedroom and hung it over her bed. If Jesus made Mr. Donovan's marital duties more frightening, if Jesus made him worry about his lustful thoughts about his own wife, nothing was said about it. The child Jesus remained in the living room, where, at nine months, Marcel would toddle over, climb onto a chair and press his forehead onto the cold glass of the frame. "Baby," he would say, "baby." On the other hand, lovemaking in the Donovan bedroom had become rather more quiet; Jesus watched. One night, Mr. Donovan had an impulse to turn the picture to the wall and was up half the night begging forgiveness. That Saturday he was given a rather stiff number of Hail Marys as penance. He never mentioned any of this to his wife, because, as is well known, men in general are not talkative, and Irishmen hold the record for silences inside the home and out. And so it happened that, at ten months, Marcel had come between his mother and his father. In his own way, and without any knowledge of it, he had, like a pimp, brought Jesus into their bedroom, and although a second brother arrived, and then a third, and fourth, things were never the same for his parents again (or for him) and no one (except, perhaps, God, whose station had been changed) would ever know why.

* * *

Marcel is older and life has become very serious. He has been sent to a Jesuit school where the teachers are priests and have the God-given authority to beat the children who misbehave or do not learn their lessons. Marcel has been sent there after a particularly outrageous explosion which took place, as do all the explosions in the Donovan household, in the kitchen. Mr. Donovan came home drunk sometime around twelve o'clock at night and was surprised to find his dinner in the refrigerator and not on the table. What was more, his pork chops were cold and there were no red spice apple rings decorating the margin of the plate since Marcel and his brother Shawn had eaten them in their own ingenious way. First, Marcel dissected one small slice and fit the apple ring back together again. Then Shawn did the same thing. Then Marcel was possessed by a desire for more spiced apple and ultimately there were three rings the size of eyes staring accusingly up from the plate. At this point, both Marcel and Shawn knew they were caught and each ate one ring, flipping a coin for the third. Shawn won. When it came to flips of the coin, Shawn always won. It is only fair to mention, however, that dissecting the apple ring and putting it back together again was Marcel's idea, as are all the other genuinely new ideas in the family, although the brothers so religiously copy them that they seem products of genes, not intelligence.

Thus it was that Marcel woke to an inconceivable roaring in the kitchen and immediately grabbed his schoolbooks lest they be burned up in the fire, and ran down the hall to wake up his brothers so they would not be burnt to crisps in their beds. Upon arriving in the kitchen, the four boys were astonished to find, not smoke, but their father thundering about the room, their mother backed into a kitchen corner right under a picture of the Virgin Mary (who was now fit to appear in company), her wide frightened blue eyes matching the color of her chenille robe, which appeared to have been pulled open by a large-knuckled red hand. Mr. Donovan was snarling at the top of his lungs about the impossibility of getting a decent meal "around here," and finished the sentence as everyone knew he would by hurling the plate, meat and all, across the room. This time, however, he varied the routine by throwing the plate at their mother. Its blue onion pattern smashed on the white tiles just above her head, a pork chop dropping onto the part in her hair like a wounded duck. The sight of the falling pork chop loosened something in Marcel, who began screaming at the top of his lungs, "I hate you, I hate you, I hate you," all the time pointing at his father, and finally catching his breath long enough to change the refrain to, "You damn filthy animal you, you damn filthy animal you." Mrs. Donovan's hand flew to her mouth in horror and Mr. Donovan turned white, leaving only his nose red enough to testify to the amount of alcohol he daily consumed. There was an absolute silence in the room into which these screams, "You damn filthy animal you!" entered like the blasts of the last trumpet, bone-riveting and absolutely silent. Marcel advanced on his father, both fists clenched, still screaming, and then turned around. His intention was to throw the television set at his father, but the thought that his father might escape before he could complete his mission flew through his mind like a demented bat and instead he seized upon the other prize possession of the family: the Osterizer.

It crashed like a bomb at his father's feet, Marcel still dancing up and down and screaming like a maniac in front of his three speechless brothers and his two astounded parents. "Show your father respect, boy!" Mr. Donovan gasped out as if from the middle of a fatal heart attack and, to his immense astonishment, Marcel saw his mother nodding her head in agreement. How could he know she had spent two and a half years saving green stamps to get that Osterizer, that she had just had it in her possession for two weeks, and that her dreams of healthy eggnogs, fine tall sons, and a rejuvenated, reformed husband were lying in slivers all over her linoleum floor? A real silence fell over the kitchen. The second hand of the clock swept past its white cheek and its numbers, neither faster nor slower than it had ever moved, doing nothing to bring this moment to a merciful end. "The boy has to be beaten," Mr. Donovan announced, simultaneously advancing and picking up a stick the four boys used for their version of baseball; "he has to be beaten." Mrs. Donovan nodded her head in agreement. The Osterizer was dead on the floor. "Don't lock that door or I'll kick it in!" his father roared drunkenly after him, and Marcel, who still heard the sound of the Osterizer smashing, suddenly stopped and stood in the doorway waiting. He was white as the face of the clock, and he was nine years old. He climbed onto his bed as he was instructed and waited out the beating. It was a vicious one. As he fell asleep, the only comforting thought he could find was for the eggs in the egg carton on the bottom shelf of the refrigerator. At least they would not have to suffer those blades. The Osterizer terrified him. He was terrified of his mother's devotion to it. It was a dangerous machine. At least *it* was dead. That Saturday the priest read him a long lecture at confession. There were other voices audible, monotonously confessing their sins, but Marcel was sure none of them had Osterizers to atone for. He was not sure he wanted to repent, but the priest reminded him that he had to honor his parents, and he was forbidden, as part of his penance, to take part in baseball after school. Thus the stick that had afflicted his bottom was now denied his hands. But there was no appeal: the priest spoke for God. It was a week after this incident that the Donovans decided to send Marcel to a Jesuit school.

The Donovans lived in a small town in Massachusetts, not unlike Marblehead, where many of the houses, and especially the "tenements," wended their way along the rocky front of the ocean. Marcel wended his way with these rocks to the Jesuit school, which was hidden behind the white frame church, whose startling spire eternally jabbed the brilliant blue sky. Marcel had once been very relieved to learn that the church was built in the shape of a cross, presumably because God could more easily find it, and began to worry because his apartment building was a mere, indistinguishable square and his apartment, which he called his house, was one long line. It would be easy, he thought, for God to overlook it altogether. This revelation in the damp white church led to another inexplicable recitation of Hail Marys since he had apparently and without knowing it (although this made no difference) questioned the omnipotence of God. At the time, Marcel was unsure of the meaning of the word. However, at nine, he was still relieved to catch sight of the church, which was built in the shape of a cross, and when sunlight struck the spire, he was certain God had his eye on him and was going to do something. He privately believed God, unlike his parents, was going to do something helpful.

Marcel's life has become more serious because he has discovered education. One of the Jesuits has taken him on as his particular problem and is giving him private lessons in mathematics, theology, and Latin. Marcel is only required to sit patiently through the blunderings of the others and not to show off, and even a prejudiced observer would have to admit that, given his usual behavior, he does an unexpectedly good job of living up to these expectations. The Jesuit priest is not married, and is not allowed to marry. He may not be a "full" priest, but only a beginner. If this is true, Marcel does not want to know about it. Solemnly, Brother Joseph explains to him that priests have to be better than other people. They do not have families so they can understand those who have families better. They give up family life so they can be more pure. They are members of God's family. God is their father. There is no doubt that, even though Marcel leads a small gang of rowdy children whom the housewives call monsters, he is impressed by Brother Joseph and would like to be like him, especially since Brother Joseph has carefully explained that God the Father is not like Mr. Donovan the father and is always just, merciful, and forgiving. What are Osterizers to him? Marcel would like to ask, but he is almost certain of the answer, so he does not, whether there is anything in the Bible about God taking a drink. It appears Marcel has a theory that God flooded the earth because he was drunk, and Marcel worries more than once a day about God's threat to end everything in fire. This is one theory that Marcel does not dare voice, even to Brother Joseph, although the ambition of his life (at least while he is in school) is to exorcise it. Marcel admires Brother Joseph, who wears long robes with a tassel swinging from his waist, and would like to enter the family of God also. He would especially like to enter it before he has an opportunity to throw the television set at his father. He gains comfort by telling himself God has protected him, is protecting him, by keeping him too weak to pick up and throw the television set anywhere at all. He has now confided to Brother Joseph his ambition to become a priest, and Brother Joseph has inadvertently challenged him by telling him not all men are fit to be pure, or hardy enough to give up families, or worthy enough to endure the confessions of others, which means seeing the lives of others, accepting and understanding them. And, of course, Marcel, climbing into the back of a milk wagon, to steal empty bottles he can return for deposits, has a sad premonition that Brother Joseph is right. Nevertheless, he continues to hope. He is still hoping when his father comes home and throws a cold plate of spaghetti at his youngest brother, Nathan; by now Marcel is thirteen and the television set is lugged in from the living room, and thrown, and splinters all over the kitchen, a sliver of glass sticking in his father's wrist, another in his ankle, and Marcel sits cross-legged on the floor beaming with satisfaction while his mother screams and fusses and cries and calls his Uncle David to come over to drive Mr. Donovan to the hospital. Not much longer after this event, Marcel (and Brother Joseph, who cannot avoid showing his horror at the thought of a flying television, and even mentions the cost, hurriedly adding how long it took his father to work and buy it) finds himself deciding he will never become a priest.

Marcel now goes to bed asking himself openly whether there is a God, and if there is, why people are not attempting to throw televisions at him. By the time Marcel is fifteen, his attempts to save money and his applications to colleges no farther than California and no closer than Chicago are enthusiastically supported by his mother, who nevertheless starts crying uncontrollably at the thought of her "baby" leaving the house and going to live on his own in a strange city. His father says nothing to him, nor he to his father, and it is evident to a visitor who has not been to the house regularly that Mr. Donovan sits abnormally close to the television set, almost as if he intends to embrace it and hold it to him. Mar-

cel now considers himself unregenerate and smiles whenever he
remembers his father is now afraid of *him*, although he is having
nightmares of greater frequency and intensity than ever before. In
them, he is the father of a small boy who keeps trying to wrap his
toy telephone cord around his legs on the third floor of the Catholic school right at the top of a steep flight of stairs. On the day he
packed to leave for college, he remembered how, when he was a
child, he was taken to see a cousin who was three, and, as a much
smaller child, he mistook the cousin for an adult and raised his
arms to be picked up, and the cousin flew off howling in fear. He
actually does not remember the event, but he remembers his
mother telling him about it. It is one incident of his childhood she
seems to find thoroughly amusing and she tells whoever will listen
all about it.

For some reason, this memory causes him to stop packing and
lock his door so he can sit down on his bed and cry. Marcel almost never cries and this is perhaps the third time he has cried
since he entered kindergarten. After today, he is going to claim he
really remembers nothing of his life prior to his University days.
The first girl he sleeps with gets him to confess he remembers a
"handful" of incidents and glimmers of this and that, but even
this confession is extorted from him. "I really don't remember
anything," he insists to her angrily, sitting up in bed, throwing the
covers off them in the middle of an unheated Chicago winter; "if
that's all you remember about sixteen years, you don't remember
anything." Since the girl is Jewish and a psychology student she
refuses to accept this, although for the time being she lets things
go, but no matter what she tries, or who she asks what to try, she
can never get Marcel to admit to remembering anything. He remembers, he says, going to the Jesuit School, Brother Joseph, who
his brothers are, and his parents, what a town like Marblehead
looks like, and *"nothing else."* Sometimes when he says this he
slams the door so hard bits of plaster fly from it and then he sits
on the couch with his head in his hands. When he raises it, it is
invariably to ask if his girlfriend (the word is a marvel in itself)

would like to go to Larry's, the college bar. There, he melts into the warmth and smoke and knows that she belongs to him the same way he once believed the Jesuits belonged to God.

* * *

It is an unfortunate truth that anything once warmed can be made to cool. As the Chicago winter wore on, this began to happen to Marcel, who began to dread the coldness more and more, and when he dreamt of it (although of course he never remembered his dreams) saw the cold as two bedsheets which invited the sleeper like snowdrifts. But the sleeper, knowing himself already half-frozen, refused to fall asleep, knowing only in wakefulness could his life be preserved. It was at this time that Marcel began to suffer simultaneously from insomnia and impotence. The first, his girlfriend (her name was Rachel) was quick to ascribe to nerves, the second to "coldness." "You're cold," she kept accusing him like a thermostat that was not doing its job in her room; "you're cold." Then she would invariably add, "All you ever do is think." "I never think," Marcel responded automatically, and in fact he really believed this. Rachel did not believe it, since she remembered one of their early confession sessions at Larry's, these being the mark of true love at the University, both partners opening old wounds for the delectation of the other; Marcel had told her (after his sixth beer and third trip to the men's room) that when he was young, he came to believe he had to confess "everything" to the priest. He found himself censoring his thoughts as he was thinking them and began to wake screaming at night, convinced the only way out of his dilemma was to find a kindly priest who would accompany him everywhere while he constantly uttered everything that came into his head, doing penance and confessing simultaneously.

"You're always thinking," Rachel sulked; "that's why you're doing so well at this damn school." It was true Marcel was doing extraordinarily well at school, but it was also true he never thought, at least not about events around him. Or perhaps it

might be more correct to say he "thought" about events happening to him as he "thought" about passages in Kant. And on the
night they had their final fight (Rachel storming out of his apartment with her shampoo, her toothpaste smudging itself all over
her battered wallet), it was absolutely true, as she shouted at him
over her shoulder from the second-floor balcony while he leaned
over the railing on the third: "You care more about Kant than
me." "What was wrong with that?" Marcel wondered idly, at the
same time stifling an inappropriate impulse to cry. Rachel was
going to make someone a fine wife, nag her children to death, and
lead, in essence, the life of an electric blanket. Some men liked
to be married to electric blankets, but in the ultimate scheme of
things, with which he had become concerned, Kant seemed to
have more importance and intrinsic worth than an electric blanket or, in fact, central heating. Marcel wondered if that was absolutely true, and if so, how one would prove it, and so much was
Rachel mourned.

* * *

As a child, Marcel had been much valued by his family, primarily
for his charm. He could make anyone laugh from the time he was
fourteen months old, and the stiffest spinster could not come into
the house without feeling as if she existed for the sole purpose of
lighting "the poor child's" life. Relatives of all removes showed
concern for the child's health, plying him with white sugared al-
monds, which, for an Irish family in the land of American cheese,
white bread, and mayonnaise, was in its way quite remarkable. As
Marcel grew, it became evident that he would never be very tall,
but then his father was not, nor very strong and bullish, as his father was. Still, he possessed considerable wiry strength, which his
father never saw, or certainly never appreciated. His mother saw
it, however, and had him lugging furniture up and down, and, on
one memorable night, had him at one end of the paternal bed tilting it upward so it would go through the bedroom door. If anyone had thought to ask, Marcel's mother would have been

considered the more lovable of his parents. She was one of those short, amply busted women who in old age seem to have, when fully dressed, bosoms literally feathered, and which convince anyone in need of mothering that there was once, indeed, such a thing as the nest. Nevertheless, if anyone had been able to extort an answer from him, Marcel would have answered that he preferred his father. His mother did, after all, have almost everything she wanted out of life. His father was too inarticulate to voice, even to himself, what he missed. So it was that whenever Marcel came home from the University he would anxiously and eagerly attempt to explain to his father, not his mother, what he was doing there.

His parents had come out to the University and were, in fact, so impressed and overwhelmed by it that they were not inclined to ask questions, especially since Marcel had a scholarship and his attendance there cost the family nothing, only occasional worries when there were tornado warnings for Chicago. The University had been built in exact imitation of an English University, and to the Donovans it was indistinguishable from Notre Dame. It would never have occurred to them to criticize it. Both his mother and father were perpetually puzzled by their son's presence there, saying that if they had to "do it over again" they could never pass the second grade. The fact of Marcel's intelligence was accepted, as if it were a hallucination which would not go away. They did not really believe in it, or see what it had to do with real life. Hallucination or not, its consequence was obvious enough. It removed their son for at least ten months of the year and restored an unfamiliar degree of peace to the household.

Marcel, who, in his second year, had joined the "Faculty and Students for Intellectual Endeavor" instead of a "department," was now, in his first year as a graduate student, still trying to explain what it was to his parents. It was Christmas and the thick snow was falling into the black water outside and the sharks had presumably fled back to the heart of the great ocean which touched the shore near the house. "The Group," as it was called at the University (whose members could not endure long titles for anything), was an interdisciplinary faculty drawn from all the departments. The Group and its students then attempted to investigate those deep gray areas where disciplines overlapped, and the light leaking from the central discipline could be combined with light from another to investigate what lay between. In concept, this was a marvelous department, but within the University itself, students who were members of the Group were known for being the most eccentric and unstable. They were also known as the most intelligent; their courses were the most difficult, and they were regarded with a mixture of fear and amusement by the rest of the University.

Marcel had entered the Group as soon as he discovered its difficulty. The truth was, his intelligence was as unbelievable to him as it was to his parents. He believed, along with the philosophers he studied, that everything must have a source, and the source of his bones and genes was his parents. No matter how well he did within the Group, he felt like a fraud, perpetually in danger of public exposure and disgrace. As of his second year in graduate study, this still had not happened; instead, he had been asked to teach a seminar with three of the marble figures he had revered for six years. In this time, two of the University's great thinkers, one a woman and one a man, had become close friends. In magnitude of achievement, the woman promised to rival Samuel Johnson in her own century while the man promised to give Jane Austen a run for her money in his uncanny ability to get at sets of truths underlying human interactions. Marcel, however, did not regard them as close friends, but as new parents he had chosen for himself, who had allowed him to be born again, and to accept himself in his new guise, and this caused him to feel a considerable guilt when he attempted to discuss them with his parents.

"The Group," Marcel earnestly began again for the hundredth time, tireless as a preacher, "takes a little something from Math and from English and from Linguistics and from Geology and from Anthropology and from Painting and from Literature and then tries to fit them together to form a new picture. You couldn't see the picture any other way," he earnestly finishes, no ticing the frantically befuddled look on his father's face. "Like a jigsaw puzzle?" his father volunteers after much thought. "Exactly!" Marcel exclaims in rapture, not realizing he sounds as if he is congratulating a retarded child; "exactly!" His father doesn't realize this either, because he beams like a schoolboy who has just been informed he will not be left back. "Then what do you do with it?" his father asks; "take it apart and start over?" Mr. Donovan is now actively interested. One source of his interest is his infinite puzzlement about what the Group can teach a grown man about how to earn a living. In amazement and horror, Mr. Donovan sees his son's face fall and realizes that he has gotten it wrong again. Marcel too is heartbroken, and sits quietly a long time, picking at the threads of the tweed-covered armchair. He has seen them often enough abandoned on the streets of Chicago, their thin wooden elbows sticking through the cloth. The chairs are angular and cheap, and almost everyone, even the students, manages to afford replacing them. A lump is beginning to form in his throat. To loosen its hold, he finally asks after his Uncle David. "Goiter," his father says, his voice full of organ music and loss. The phrase "lace curtain Irish" floats through Marcel's mind like a refrain from an old song, and his skin feels too tight for him. He would like to get up and hug his father, but his father would never understand, and would be filled with foreboding. "I think I'll find Shawn and go for a walk," Marcel sighs. "Why don't I just come along?" his father suggests jovially. "Sure," Marcel assents, without enthusiasm or lack of it. His father does not move, and his mother enters the room. "I think I'll just stay here with the old lady," his father wheezes, looking down at his shoes. Marcel returns to his room, sits on his bed, and fights an impulse to cry. It takes him so long to fight that by the time he looks for Shawn, Shawn is already asleep and he goes for a walk in the Marblehead winter alone. Marcel has also found the girl he wants to marry.

* * *

In the University's main building there is a coffee shop known characteristically as "the coffee shop." Members of the Group tend to gather at a huge table in the middle, something which really distinguishes them from the others, since almost every other student seems to have a tropic response to dark corners. Now that Marcel has begun teaching courses for undergraduates, he not only has his colleagues in the Group to talk to, but a following of devoted students who hold to his every word as if to a lifeboat rope, and it seems his life is quite full. Sometimes it seems his life is *too* full, as on occasional mornings when he finds an innocent-eyed female student sound asleep on the welcome mat outside his apartment door, resembling, in the memorable mistranslation of Immanuel Kant's text, a snail "curled up in defiance of all probability." Marcel and his roommate, Jim, then make coffee, wake up whoever it is, invite her in (it is always a her), give her a cup of coffee and a lecture and directions for the shortest way back to the dorm. Then Marcel goes back into the living room and sits down on the overstuffed navy blue plush couch from Catholic Salvage while his roommate, Jim, who also teaches, but rarely wakes up to find students rising from welcome mats with the dawn, lectures him on his seductiveness. "I'm only being myself," Marcel argues defensively. "That's the whole point," Jim says emphatically, stirring his coffee. "Why the hell don't you drink it?" Marcel demands petulantly. "Because I can't drink hot things," Jim answers as he has countless times before. The two of them have discussed everything from Kierkegaard to Marcel's sex life, and while Marcel finds Jim inadequate on the subject of Kierkegaard, he finds him surprisingly acute on the subject of his sex life and its infinite problems. "Too possessive," Jim diagnoses; "too possessive. You can't leave anything alone. You want to make everyone over into your own image. That image isn't so great, either," he finishes. "All I want is a good lay and a friend," Marcel argues. "Shit," Jim says calmly, "all you want is a good lay and an identical twin who happens to be the same sex." "Why do you think that?" Marcel demands, enraged. "Because, for some reason that escapes me, you have a Florence Nightingale complex, and no sooner do you get someone in here who you think is good for you than you have to show how good you are for *them*. And they, meaning Phyllis, and Edna, and Marge and Joy and Lenore, don't happen to think they need anyone to be good for them. Also, you don't pay any attention to them unless you think they're going to sleep with someone else." "Do they?" Marcel asked, his face on fire. "Not with me, they don't," Jim answers, getting his coat and book bag. "I don't go for the type that wants a sadist." Marcel does some spluttering. "I know you're not a sadist," Jim says unpleasantly; "they're just all masochists. It's funny how they pick you out, or vice versa: who cares!"

When Marcel's love slept with his best friend from the Group the weekend he went home for his uncle's death, Marcel decided there might be something wrong with his sex life and that he would give himself ten years to see what could be done about it, and at the end of that year (on March 15) he would try to see how the other half lived.

He now believed this existential experiment would be unnecessary because someone new had shown up at the table in the coffee shop and, as with each of the women he met, Marcel thought he had met the answer to his problems. Everyone else thought she was, as one of the Group put it, the true embodiment of problems, but this was not how she appeared to Marcel, and he had decided to marry Charlotte.

Charlotte had walked into the coffee shop one day and pulled up a chair and then sat there watching the rest of them as if she were at a movie and her only hope was that it would end before she fell asleep. They were discussing, as usual, Kierkegaard. Marcel notices her immediately and begins to hold forth even more enthusiastically than usual. There is no doubt about it; when overexcited he has the revivalist preacher's indomitable energy and seductive powers. At the same time, he is completely conscious of Charlotte's face. By no standard can it be considered pretty. She is so pale she appears to have missed her last two transfusions. Her hair is so white it seems not to exist except to round out the shape of a skull and suggest she might still be alive. Her mouth is her most peculiar feature, discounting her two pale eyes, which seem made of glass, so that looking into them, as Marcel finds himself obsessively doing, is like looking out of a window onto a remarkably cold day when the temperature is below zero but no wind blows. Her mouth is a thin white scar in her face and when she talks it moves stiffly, as if pulled by invisible strings. When she smiles, which she does rarely, her mouth pulls down at the corners as if thin wires are tugging at her lips. She is smiling now. "You don't understand Kierkegaard," she says quietly; it is clear she is absolutely positive she is right and is not showing off, and she proceeds to give a fifteen-minute lecture on the logical fallacies in the argument Marcel had so carefully constructed. This causes love at first sight. Marcel, who never tires of arguing, does not want to argue with her, but to take her off to his apartment and keep her there. All of the edges of his mind are unrolling, changing a globe of his inner world to a flat map of it, a topological impossibility, but it is happening nevertheless. He wants to feel the print of her mind's feet on the carpet of his. He has an intuition it may be possible to worship her.

"What do you do?" he asks her, walking past the science building. He is still getting over the shock of seeing her get up from the table and pick up a walking stick, which she clearly needs. "Paint," she smiles, the corners of her mouth testifying to the existence of gravity. "Paint houses," she adds to the silence; "it's how I keep myself alive." "Insides or out?" Marcel asks, feeling like a fool. He is already wondering what he likes about her? He knows she is not sexy, but she seems overpoweringly so to him. "And teach Russian," she adds generously. "Then why didn't I ever come across you?" Marcel asks suspiciously; "I've taken all the Russian lit courses." "I teach the courses in the original," she says with a shade of contempt; "Kierkegaard influenced Dostoevsky, you know." "Did you read him in the original?" "I read everything in the original," she answers, without bothering to clear up the minor problem of pronoun reference. "Would you come up for a cup of coffee?" "Why not?" she asks, her cane tapping against the cement. "Please get off that damn mat," Marcel growls at one of his students, who looks at him with big hurt eyes. He is aware he is not himself and that all of his charm is gone. "A pet?" Charlotte asks, the corners of her mouth turning down. Marcel becomes aware of a vague southern accent. "South Carolina. Poor white trash," she says, cutting him off.

Marcel's charm does not work on Charlotte. She is irritated when he tries to use it on her and is willing to get into bed without Byzantine approaches. Furthermore, there is no one else she wants to sleep with. On the other hand, it is questionable how much she wants to sleep with Marcel, or cares about him. Perhaps this is because she takes so many pills and drinks constantly. "I told you. Poor white trash." She smiles, finishing a bottle of vodka one night while they talk. Marcel has been dismally watching the level sink and sink in the bottle. Even as an Irishman he can't keep up with this. Charlotte takes out another bottle. "When I'm half through with this I'll feel like the dead feel, or the newly dead, to be precise," she says, emptying a glass. Jim walks into the living room, looks at both of them, draw his cheeks and lips into a whistle without making a sound, and walks soundlessly out. Marcel asks her to stop drinking, but Charlotte says she drinks when she wants and what she wants. Marcel sighs because he knows it's true. "How much do you care about me?" he asks her. He wants to protect her, to suck the alcohol out of her blood, to get her to talk about her past. "Oh, I love you," Charlotte answers, filling her glass to the halfway point. "Then will you marry me?" he asks desperately. "When?" Charlotte asks, sipping the vodka as if it were soda. "Christmas vacation. I'll be finished with my papers then." "Sure," Charlotte says, "but we have to get married in South Carolina. It's the one promise I made my mother I intend to keep. You don't ever wonder if I have Negro blood?" "Do you?" Marcel asks, shocked. "Of course not," Charlotte answers;

"I just wondered." "You wonder about some pretty strange things," he observes. "Don't you like it?" she asks him, eyes narrowing; "you're not so normal yourself." "What do you mean?" "You know what I mean," she answers, emptying the glass and walking steadily toward the bed, limping; "all you ever do is think." "All *you* ever do is think," he answers. "That's what I mean," she smiles, her lips forming their smile; "we're both crazy." "I'm not crazy," he says quietly. "Then why do you want to know about everyone I ever slept with, and what do you care about what kind of little girl I was?" "I care about everything about you," he answers, and it is true. "Too bad," Charlotte says; "oh, too bad," she says, pulling off the knee socks she wears under her jeans. "What do you mean?" Marcel asks again. He has visions of Jim coming in one afternoon just as Charlotte wakes up from one of her drunken sleeps, the two of them in bed, his walking in and finding the two of them there; "are you sleeping with anyone else?" "No," she answers. "Do you want to?" "No," she says, "and that's the end of the catechism. I'm going to bed." "What religion are you," Marcel murmurs, half falling asleep. "Virgin-pagan," Charlotte whispers. Now Marcel does really start to cry, although he convinces himself he has a cold and his eyes are tearing, but Charlotte has already fallen asleep, or if she is up, she is pretending to be asleep, as she would do if she were, in fact, awake.

* * *

At the University, time passes suddenly, as do the seasons, summer converting itself into its opposite, not bothering with fall, and summer vacations, especially Christmas, arrive for Instructors in a snowstorm of recently finished, exhaustive and exhausting term papers. This Christmas, Marcel was not going home since he was going to South Carolina to get married. He had not thought much beyond the actual event, and did not care about the ceremony itself; what he cared about was attaching a gold ring to Charlotte's rather bloodless finger and having someone he could refer to as "my wife." Perhaps this seems odd in a character like Marcel, who has now spent most of his adult life studying the nature of good and evil, and is generally acknowledged to be among the finest minds at the University. But when Marcel was a child, he already thought as many philosophers do, that if something existed, its opposite could also exist. His family existed, and he had pronounced it dreadful. For this reason, if for none other, he had come to postulate (without realizing it) the existence of a perfectly happy family, in which the children thrived and sat at the wise knees of their father, while their mother, his wife, whiled away her days in tatting, or polishing silver, or in writing a doctoral dissertation on the linguistic implications of infinity. Probably if Marcel was really pressed (under anesthesia) for memories of his early life, some of the most vivid would show schoolmates he had walked partway home walking into whole houses which belonged only to them, not to boarders or to landlords, where they were greeted by their mothers or sisters, or not greeted at all, but from the confident, springy step of their legs up the front steps, it was evident that they expected a welcome and had no sense of dread about what was lurking within. How Marcel came to believe such a structure could be built upon the cornerstone of poor Charlotte would be an eternal mystery (and in some sense must remain so) were it not for his horror of the flesh, so thoroughly driven into him in Catholic school, and so neatly embodied in the drunken demonstrations of his father, his own outbursts with his accomplice the television set, and his mother crying soundlessly, asking for no pity, already pressing her hand over her eye, anticipating the swelling, the black and blue eye which would predictably fade to green, then greenish yellow, then a shadow, then nothing at all. Charlotte, Marcel felt, was all mind, and, moreover, she needed protection. Finally, he was in a position to give it.

Before Christmas, Charlotte gave him careful directions to her town in South Carolina, warning him to slow down if he saw a straw hut because he might not see anything else of the town, and to dress respectably, because the hillbillies didn't like strangers and would tear him apart if they thought he was a hippie. "If you don't like my directions, you can always call AAA," she said sarcastically; "I don't see that we have to waste our time discussing the shortest distance between two points when there is only one road." She was methodically giving him directions to the Baptist church in the town of Demby. Marcel knew better than to ask why he wasn't being given directions to her house. Charlotte hated questions, and, if forced to answer them, would invariably create a new context for both question and answer, one which made him wish his mouth had been sealed shut by molten lead.

So it happens that at Christmas, Marcel gets in his '46 Pontiac (of course its windshield wipers don't work; neither does the door handle, so that he has to get in the passenger side and crawl over, and no one is sure what his brakes are for) and sets out with a small gold ring wrapped in toilet paper and a huge manila envelope filled with term papers on Nietzsche which he intends to correct at the diners in which he will stop along the road. He is taking no one with him. There seems to him something sacred about this moment, although to others, his actions might seem impulsive, furtive, and perhaps even obsessive, obsessive in the way Dostoevsky's characters are obsessive, so that their obsessions always seem to make the events which generate them seem entirely inadequate to the effects they produce. Yet there is no doubt that if anyone attempted to stop him from getting in the car and speeding off with dubious brakes to Demby, South Carolina (which of course is impossible, since no one, not even his favorite brother, Shawn, knows where he is going), Marcel would physically attack him and would drive off into the blizzard without a twinge of the frontal lobes.

The miles pass and pass and Marcel drinks cup of coffee after cup of coffee, taking care not to spill a drop on the carefully typed term papers of his serious students. He is also careful not to spill a drop onto the Formica. Once in the ancient past his father beat Shawn for spilling a glass of milk for the second time in one day.

Whether this has anything to do with his treatment of the coffee cup is of course open to question. As the miles pass, Marcel has to lean less and less frequently out of the car's open window to shovel the snow from the windshield with his hand. Finally, it is getting positively warm. In his methodical way, which he will never get rid of, he asks how to recognize Demby fifty miles before approaching it, and is told it has the only church around with a roof shaped like an onion. He presumes, and rightly, that the church is an imitation of a Russian building. Marcel arrives in Demby exhausted and shaking all over with excitement. Flushes pass over his face like waves, turning him red and hot, then cold and spent. He is supposed to meet Charlotte at the church at nine, but it is only six-thirty. He finds a diner and sits grading papers, although he now looks up after every sentence in the semiconscious hope Charlotte's face will appear at the window or her body at the door. At eight-thirty, after having ordered countless courses he does not want to eat, but which permit him to remain in his Formica heaven, he leaves and starts out for the church. The wedding is not until eleven, but people are already there. His heart swells like an organ playing the B Minor Mass. The people, however, seem to have something odd about them. As he gets out of the car and walks closer to them, he sees that one of the women in a flowered chintz dress is waving wildly at him, shouting something, and that her eyes are very red. Behind her is a man twisting his wedding ring, shifting from foot to foot, also with red eyes, not making a sound. He comes up to them as if they were giants and he were a pygmy who had just shrunk in the rain. "She's not here!" the woman wails; "she's not here. Oh," she interrupts herself, suddenly becoming a reasonable facsimile of a polite lady, "I'm Charlotte's mother." Immediately, she begins wailing again: "She's not here. I don't know how she could embarrass us like this, not staying to tell you herself. I don't know how she could do it, I just don't know how she could do it." "I don't know what she was thinking of," her father murmurs disconsolately. "That's nothing new," Charlotte's mother says bitterly. They prevail upon him to come home for breakfast and to "warm up," but Marcel is nauseated and dizzy. Charlotte's mother, who insists she be called Priscilla, grabs him under the arm and they steer him to their vehicle, which is a farm wagon pulled by a pair of dray horses. Once home (home is a white frame house, the windows covered with something resembling oilcloth) Priscilla puts Marcel to bed. The mattress feels funny and Marcel realizes it is stuffed with straw. "We have to sell off the feathers," Priscilla apologizes. "I think I'm sick," Marcel murmurs, and indeed, his head is burning hot to Priscilla's palm. They send for the doctor who says, "Leave it, it will run out of him in a few days," and in a few days he is better. He kisses Priscilla goodbye because she insists, although he is repulsed by the feel of her cheek. It is slippery and has a salty taste. Her husband contents himself with wringing his hands. Both of them are in real despair. "I don't know why she did it, I don't know why she did it," Priscilla keeps repeating, even after he has gotten into the car; "I don't even know where she is." There is still some sickly blond hair left in her iron-gray bun. Marcel nods because he finds he cannot say goodbye; instead he finally manages to say thanks. He drives blindly for the first fifteen miles, because the tears are covering his eyes like rain on a windshield and at the moment he would not care if his car ran into a tree or a cow or even another person. But by the time he gets back to the University he has finished the term papers; there is the usual student curled up on his welcome mat; Jim helps him send her back, and Charlotte never reappears in the coffee shop. A roommate he never knew Charlotte had materialized to say she was "very mixed up" and that "it is just as well." For weeks a sense of loss, irreparable loss, gnaws at him like a live animal, and then he forgets it. The time has come to take his comprehensive examinations, and he is going to do the best job any student in the Group has done in thirty years. Thirty years, thirty years, he keeps repeating to himself, turning the pages. He is twenty-seven, and probably he is going to succeed in this.

* * *

The University has long been known for its fiendish system of examinations, and Marcel has coped brilliantly, and with apparently little toll to the nervous system, with the six-hour comprehensive exams which, given at the end of the school year, determine the grades for the entire year's work. But the Group's examination method was the most spectacular; it assembles its faculty and students in the same Gothic amphitheater where *The Play of Herod* was later to be staged and there the candidate, as a preliminary to beginning his thesis, must give an hour-long speech to the assembled venerables. The only proper analogy is that of the Christian thrown to the lions, but it must in all fairness be observed that in choosing the Group, the candidate has chosen martyrdom, not had it inflicted upon him. Marcel has his speech prepared, having already taken the three six-hour written exams in the three related fields of his choice and having managed a "high pass" in ancient and modern German as well as Greek. He has also been working with the two most important members of the Group Faculty, Frieda Hofstadter and Ernst L. Hourbach. It is on Ernst L. Hourbach (who out of sheer nerve and gall Marcel insists on addressing as Ernst, although the last person to do this was probably Hourbach's mother) that Marcel's attention focuses. He wants to stun Hourbach, to show him once and for all what he can do. He does not intend to have the same effect on Frieda Hofstadter, and believes his lecture will be a tribute to her and the intellectual endeavors she has inspired. He begins his lecture in the most radical manner possible, dissecting in fantastic detail the commentaries of Hourbach, Eliot, Maclean, and Newman on Kierkegaard and Kant. His thesis is that, as Kant foresaw, all perceptions are necessarily subjective; this of course is nothing new. What is new is his explicit investigation of the subjective prejudices of Hourbach, Eliot, Maclean, and Newman, which, he claims, force them to see Kierkegaard by their own light and thus to distort entirely the reality the old master fought so hard to unearth from the dust of individual thought. There is no doubt that this *is* a brilliant lecture,

both in the treatment of its subject, and the treatment of its vic-
tims, the venerated members of the Group. Afterward, there is indeed a stunned silence. To his surprise, Mrs. Hofstadter avoids his
eyes. When he finally manages to catch her steely gray gaze he
sees unutterable sadness. He is surprised at this because, of all people, he believed Mrs. Hofstadter selfless, a solid self without an
ego, or, to use the correct terminology, without egoism. She picks
up her large cut-velvet bag with its two curved wooden handles
(the students affectionately call it her carpetbag) and slips
through a small back door in the auditorium. No one knows the
auditorium better than Mrs. Hofstadter, who is called upon almost weekly to address one delegation or another, many delegates
flying by chartered plane to the University for the sole purpose of
hearing her. When Marcel finally sees himself moving toward the
assembled Faculty, who will record the worth of his performance,
and sees them moving toward him shocked and surprised, as he
intended them to be, he knows he has succeeded in his ambitions,
although unaccountably, he is stifling an overpowering urge, not
only to cry, but to wail like a helpless infant who has rolled over
onto something hot. "That will get you a degree with honors,"
Timothy Maclean says to him. "Yes, we all agree on that," Ernst
Hourbach says in an inexplicably soft voice. Ernst stands there
thinking. "Frieda would say that an event cannot be judged apart
from its motives," he comments. "She left," Marcel responds in-
anely. "She would say an event cannot be judged apart from its
motives," Ernst repeats gravely. "You have shown us," he says
slowly, "that your mind is at least equal to ours and that ours are
often unequal to the occasions they must meet. I offer you con-
gratulations." Marcel is by now glowing with pleasure, although
there is a hot edge to the glow. "I wish you good luck on your thesis," Ernst concludes. "But you'll be supervising it," Marcel crows;
"wish me luck later." His charm has never been so evident, or his
seductiveness so hypnotic. "I am afraid I won't," Ernst tells him
gravely. "Frieda, I am sure, will keep her word. She is a remarkable woman," he says almost under his breath. "She'll persuade you

to do it," Marcel insists. "On the contrary, I shall not persuade her not to do it," Ernst replies. Timothy Maclean's face begins to show embarrassment. He shakes his lion-like head. "I will take his place. If you have no objection," he adds in his English accent. Marcel wants to argue and to press for an explanation but suddenly is too exhausted to do so. "I don't know if the academic life is for me," he says suddenly to Ernst Hourbach. "Perhaps not." His tone is totally unsympathetic. It occurs to Marcel that he has been uncomfortable in the academic world for a long time, and that his hungers and dissatisfactions hide a craving for the real world. He does not have to ask whether or not his thesis, on the nature of manners, can be completed in absentia, because he knows the answer is yes.

After he announces his decision to resign from academic life and to find a job in the "real world," only Frieda Hofstadter attempts to dissuade him. "There is no real life," she tells him gently; "not unless you make it one. That speech of yours was real life. It was a stabbing outside Billings Hospital." Marcel prefers to misunderstand her, and attributes her choice of metaphor to her unfamiliarity with figurative language and the English language in general. "But what will you do to yourself?" she asks. (She means "with yourself.") "Something to do with books; that's all I know about," Marcel answers. "Well, then," Frieda answers, "you must wear yourself out. But you will keep in touch?" For Marcel there is no question of keeping in touch. Losing Frieda would be like losing his own mother; worse, he thinks. "I think I'll take the job with Holten Hill that Jim wants to give up." "A big executive," Frieda smiles indulgently; "I hope you succeed there as well as you've succeeded here." She sees something disturbed and disturbing in Marcel's face and adds, "I hope you succeed differently there than you have succeeded here." "I have not succeeded so well here," Marcel says. "I can't stand coyness," Frieda says in her thick accent; "you know what you did." But Marcel cannot or will not understand her.

Three days after the semester ends, he packs all his belong-

ings, many cartons of books, one suitcase, and one beloved cat
into his '46 Pontiac and heads for Holten Hill, Inc., and New
York. His cat, Pinto, screams with fright for the first day and Marcel himself holds so tightly to the wheel his knuckles show white.
He is terrified and knows it. On the second day, he is less terrified.
On the third, he has the resigned exterior of a condemned man
who has run out of energy and is awaiting the police with per-
ceptible relief. At ten o'clock at night, Marcel rings the doorbell
of his friend's apartment. It is on a grimy street which looks
better, and more ominous, by street light and which evidently
has something to say for it, for it boasts an extraordinary number of drunks, all apparently fixtures of the street. Jim Callahan
comes down the stairs, takes the scratched, grayish-blue cat box
out of Marcel's hand (Pinto has resumed her helpless, rhythmi-
cal screaming), and grabs a bag of books while Marcel lugs
his overstuffed suitcase up the stairs after him. "Welcome to
Shithole and West End," Jim says, opening the door with a Drac-
ula flourish; "you are now a sacred citizen of the Big Apple.
How's Second City?" he asks casually; it is clear he is not really
concerned. He is leaving in the morning for France, taking his
typewriter and his wife; he is going "to write a novel." Marcel
wonders fleetingly if this happens to editors as a matter of course.
He himself has no impulse to write anything fictional. The two of
them stay up all night discussing "life" as only old friends can,
one passionately interested in every word, the other (in this case,
Jim) bored to death. Marcel is elaborating on his new theory of
Life as Adventure, which has the unfortunate sound of a University course listing. He elaborates at length his theory that if one is
open to all experiences, no matter how varied and contradictory,
one will soon be in contact with one's real feelings. He brings
many philosophical arguments to buttress this new, picaresque
view of life. It is a tribute to his desperation that he can hold
forth so energetically in the midst of his exhaustion, Pinto cower-
ing on his lap. She has already peed twice on his pants in the
car. "Well, there'll be plenty of adventures here," Jim says, not

bothering to stifle a yawn; "I'm glad to be getting out. Let me show you where to sleep," and he leads the way to the couch in the glassed-in dining room. "Don't eat in bed," Jim advises him; "they're not cockroaches; they're cannibals. Here," he says, giving Marcel a sheet and a small pile of towels. "Sleep tight. This is New York. Scream if you hear anyone at the window. You won't blame yourself afterwards," he yawns, "when you're looking back on this from the next life. You can say you did the right thing." Marcel falls asleep in a feverish mixture of expectation of adventure and unnameable dread. When he wakes up in the morning, New York is standing outside his window, and when he blinks, it does not go away. Jim is packing faster and faster, and Marcel has never felt so alone. He begins planning how to get in touch with his brother Shawn, who, according to his parents, is in some kind of mysterious big city trouble, and he begins to worry about how to get his one suit pressed for his first day at work. Jim gives him quick and sloppy directions to the dry cleaners and he ventures out like a cat thrown from the car by its careless occupants.

* * *

Marcel has gone to work at a rather peculiar publishing company, and after six months coincidence, the only deus ex machina we have, and which is undoubtedly a very small nasty animal covered with warts, is about to take a hand. The publishing company has an unfortunate tendency to judge people as if they were living bank accounts, and Marcel understands this fully, knowing that a publisher as large as Holten Hill is a commercial entity, subsidized only by its diversified stocks, which include supermarkets and flocks of sheep, and must make money. Still, he is not used to being inspected as if he might be a counterfeit bill, and the fulfillment of a long-hidden dream, to be judged not for his mind alone, is having dubious effects. His mind, which the upper echelons seem to visualize as clearly as if they were viewing it in embalming fluid, is a distinct disadvantage here because "it" might come between him and the pulse of the public. Marcel has trouble coming to terms with this new image of himself as a clever diagnostician of a healthy patient whose cure takes the form of emptying the contents of the patient's pocket into the doctor's wallet. It seems to him he is forever trying to convince someone he is not "too" intellectual, while on the other hand he greatly resents anyone who does not immediately recognize his intellectual abilities. He is also more or less stalled in his talent for Byzantine machinations since the Editor-in-Chief of the Trade Division is a man named Pane who is seen only by his secretary, and, on rare occasions confirms the fact of his physical existence by scurrying hurriedly out of the men's room. No one there knows whether to describe him as a mole or a vampire, and different factions discuss this question a good portion of the working day. Marcel, as one of the youngest editors, has inherited a grab bag of unfinished products, and finds himself submerged in a tide of domesticity and family life he prefers not to know exists. He is completing books on the proper treatment of plants, the proper treatment of toddlers, the improper treatment of the Second World War by the Air Force, one hundred and fifty famous photos of the mushroom, with an elaborate commentary by a well-known botanist and is getting used to, he says, "Morgue Day," Wednesdays in which all the editors go down to the receiving room and start opening the unsolicited manuscripts which invariably deal with one man's experience with his wife's cancer, or his own heart attack, and represent the last, heartbreaking attempt to wrest meaning from a life gone bad from every imaginable engine in the world. He has also begun living with a feminist he met in the course of corporate duty, and is not used to feminists, rather redundant and unnecessary objects at the University where the women were "above" feminism, and apparently above everything else as well.

This new woman in his life, named Max, does not seem to be working out much better than Morgue Day. She spends a great deal of her time ferreting out all Marcel's prejudices against women, all of which he is eager to admit to, her accusations hitting on the old nerve of guilt, which once prompted such voluminous confessions so that one old priest, after an hour of tearing his hair behind a partition said gravely and kindly, "My son, it is enough. You need not say more. All is clear. I can see the rest as if it were written out before me. Go and begin again," the old priest instructed, and Marcel left the church with a light heart, feeling, for the first time, profoundly understood. "If only they allowed televisions in there," the old priest muttered to himself in his room, savagely yanking off his collar before his shower; "if only they allowed radios, even a puppy to pat. O God," he asked in all seriousness, casting his eyes up to the cheerful heavens, "is it too much to ask? A radio? I wouldn't really listen, but I would hear it in the back of my mind. It would relieve my sufferings. This arthritis is impossible," he added peevishly, over the years having become accustomed to addressing Him as a valued but very familiar relative.

However, no matter what Marcel admitted to, Max's capacity for affection remained unaltered. She expected affection as part of her natural right to live, but regarded Marcel's demands as babyish and the result of conditioning. "You expect to be coddled like a baby," she shouted at him vituperatively the day he came home sure he was going to be fired and sat down next to her on the couch and wanted her to put her arm around him. Then one day she gave a speech at a women's group, and Marcel stupidly agreed to go. "What did you think? What did you think?" she kept asking him again and again, and he told her she had done beautifully and in fact he was very impressed. "You don't have to humor me just because I'm a woman," she pouted; "you can tell me the truth, no matter how bad it is." "But it *wasn't* bad," Marcel insisted; "you were great." "Was I as good as Frieda Hofstadter?" she asked finally. "Well, no," Marcel answered honestly; "nobody is, not before they're fifty, anyway." "Oh I see," Max answered icily, drawing out the last word as if it were a thorn in her paw; "I see. Come right out and say," she demanded, "how much you didn't like it." "I liked it," Marcel pleaded. "You *hated* it," Max insisted; "go on, come on and say it." "I *didn't* hate it," Marcel insisted, feeling as if he were trapped in some incredible Chinese box from which only a termite could hope to free himself. "That does it," Max announced, heading for the closet; "I'm leaving." "For what?" Marcel demanded close to tears. "I can't live with someone who doesn't respect my work," Max answered haughtily. "You're crazy," he said, beaten. "Or with someone who calls me crazy whenever I have the courage to be honest," she added, rummaging in a pile of shoes.

Marcel began to wonder if Max had something there; maybe all women were crazy. Half of them had to be to put up with men, and the other half drove the men mad over toothbrushes and razors, imagined betrayals, forgotten anniversaries, and remembered transgressions. He remembered his father fleeing the house in Marblehead one Saturday morning without any explanation, plunging down the stairs like a stone. Apparently, it emerged, his poor father thought the day was his anniversary, and he was so terrified of not having a present, he searched not only Marblehead but three of the neighboring towns. In fact, the anniversary was the next Saturday, and Mrs. Donovan was so enraged by her husband's error that she took the vase he bought her and threw it down right in the middle of the kitchen floor. The remainder of the story should by now be an old one to anyone who has even a passing acquaintance with this family.

So it was that Marcel once again found himself alone, and found many men inside the company and out comforting and affectionate, if not downright maternal. Moreover, he had just received a book proposing to discuss in detail the new movements in the gay world. The book was intended to introduce the average citizen to the world of the homosexual, the "gay man," the gay bar, the gay affair (which he compared to serial monogamy), and was to do this through a series of semifictional documentaries. It developed that Holten Hill was not ready for such an advanced book, but by the time the senior editors made clear to Marcel the magnitude of his misunderstanding of company policy, Marcel himself had reached the point of wishing *he* were a case history in that wonderful book of happy people. It seemed to him that he had found the new *Decameron*, and the only pity, he thought, was that it had taken so long to come into being. As the book made clear, the gay world offered the most genuine and varied hope for a life of adventures, and it was not long before he had discovered the Continental Baths, monks who wanted their monastery assignment changed so they could be with their lovers, disinherited members of royal families, who, according to all reports, spent their vacations riding white horses across blue-crested mountains of Bavaria, women in feathers who were really men, a gay couple who intended to adopt a gay child but were having their troubles, because, according to them, it was so hard to know in advance if a newborn infant was gay. It all had the unutterable charm of an Isak Dinesen story. Life had become a story within a story within a story where the characters changed every night, and no one was ever lost. Sooner or later, they all showed up at the gay bars.

On the same day that a friend at the company had warned him to be more reticent about his personal life (someone had told the Editor-in-Chief they thought the art director's assistant was gay, and the man replied, "Do you think so? He always seemed so very glum to me."), Marcel got a strange phone call from a female who sounded familiar and who was evidently calling on a phone she had commandeered from a shoe store clerk on the Lower East Side. It appeared that she had written a novel, and was from Chicago, and had a friend who was also from Chicago, who had an aunt who worked in the company's shipping department, who had told her niece, this female's friend, that there was a new editor from Chicago at the company, and the niece had repeated this to a friend of the female calling (while she was in the ladies' room before giving a reading in what she called the "cockroach circuit") so that the novelist overheard them and made a mental note and was calling to find out if she could send the novel in or not. Marcel, who had been ordered to sign up some successful books, as if they hung around like actors out of work, said she should send it in, but probably it would not be any good or, rather, he added more tactfully, "work out here" (a phrase he had absorbed with indescribable relief), because, he said, everyone he knew from Chicago sent him novels, and they had all turned out to be terrible. "Oh," said the voice. "But send it in anyway," he said tonelessly. "Are you sure?" the voice inquired solicitously; "I have to wrap it up and everything and it's three hundred pages long." "Send it in, send it in," Marcel repeated. He was beginning to pick up certain Jewish intonations and patterns of speech and would have been very satisfied with himself if he could bring himself to believe this was actually happening, because, as had been impressed on him over and over again, Jewish intellectuals ran the establishment, because, his mentor told him, they could deal with guilt, and even make it work for them, whereas Protestants and Catholics could not cope with it at all and had to rely on other strategies, as, for instance, Marcel's famous charm. His charm was getting full exposure, but he was, on the other hand, rather tired of it, and now felt that although people definitely did not love him for his mind alone, they did love him for his charm.

It is at this point that the manuscript from the nameless female in the shoe store arrives, and seen cynically, could be described as a work extolling the joys of sex, family life, and standard commitment, all values extolled monthly by *Redbook, McCall's,* and *Ladies' Home Journal.* Moreover, the book advocates psychoanalysis and clearly assumes the value of doctors, even witch doctors. (Marcel has been told belief in doctors is another Jewish trait.) Marcel falls in love with this book and immediately assumes the company is conspiring against him to prevent its publication. Every night in the gay bars he discusses with gay critics how this remarkable novel must see the light of day appropriately dressed in simple print, and finally, he prevails in having the book accepted while the author is recovering from a postpartum depression in Brooklyn Jewish Hospital and the news of the acceptance seems to demoralize her even further. Still, it is clear that Marcel's role as midwife has endeared him to her beyond reason and she now considers him a blood relation. Between these two, an extraordinarily uneventful and peculiar relationship begins to grow up, although fortunately for both neither notices its existence for five years. Diana Cotton is excessively vulnerable to people she likes, and although she becomes more involved with them than thread caught in the works of a sewing machine, for her own protection she insists no involvement exists. Nevertheless, should anyone say anything even vaguely unpleasant about her editor, she suppresses an impulse to claw out the offender's eyes, as she used to do when anyone attacked her younger brother, and instead attacks them verbally, usually smiling, with about the same results. At the company, Marcel and Diana are invariably thought of together, first because Marcel "discovered" Diana, who has now written novel after novel (one for each baby), and because she will go nowhere without her editor. If he does not physically accompany her to literary events, she lectures all and sundry on his extraordinary merits, and, no matter who they are, refuses to converse with them unless they agree. By now, people have gotten used to this, although when Marcel and Diana first began working together eight years ago, the Publicity Department was certain this peculiar behavior would be the end of both author and editor. Nevertheless, Diana has survived with her husband and three children, continues to work at designing hats and her own huge house, to get up in the mornings to feed the children whom she hands over with a mixed sigh of relief and guilt to the housekeeper, and Marcel continues to have his adventures. Diana refuses to hear about them, theorizing that if they are so much talked about, they are valued more as conversation pieces than parts of life and this convinces Marcel she is prejudiced against homosexuality. She has denied it so many times she has lost count and ceased to care what Marcel believes. Nevertheless, they remain very close, although Diana keeps Marcel at long-stem rose distance, primarily through her sarcasm and teasing. Marcel does the same with Diana when he insists on attempting to narrate his latest adventures. A cool silence and telephone alert at the Cotton household invariably follows one of these exchanges. Recently, however, Diana has begun to feel that things have changed, the old balance has shifted, and that something is wrong. She finds herself dreaming about Marcel, who continues to appear in the guise of her youngest son, dressed like Julius Caesar in flowing Roman robes, but perpetually making washing motions with his hands, like Lady Macbeth. When she questions him in dreams, he mumbles about Banquo and not getting enough sleep, and in her latest dream, Diana has pursued him, in the middle of the night, to the top of the Empire State Building, where he insists on climbing the tower to swat at planes. "It's past your bedtime," Diana keeps pleading; "get down here," but he escapes and goes off to hunt for alligators in the New York sewers for the rest of the night. Diana herself wakes up exhausted after one of these ludicrous dreams and now has a favorite vision, which she can instantly conjure up. In it, she is putting Marcel to bed (the bed has high railings) and she is securing his blankets by means of a staple gun. "Ah," she sighs with satisfaction, feeling the jerk of the staples going into the blanket, "the staple gun, what a wonderful invention, second only to heatable hair curlers." With this vision preceding her up the stairs, she goes back to work on her latest novel. She is interrupted by a call from one of the salesmen's wives whom she has met at a party. "Doesn't Marcel look *terrible?*" the woman asks, and instantly Diana is in a panic. "He looks perfectly fine," she says huffily, and asks the woman what she does when her toddlers refuse to stop hitting and scratching her. "Does the whole world have to notice?" Diana asks herself, hanging up. On her way back to her desk, which is three feet from the phone, she says out loud to herself, "I have to do something about this."

* * *

Marcel has become more and more emaciated, although he regards this as becoming fashionably thin. He also looks ten years older than he did five years ago. Diana, on the other hand, looks considerably younger than she did when she was twenty-six and has become world-famous for her novels of good and evil. The lives of these two people have become inextricably bound, since, in a sense, each has helped to create the other's destiny; without Marcel, Diana might not have been published. Without Diana, Marcel might still be earning less than an English chimney sweep. After five years, neither is clear on how much of their lives depends on the other, but both have a rather resigned nagging consciousness that some kind of dependence exists. Both Marcel and Diana prefer to think professional dependency ties them together, although by now it would be clear to anyone that Diana did not need any particular editor, nor Marcel any particular author. However, they have both been trained at the University, and are beginning to become uncomfortably aware that they are more similar than they care to admit. This realization begins to dawn on Diana first. She has just published her fifth novel and there is no reason to assume it will not have a magnificent critical reception; in fact it has already *had* one, but as long as the *Arkansas Cow Digest and Literary Magazine* has not been heard from, Diana remains on the lookout for disaster. It is also true that during these postpublication periods Diana comes closer to psychosis than she ever would under any other circumstances. She is given to picking arguments with friends, suspecting the maid of hiding her stockings before interviews, taking seriously rumors that everyone she knows at Holten Hill is about to be replaced with her worst enemies, and fearing fire on the third floor. She is also certain her children are coming down with measles, hepatitis, and polio, which she is sure she has transmitted to them, because even though they have had their inoculations, she has not had hers in some time, and it is always impossible to say with assurance that an inoculation took. "I can't stand the reviews anymore," Diana announces to Marcel one Wednesday afternoon; "they're making me clamp my teeth together at night. I'm going to call up that man and tell him he's a monster and if he has any children they're probably on drugs." She continues in this vein for half an hour, wears herself out, and concludes wearily, "I'm probably depressed." "You'll get over it," is Marcel's standard reply. "Easy for you to say," she replies on cue; "wait until you write a book." "Oh, I'll never do that," Marcel answers in his light chirrupy voice. "Nothing you do surprises me," Diana says; "I'll talk to you tomorrow. I don't want to talk about this anymore. I really don't." "All right," Marcel answers, although Diana always wants to talk about everything.

But later that night, after Diana has fallen into a depressed sleep, resembling a coma, from which even her husband would not attempt to rouse her, something extraordinary happens. The phone rings and Marcel's voice comes over the speaker of the answering machine. Diana wakes up immediately; that voice affects her as the bell did Pavlov's dog. "I know you're there, Diana," Marcel is saying; "I know you don't go out for three weeks after a book is published." Viciously, Diana picks up the phone so that the answering machine will shriek into Marcel's ear. "Hello," she says thickly. "Are you awake?" "No." "Are you going to wake up?" "I don't know. What do you want?" "Well," Marcel begins in a concerned tone, "I don't like the way you sounded before." "So what, I hate the sound of my own voice," Diana mumbles agreeably, starting to fall back asleep. "No, I mean the way you were talking; it sounded ugly." "What are you talking about?" Diana demands, "the monster from *Library Chronicle?*" "That's what I mean," Marcel pounces; "it's not fair to call a man and tell him his children are drug addicts." "Oh for Christsake," Diana mutters, beginning to wake up, peering at the hands of the clock; both hands are on the twelve. "I don't even know the man. I don't even know if he has children. He probably owns the Continental Baths. I'm going to call him up and tell him his children are heterosexuals." "That's what I mean, Diana," Marcel patiently explains; "you don't usually talk like this." "I talk like this all the time, especially when I'm frightened." "But you don't have anything to be frightened about," Marcel insists. "That's what you think," Diana answers. "What are you frightened about, if you have something to be frightened about?" "All this publicity," Diana says, hoping he'll go away or turn into a Bugs Bunny commercial. "What publicity?" Marcel asks, "this is your fifth time around." "It gets worse each time." "That's what's wrong," Marcel tells her; "by now you should be getting used to it." "You're right," Diana agrees; "now can I go back to sleep?" "I'd rather you told me what was bothering you about the publicity," Marcel says rationally; "don't you like your book?" "No, I don't like the book; I meant to tell you my mother wrote it, but she's even shyer than I am. Can I go to sleep now?" "What's the matter with you?" Marcel demands, irritated. "I don't like being successful," Diana says finally. "Why?" Marcel asks quietly. "Don't ask me. I tell you what, I'll think about it and we'll have a long talk about it later." However, they do not talk about it for some time.

In the morning, Diana wakes up and remembers the phone call with a shock. Marcel sounded worried. For Marcel to be worried, and to know what to worry about, she reasons, he must be having similar problems himself. "I wonder why Marcel is afraid of success?" she thinks to herself. She gets dressed, goes to work (she now works only part-time, still designing hats), and when she comes home, and finishes with the chores and the hugs and the kisses, goes to work on her sixth novel. "The albatross is back," she tells her friends with a mixture of resignation and satisfaction. When she writes, she loses all interest in calling people, visiting people, and in how her last book is selling. In fact, it is selling extremely well, and she fails to notice this until with a certain annoyance and cheery satisfaction, she sees that it is climbing the best-seller list. But it might as well be someone else's book and someone else's beanstalk. Diana's mother wants to know what she'll find to complain about if she ever wins the Nobel Prize. "I hate plane trips," Diana answers; "they scare me to death."

* * *

It is two years later, and with minor variations the above scene has been repeated. There are certain flourishes, however, in Marcel's department. He has taken to blacking out and to taking an experimental drug affectionately called, by the drug companies, PxY8. Diana has already looked this up and found out that one of the minor side effects is instant death, and that a fairly common side effect is massive swelling of the tongue due to progressively severe allergic reactions which results in the self-strangulation of the patient. Diana privately believes that it would serve Marcel right to be strangled by his own tongue, but by now she is too attached to him to contemplate this fate with any equanimity.

It must be mentioned that, after Houdini, Marcel is the greatest escape artist when it comes to avoiding discussions of his own problems. As far as he is concerned, he never has any. It is always "a passing thing," "something I'll get over," "something you don't understand because you're such a prude," or, as the ultimate resort, "none of your business." Under the circumstances, trapping him is no easy business. Marcel always reminds Diana of certain raccoons who drive farmers mad by eating the corn in back of the front rows so that the field looks undisturbed, but when the farmer gets around to inspecting it, finds he has been watering four rows of corn and many acres of manured earth. Today, however, they are standing in the middle of a snowstorm in front of Holten Hill waiting for a limousine to take them to a publication party. "You know who died?" Marcel begins. "Never mind who died," Diana answers; "I want to talk to you." Marcel immediately dives into the front seat of the limousine, volunteering Diana for the company of the Editor-in-Chief. "Oh dear," Diana says innocently (her husband calls this her Baby Snookums voice, and it should be mentioned that Diana is an extremely beautiful woman), "I *have* to talk to Marcel about my new book; he's so busy you know, what with all the big authors coming over to the company to work with him, I hardly get a chance to talk to him. *We* better sit in the back," she ends, glaring at him, and winding up in a steely tone. Everyone scrambles about without looking at one another. Marcel looks as if he is considering throwing himself out of the car into midtown traffic. "Now," Diana grins, settling back and fixing him with a look he has learned to know and dread, "I want to talk to you. I am worried about you." "Shhhh," Marcel murmurs desperately, pointing at the people in the front of the car. In business, as in politics, it is unwise to let people suspect you have so much as a cold. "Don't point," Diana says sweetly; "it's not polite." One of the women in the front seat turns around and smiles as the car pulls out into traffic. "Ah, the roar of the buses," Diana croons at him; "no one can hear a word we say." Marcel is turning pale green. "I am worried about you," she says mournfully; "according to all reports you get two hours' sleep a night. Even a bat sleeps more of the night than two hours a night. You are sick all the time and you think it has something to do with your kidneys or your medulla when anyone could tell you that two hours' sleep won't keep a geranium alive. In the meantime, you take something called Xyz9 which would kill off any healthy person. I think you need some help. I think you're frightened to death. I know you're frightened to death or you wouldn't know *I'm* frightened to death." Marcel looks at her questioningly. "Your intuitive powers have never really woken up," she continues, "so, for you to know I'm frightened, you must be frightened, or you wouldn't know I'm frightened. I'm sick of the sentence," Diana sighs; "you get the point."

"What frightens you is success," Marcel says tonelessly. "What frightens you?" Diana asks. "Success," Marcel answers, stunning them both into temporary silence. "Are you about to become more successful?" she asks. "You know I am," he answers grimly. "How do you know? Are you getting a raise?" "The signs are there," he sighs. Then, surprisingly, he continues of his own accord. "The last time I was a success, at the University, I practically broke down."

In the ensuing conversation, Diana warns Marcel approximately twenty-five times that she does not want to hear theoretical explanations of his behavior or philosophical rationalizations for his life. She just wants to know if he is happy. No, he isn't. Is he getting unhappier? Yes, he is. "I can take care of myself," Marcel says automatically. "But you're not, so that's that." Silence smothers the back seat. "Well," Diana says, "talk. No twenty minute pauses between sentences while you quote mentally from Kant. Just one sentence after another." Marcel begins to talk wistfully about Frieda Hofstadter and Ernst L. Hourbach, two names to which Diana is by now allergic. However, this time she does not interrupt, comment, or make sarcastic remarks. For her, this is a remarkable exercise in self-discipline. "You see," Marcel is saying earnestly, "for them it was all accidents. If ecology hadn't come along as an issue, Frieda would never have found her main theme; if Watergate hadn't come up, she wouldn't have been able to be brilliant about it; if Israel hadn't been bombed, she couldn't have gotten involved in distinguishing morals from patriotism in politics. And if Ernst hadn't come across the Bloomsbury letters and then the Manson letters, he could never have developed his theories of social dynamics." "Do you mean to say," Diana asks after some time, "that if there was no ecology problem, or Watergate, Frieda Hofstadter would be some poor hack academic?" "It's possible," Marcel answers. "It's not possible," Diana says; "the things she's written on are all different. The world is a series of accidents. If these hadn't happened, others would. She's open to events; some appeal to her more than others, but she doesn't have to depend on some specially tailored wrinkle in history before she finds something to interest her." No answer. Diana thinks some more. "I think," she says finally, "you want what Frieda Hofstadter and Ernst Hourbach have, but you don't know how to get it, and you know you can't get it by copying them, and besides you're afraid of what would happen to you if you got it." "Then why are you so afraid?" Marcel asks. "I'm always frightened of something," Diana answers; "besides, I know what makes me frightened." "What?" "My parents and competing with them. You wouldn't like to hear about it. It has to do with that Sigmund Fraud whose name you revile so much." "I don't believe in the theoretical assumptions of psychoanalysis," Marcel reminds her. "Who cares what you believe in as long as it works." "You can think that way," Marcel retorts huffily, "but I'm an idealist." "I suppose you're an idealist when you decide to publish a songbook for African plants," Diana snaps; "you're not an idealist, you're an idiot." They sit in hostile silence. "Will you think about it?" she asks. "What?" "Going to see a psychiatrist. You owe it to yourself to see them behaving stupidly for fifty dollars an hour. At least afterwards you can have the authority of an eyewitness instead of sounding like a brain-damaged Platonist. Will you think about it?"

"I'll think about it."

"Not like last time?"

"Not like last time."

"Promise?"

"I promise."

Diana represses an urge to ask him to cross his heart and hope to die. She is sure he will not think about it. Nevertheless, he grabs her in the middle of the party and drags her out into a blizzard for a walk. "Now what's up?" she asks; "did you try to pick up Hugh Hefner?" "Stop," he pleads. They walk along in silence. Snow glitters like dead fish scales. From some angles, the campus is a vision of heaven. "I wonder," Marcel says softly, "what it would be like to sleep with women again." In the dark Diana's eyes fill with tears. "I'd like to finish my book"—he is writing on manners—"so I could give it to Frieda Hofstadter. I'm doing it for her. I want to give it to her for a present." A tear falls out of Diana's eye and ices down her cheek. She is always trying to give away her books, to blame their genesis on someone else. That way she never has to take responsibility for them, or for their success. "That's the story of my life," she murmurs, holding Marcel's hand; "that's terrible." "What's so terrible about it?" he asks, puzzled. "You can't have anything for yourself. Why did you say that?" "What?" "That you'd like to sleep with women again." "I'm happy the way I am," Marcel answers; "we can't have children. Sometimes I wish we could resolve the problem by adopting one. I don't know," he says, "I just wonder, sometimes, what it would be like to sleep with women again."

"Thank you," he tells Diana at the end of the night. "For what?" she says. She cannot bring herself to smile. "For what?" she repeats aloud to the empty back of the cab.

Marcel's friends now close around him, see that he sleeps, goes to a normal doctor, and stops taking PxY8. Astonishingly, his kidneys recover spontaneously, but nevertheless, he continues to worry all his friends who are sure something is very much the matter. Everyone is sure something is very much the matter except Marcel, who is sure he has solved his problem by getting more sleep.

*   *   *

Of course, things change. Marcel gets older and acquires gray hairs, which do not give him a distinguished look, but rather that of a child whom nature has decided to blight itself too early in life. He has, as he has threatened to do many times, changed publishers; over the course of twenty years he has now worked for three companies. He does not put on weight because he is conscious of how much appearance counts in the new world he has selected for himself. While long ago he used to fear that his young lover would reach the age of twenty-six, the magic year for homosexuals when they often choose to become straight, and then leave him, he now fears he will soon be too old to attract anyone. He is still living with the same man he was with thirty years ago, but to outsiders they often give the appearance of a nagging couple prematurely retired to a condominium in Florida. The multitudes, the one-night stands, have dried up, partially due to boredom, the lack of energy that comes with the approach of the fifties, continuing days of hard work, and a suspicion that there is something to be done that has not been done. It may be this last which is the most wearing. Marcel now looks at his life with considerable dissatisfaction, although by now there is little he can do to change it. He has had the adventures of syphilis scares, visits to syphilis clinics, group sex (when he often wanted only one of the group, but the majority won), bishops who wanted to build their dioceses by making real estate investments and who threatened to ruin the advancements of archimandrites who were "into" leather, Peaches La Plum, the queen of the transvestites, who, unlike many transvestites, is really homosexual, visits to Switzerland on the spur of the moment to visit the last physical incarnation of his classic male ideal, the endless stream of reincarnated Michelangelos. He has lived the life of eternal youth in the land of the Perpetual Crush, where every love is new and the mention of the beloved's name brings trembling hands, burning cheeks, and a suspension of time. Several years ago, even Diana (he still reads her books in manuscript although he is no longer her editor; she claims she cannot leave Holten Hill because she is incapable of finding her way around the city, and by now, if she got lost, would return to the company like an old horse lost in a storm) has admitted to envying him this aspect of life, for as she well knows, married life is not an unending series of crushes, those debilitating fires of adolescence, not the heartbreaks she still remembers with such detail and regret from her early twenties. She suspects, however, that all gay men do not live like Marcel and that many are really gay in the old sense, and she does not mention that even old married women periodically develop crushes on their own worn husbands, who suddenly appear to them in a new, blinding light, which is the same blinding light in which they stumbled to the altar. Diana does not mention this because by now she knows they are stalemated. Time has taken what he wanted from both of them, and in the face of sadness, she prefers to let what remains, remain. In her adult life, Diana has said, "I told you so," seven times, each time to one of her children, and each time the sight of their faces has prevented her from ever saying it again.

* * *

Time, the passage of time, Diana thinks after her husband dies. She is seventy-two; so was her husband. Marcel is seventy. She and her husband had always assumed they would die together, picturing the occasion, if they pictured it at all, as a bedroom filling slowly with heavy smoke. She does not like the way the children

look, all dressed in black; they remind her of crows about to settle
on a branch or a body. Marcel has insisted on coming to the funeral, although Diana does not want him there since she knows
he secretly believes that, even at her age, she will soon find someone else. She does not hear a word of the service. She is remembering her grandfather's funeral, her grandmother's, her mother's,
her father's; she is remembering how she did not feel anything
when her grandmother died and how she still mourns for her now.
Now she feels everything. She sees the body asleep in its narrow
bed; she wants to get in and cuddle up. Success, what is it? The
sound of the dirt on the coffin jars her so that she jumps and her
youngest daughter holds on to her wrist so hard she hurts her. She
is crying steadily but she doesn't make a sound. She thinks of a
great many things. She wonders why she feared being more successful than her parents when they thrived on the fuss and the
flurry and she thinks the one thing she has really succeeded in doing is duplicating the life of her mother. She now realizes she can
never live long enough to know if she has succeeded, or found the
kind of success she was born wanting. She is now like her own
grandmother. She thinks to herself that it is not true that your own
life flashes before your eyes when you die, but that this does happen when someone else you love dies. Her own life is flickering before her, the arguments, the competition, the cancer scares, the ap-
pendicitis, the bad backs and all that was called daily life, so that
now in her seventies she finally knows it is called love. She does
not, and really would not, mind death now. Yet there was a time
when the news of a friend's terminal illness would have her at
the doctor in minutes. She has changed, she often says, into a
taller version of her mother, although this is not really true, and
yet it is. She lives by the values her mother lived by. She leaves
people alone, as her mother told her to, "because they cannot
help it." As she simultaneously thinks this and looks at the coffin
she begins to sob.

Marcel's roommate, as Diana has insisted on calling him for
half a century, is also very sick, and given his past history, the doc-

tors had tentatively diagnosed his illness as a recurrence of gonorrhea. As Marcel's life has ticked on, he has tired of the novelties
of illness, and it now appears what is wrong with his roommate,
Saul, is not gonorrhea but a rare disease of the lymphatic system.
This means that Marcel is constantly surprised to find himself at
Diana's house, but Diana sees him there without the slightest
surprise. He has become an alternate godfather to her children,
many of whom have been locked in their rooms, forbidden des-
sert, had their mouths washed out with soap, all the old family
remedies, until they learned "tolerance." It is questionable
whether they have ever learned it any better than their mother, although, like her, they have learned love.

* * *

Diana has recovered and continues to write, and from her studio
window over the garage watches Marcel wandering around her
flower garden like an old gray bee. He nods his head in the direction of the yellow roses, suddenly sticks his hand out like a child
stealing candy, takes off a petal and eats it. For some reason, this
reminds Diana of the time she was on the floor playing with her
first child when he suddenly decided to feed her his zwieback. Before that, he had never shown the slightest inclination to give
away anything, and Diana feared he would grow up to be Eben-
ezer Scrooge. Suddenly David, who was ten months old, put his
zwieback to her mouth and regarded her seriously. She took a little bite. He put it back to his mouth, touching his tongue to it,
pretending to eat it, then back to her mouth. Diana was surprised,
because all along she thought David had been fooled by her pretending to eat his horrid food so he would finish up his jar. At the
time it was happening, she knew it was one of those odd irrele-
vant moments in life that would become a fixed, governing point.
She had often told herself it was just as well Marcel did not have
children, because he had spent a half-century telling her he didn't
want any, and anyone who says something for fifty years, Diana
reasoned, must mean it. Besides, children have a way of staying on

and on, like the man who came to dinner, and Marcel has never shown any tolerance for that concept of permanence, although it now occurs to Diana that he and his roommate have been in the same apartment for over fifty years, although daily each reports detailed plans for packing, flying to Puerto Rico or Brazil, where one or the other has suddenly remembered an old and very important acquaintance. What is she writing about anyway? She doesn't know, and gets up and goes into the garden.

"How are things, kid?" she asks. This has been her standard greeting for so very long that even Diana, who adores old people (and even herself, now that she has become one), doesn't like to think about it. Marcel shrugs his shoulders. They stand there looking at the roses. "Liver for supper," Diana says. "Fine," Marcel answers. When ten o'clock comes, he gets ready to go home because he does not like to take the trains any later, although as usual, someone objects. "Come on," Joan says; "I'll drive you." She is Diana's oldest daughter and close to fifty herself. "Not unless Alex goes with you," Diana warns. Alex is going. "Don't bother," Marcel pleads; "you have your thesis to finish." Alex is in his middle twenties. Diana had her last child at forty-eight, to the infinite surprise of the family, Holten Hill, and Downstate Medical Center in general. "I'm finished," Alex says, "and I'm not working on anything Mother lets me mention. Mother's a prude, didn't you know?" "You mean the crones," Marcel jokes halfheartedly. "Watch it," Joan warns him, jabbing him in the stomach. She looks and acts like the Diana of almost forty years ago. With relief, Marcel lets them stuff him into the car. He wonders idly why everyone in Diana's family loves to drive. Diana pretends she wants to go off to write, goes into her studio, turns on a light, hides from it behind the screen which shields her little couch, and starts to cry. Suddenly, she thinks of a forty-year-old photograph taken at her first publication party. In it, Marcel is beaming, his smile radiant as sun on a coin. He looks as if he simply has to stand there and Apollo's chariot will pick him up and take him away from all this. Diana looks horrible, as if the reviews of her book had somehow affected her liver. She wants the photograph back and begins searching frantically for it. She turns drawers upside down and paws through the contents on the floor. There is a frightening, stiff look on her face. She never finds it. Diana is usually an orderly person. She sits down in the middle of a pile of papers and her fingers move into the position of fingers holding a photograph. She sees it as if she were holding it. After she has been sitting a long, long time this way, it occurs to her she has never seen Marcel laugh, or cry, although he does make a choking noise meant to imitate a laugh. This makes her begin crying all over again.

* * *

Marcel's roommate is not dead, but he soon will be. The two of them have decided to move downtown to be closer to the Hospital for Special Surgery. Marcel is in a steady rage with Saul, because he has a dread of disease, and Saul is now diseased beyond imagination. Yet he feels tenderness for him, and pity. Pity is perhaps the emotion Marcel tolerates best. While Saul is resting in his room, Marcel begins sorting the papers in his huge desk drawer, the drawer on the bottom into which he has spent fifty years putting documents he never expects to want again. He has now thrown almost all the papers into an empty Carnation milk carton when he comes to the last one. It is yellowed and has been folded for so long it is white at the creases. What is it? Marcel unfolds it carefully and feels himself receding as if he were a figure seen through the wrong end of a telescope. "Marcel Patrick Donovan," the paper reads, "born December 31, 1939, at Saint Catherine's Lady of Hope Hospital." There are the names of his parents, the priest, the punched emblem of some official design chewed into the paper by the teeth of a metal seal. Marcel picks it up and pushes some manuscripts from the end of his jumbled sofa. A long time ago, Diana gave him the sofa in the middle of one of their interminable theoretical arguments about materialism. To his amazement, he begins to cry, and to his amazement, he cannot stop. It is back, that feeling of irretrievable loss he once had at a little church in South Carolina. Irrelevantly, he remembers Brother Joseph. He is saying, "Father I have sinned." "In mind or body," Brother Joseph asks. "In mind," he answers. He sits there crying until long after the sun has tried to come up in the hostile Manhattan sky. "There were no accidents," he sobs; "there should have been an accident. Something should have happened." He tries to get up but his legs won't hold him. He hopes no one will find him dead this way, with this paper, his eyes swollen.

At her home, Diana turns over in her double bed (she always sleeps now on her husband's side) and has a vision of Marcel catching his finger in the typewriter. She has had visions like this for almost fifty years. "Stop it," she tells herself, thumping the pillow. "Fifty years of worrying about nothing is enough. It's enough," she tells the pillow defiantly, as if it, or her husband, had answered her back.

The Queen of Egypt

Abigail Ida Jennings-Smith had the kind of childhood which was entirely miserable, although the misery of it was almost entirely screened from the eyes of others and virtually unknown to her parents. The Jennings-Smiths were of an old English family who had quite literally come over on the *Mayflower*, and although in most neighborhoods, this would have worked to the social advantage of a young and presentable lady, in the middle of Brooklyn where her father had chosen to live because the brownstones reminded him of the houses of his childhood, during which time he had lived with an uncle while he attended the best British schools, Miss Abigail's ancestry was definitely against her. She had once brought a friend home from school, and had to confess, upon being asked if she would like to go out and buy hot bagels, that she had no idea of what bagels were, nor did she have a skate key, for her governess took her to a private rink where her skates were

high button shoes with wheels attached to the soles, and, upon
hearing Miss Fenwick address her as Miss Abigail, the young
friend began to watch Abigail suspiciously, as if unsure whether or
not a joke were being played upon her. Finally, out of desperation, little Miss Abigail ventured that her family had come over
on the *Mayflower*, a remark she had always seen spur on a lagging
conversation in the drawing room. When her little friend asked
for an explanation, Miss Abigail, who confused *Mayflowers* with
sunflowers, and who had never been sufficiently interested in the
subject to begin with, blushing at its mere mention, assuming it
had something to do with the birth of babies, said vaguely that it
was a large yellow flower, and that somehow her family had gotten over from England on it, as if it were a raft; whereupon her
friend decided Abigail was crazy and duly reported her findings to
the children at P.S. 206. Thereafter, the children, who normally
persecuted and ridiculed anyone who did not belong as a matter
of routine, ignored Miss Abigail entirely, so that she spent all of
her recesses in the corner of the schoolyard, moving aside like a
compliant tree whenever one of the others began climbing the
schoolyard's wire fence like a bean on Jack's beanstalk. After several months, Miss Abigail resigned herself to this monotonous
daily existence and fought her increasing sense of her own in-
visibility with increased visits to her little cousins, all of whom,
with their pompous airs, and their unending talk about clothes
and Dun & Bradstreet, she found unendurably boring. The truth
was, Miss Abigail would have liked to skate on sidewalks and eat
bagels and knishes, but she did not have the foggiest idea of what
these things were, and her mention of the *Mayflower*, which had
brought her family to America, had understandably closed the
mouths of her classmates to her.

It was understandable that her parents were of very little help
to her. The Jennings-Smiths were fantastically rich, and an ac-
countant had once calculated that even if the dollar were to sink
to a value of a single penny, there would be money enough to
maintain the family and all its heirs for several centuries. Miss

Abigail's father, Charles Alexander, had attended Oxford, making frequent visits to Cambridge, and had come away with an unshakable conviction that only the scholars, the seekers after knowledge, had any real right to draw breath. After endowing every scholar he deemed worthy of his intellectual standards with enough money for a lifetime (thereby wrecking many a promising career and plunging many earnest young men from the provinces and coal mines into hopeless excesses, not to say decadence), Mr. Jennings-Smith had picked up his entire family and come back to America, the second land of his ancestors, vaguely remembering that there was some such gesture in an inordinately complicated, but probably true, novel of Henry James; America, with its newness, would be a new place to begin. Mr. Jennings-Smith, for all his idolatry of the academic (perhaps this was the source of it), was not an extraordinarily intelligent man, and when he came to America, he never fully realized he was merely continuing his life as it had always gone on, while he was indeed forcing new beginnings upon his family. Abigail, who he still sometimes found himself addressing as "daughter," knew better than to come to her father for help.

At the end of her high school career, she entered her father's dim study, all but one wall paneled in dark wood, intending to tell him she was the valedictorian of her class, but at the sight of her father, hopelessly poring over an advanced book of mathematics called *The Topology of H-Spaces*, she immediately changed her mind. Abigail went into a corner of the room and sat down in her father's throne-like leather chair, which he had put on casters, the better to move about between bookshelves with, and let her feet dangle loose; no normal human's feet could ever reach the floor from this chair. "Don't swing your feet; a young lady never swings her feet," her father droned without looking up. He had always felt these instructions concerning deportment were the principal responsibility of a conscientious father. Abigail swung her feet, knowing perfectly well nothing would again induce her father to look up from his book.

On the wall facing her was a painting in exact imitation of the Bayeux tapestry. The painting of it, which had occurred when Abigail was only five, had been the most exciting event in the history of the household. After extensive investigation, Mr. Jennings-Smith had finally satisfied himself that he had an artist capable of rendering an exact duplicate of the tapestry on his study wall; only years later did it come to their attention who the painter was: the most accomplished and wealthy forger in Europe. During that year of the tapestry, however, there was a general atmosphere of depression in the country, and Americans were demanding few Breughels and Rembrandts and van Goghs. So the artist had had to content himself with this assignment. He was bothered not so much by the nature of the task itself, for reproducing the faded colors of the tapestry was a challenge even to him, but because the work he was doing was altogether legal. There had been horrible explosions over whether the king in his castle addressing his two courtiers leaned too much or too little to the left; did his scepter tilt from his arm at exactly the right angle; did the sails of the ships carrying the fish-like sailors to battle billow too naturally, giving the tapestry an overly modern look. When her father told the painter he had none of the right spirit in him, but was possessed by Fragonard, the painter threw his brush full of dark brown paint at the wall, where it stuck, like a tail on a donkey, right in the middle of the flames a soldier was using to heat something or other, and then stormed down the stairs. Upon reaching the flight to the first floor, he lost his balance and fell to the main hall landing, breaking both legs. He was installed, at his own insistence, in the study, on a specially constructed litter, where he painted daily, and when he rested, it seemed to be solely for the purpose of glowering at her oblivious father, who was buried in Kierkegaard, whom he was trying to read in the original Danish. He had also developed the habit of looking at Abigail and shaking his head sadly, as if she were a work of art he had botched and had to get back to.

"Father," Abigail said finally, "it is impossible to read under these conditions." Her father informed her that: "Ideal conditions demand that the reader and the book be sealed together, like page and binding. It follows that the light, too, should be confined to the pages, not leaking out all over the room as from a faulty pipe." He looked with distaste at the gold light splashing on the Oriental rug. "I have often thought," he continued, "how sensible it would be to have a round straw hat, something like the Chinese coolie hat, with bulbs wired to its rim; the light would then properly be confined. However," he sighed, "my electrician tells me it would not be practical, which I claim is of no importance, but he claims further that the bulbs would overheat the head and cause heat-stroke and brain damage; that, of course, cannot be risked." "Certainly not," Abigail whispered, who knew her part as the anti-strophe of strophe. "Dinner should be on the table soon," he said comfortingly. "So it should," Abigail agreed and went down to her room. She still went out into the yard, which, unlike all the others on the block, was a mass of flowers and velvet grass and odd watering equipment that aimed streams from the small ga-rage and the back house wall as well as from little nipples under the earth. Once in the yard, Abigail always did the same thing: she fastened a pair of old-style roller skates to her shoes and tried to navigate on them. The result was always the same; her weight pressed the wheels into the earth, anchoring her in position, and, if she attempted to throw herself forward, she landed face down in a mass of pyracanthas or African violets. Once, she had suc-ceeded in advancing two steps, but the swoop and swirl of the roller skates was, she knew, beyond her. And Miss Abigail was proud; she would not begin her fledgling attempts on the streets, where her old schoolmates might see her and offer advice, and then go home and laugh, telling each other she really was crazy, to start roller skating at her age.

Abigail's mother, the former Lady Anna Olivia Reed, was little help to her daughter, although she had seemed to grasp the im-portance of Abigail's graduation, and had not only promised to come, but to see to it that her twin sister, Lady Dolores Wellington, should accompany her in identical dress; at least this time, she told Abigail, her schoolmates would finally see what was what. The idea of eclipsing the others appealed to Abigail, but she knew that when her mother appeared with her Aunt Dolores, who was, for some reason, commonly referred to as Winnie, most of her schoolmates, now all conscious of money and their lack of it as they filled out their applications to the fancy colleges which would accept her without reading past her pedigree, would feel envy only, and many of them would manage not to feel even that, having already been infected by the American craze for nature, the simple life, and burlap clothes. Lady Anna herself knew that something had been wrong with her daughter's life: ever since the day she had seen her maniacally attempt to skate more than three feet across the botanical gardens of their backyard. "The child is lonely!" she thought to herself in astonishment, thinking of the governess and the multitudes of velvet and lace cousins. Children had always appeared as ideas to Lady Anna, whose primary acquaintanceship with them came from the tapestries of her family's old mansion; in the aged, beige borders, they sat at the feet of harpsichords, at the voluminous skirts of women she had always assumed to be their mothers, busy with a book or a doll or staring idly in happy bafflement at the splendrous world around them. Lady Anna's own parents had been almost as intellectually preoccupied as her husband, and when she was once asked, by a young social historian, to give a particular account of her childhood, she immediately assumed her furrowed, intelligent look, and, after much thought, said with an indescribable expression of genuine discovery: "Why I don't believe I had one!"

When Abigail had arrived, Lady Anna had been grateful to the child for having completed the passage without annihilating either her life or her tulip-stalk figure; after that, she held the child after Miss Fenwick pinned heavy linen antimacassars over the front of her embroidered dresses. The child's crying upset Lady Anna, not because the child might be unhappy, but because the crying, as did the spitting up, the changing of the diapers, so unlike the Changing of the Guard, completely upset her ideas of the delicacy and beauty of childhood, the divine mission of women, which was to take care of the divine cherubs. "Where are the clouds of glory she trails?" Lady Anna wailed to Winnie, her sister. "Is she supposed to look like this?" Winnie gave her sister a look, which implied that she had taken leave of her senses to even think she, of all people, could expect her to answer such a question. "What is the matter with the dear child?" Winnie asked finally. "Influenza." "Influenza," said Winnie. "Not as interesting as consumption, but a great deal less worrisome, I must say." Lady Anna looked forward to the time when Abigail would turn suddenly into a version of Winnie, an intelligent, self-sufficient creature with whom she could intelligently converse. It never occurred to her, as the simplest things never occurred to her husband, that as Abigail aged, so too would she, and that the nature of the aging process would in itself cause them to differ, those she knew questing for the family tree which had its roots in the veins of Adam and Eve, her own daughter questing for the golden bagel and the potent, grace-giving skate key.

Still, Anna was disturbed by her daughter's attempts to skate among the rhododendrons, especially when she saw her fall into a peach-and-purple rosebush, cross-bred especially for the family, and named for them. Anna watched her as she sat, awkward and crying on a patch of emerald grass, pulling thorn after thorn from her arms and legs, then from her lovely seersucker dress, in which she looked like a Gainsborough painting, and very evidently having no intention in the world of asking for help or sympathy. Lady Anna resolved to pay a visit to the governess' room, although she had always held that the servants, especially those who were practically household fixtures, had an inviolable right to privacy, perhaps an even greater right than that of their masters. She knocked at Miss Fenwick's paneled door like a guilty thief. "Come in," Miss Fenwick called in her timid voice. It took Lady Anna's eyes moments to find her, located as she was in a corner of her great room, the walls of which were completely covered by bucolic scenes, centaurs and unicorns frolicking among kings and queens and princesses on lawns which spread out in front of mountains, picnicking on splendid Oriental carpets which had been brought out to protect the sanctity of the ladies' hems. Mr. Jennings-Smith had permitted her to choose the style of her murals, and she had chosen these paintings, which resembled, unfortunately to Mr. Jennings-Smith, although he said nothing about it, the Fragonard he so hated. "Ahem," Lady Anna began, feeling like a schoolgirl called up for violating the cardinal rule of her headmistress. Miss Fenwick looked up from her bed, which was entirely covered with buttons. There must have been several hundred of them, perhaps even a thousand; it was impossible to count. She had the air of a frightened squirrel. "My hobby, my lady," she stammered, caught in the act: "it has always been my ambition to create a magnificent tapestry from these buttons and present them to your ladyship and the master before I . . ." she broke off, coughing delicately. Lady Anna had long ago given over her attempts to induce normal American forms of address into Miss Fenwick's speech. She was momentarily thrown off balance, largely due to the fact that she was beginning to imagine, against her better judgment, her husband's reaction to a huge, infinitely life-consuming tapestry of buttons. Whenever possible, Lady Anna imagined nothing, since she had long ago concluded that the fewer expectations she had, the less she was likely to be disappointed. She minded disturbances very much. "Having great expectations," she had once told her poor daughter who was trying to write an essay for school, "was poor Pip's mistake." She refused to entertain any other explanation for his difficulties.

"My daughter," Anna began, "appears quite definitely lonely." "Oh, Lady Anna," the governess cried, "I spend every waking moment with her," and she looked wildly around the room as if she had somehow overlooked Abigail's presence, "but she will go off on her own sometimes." "She appears to have no friends of her own, especially not of her own age," Lady Anna persevered remarkably, since it had been some time since she had thought so long on any one topic: "I *seem* to remember," she said, crinkling her nose and racking her brain, "that I had *some* when I was her age. Surely I had *one*." "I wouldn't know, my lady." "I certainly did," Anna retorted insulted; "something must be the matter." "Perhaps it is the school," the governess whispered, feeling like Oliver Cromwell faced by King Charles; "I do not believe she likes it. The children are rough and dirty and do not understand her. None of them will speak to her." Lady Anna sank down on the tufted velvet chair near the door, but the back of her head struck a carved rose and this brought her out of her paralysis. "Why, then, she should certainly not be there." "It may seem so to *us*, my lady," Miss Fenwick said in a conspiratorial voice, "but you know the theories of the master. And this could not be a worse time for discussing it. He has been at John Stuart Mill again, and lately nothing will do but the original papers of the founding fathers." Anna remained transfixed. "The buttons are magnificent," she finally murmured; "I am astonished you have time to find them." "Abigail finds them, your ladyship. She says it is her only hobby," whereupon Miss Fenwick jabbed herself with her needle, emitted a little squeak, and fell silent. "I shall have to talk to her father," Lady Anna said querulously. "That might be just the thing," Miss Fenwick said, industriously licking her bloody finger. "Dear!" Lady Anna said again, and stood for some time on the parquet of the second-floor landing, gazing up at the door to her husband's study and its gigantic brass knocker in the shape of a lion, the knocker itself being the mane which lifted from the head and fell back into place against the door with a terrible crash. Lady Anna had always thought it a ridiculous thing.

"Charles, put down the book," Lady Anna said unceremoniously, entering without knocking. She knew the waste preliminaries involved. "It appears Abigail is most unhappy in P.S. 206." "Unhappy?" His eyes were still flickering over the pages like rapacious, slightly senile moths. "Unhappy, unhappy. The other children will not talk to her and she is lonely." "My dear Anna,"

Mr. Jennings-Smith said, "Abigail was sent to P.S. 206 precisely so that she might know trials and tribulations which we were spared. It was our privileged position which put us in our places like fruits in a gelled mold; she must suffer to be superior; she must become acquainted with the world as it is. Thomas Jefferson himself has this to say . . ." and he picked up a heavy peeling leather tome. "Charles," Anna interrupted, "she is not getting to know the world around her; the world around her will not talk to her. It only ignores her. She spends all of her time collecting buttons for Miss Fenwick, who intends to present them to you on a tapestry." "What do I need with buttons?" he asked, completely distracted. "She must be sent to a school where she will have friends," Lady Anna insisted, the old bulldog of her childhood taking possession of her; she held to the bone. "I am sorry, *Mrs.* Jennings-Smith," her husband said, as he always did when he wanted to remind her as delicately as possible to whom she owed her current style of life, "the subject is permanently closed." "You will have the sole responsibility when the disastrous consequences begin to become apparent." "My dear Cassandra," he answered, now thoroughly vexed, "I have never in my entire life undertaken any action whatsoever which could in any manner thinkable perpetuate disastrous consequences." "Is that your last word?" Lady Anna asked, but apparently it was, since Mr. Jennings-Smith had definitely returned to his perusal of Thomas Jefferson.

But for Anna the subject was not closed. She now definitely remembered that she had had a friend as a child and that the child's name was Eleanora. She consulted with Winnie. "Perhaps you ought to spend more time with her," Winnie suggested thoughtfully; "I remember mothers in some of our families did that." "I don't remember anything like that," Anna puzzled. Nevertheless, she resolved to talk to Abigail. "Abigail, dear, come talk to me," she said over tea in her sweetest and what she imagined to be her most maternal voice. Abigail looked up in terror and the little demitasse cup dropped from her hand into her white raw silk lap. "What have I done, Momma?" she quavered as they went into her mother's sitting room. "Nothing, my dear, nothing; how can you imagine anything of the kind? Can't a mother want to talk to her own daughter?" Abigail, who privately thought this impossible, looked furtively around the room, wondering where to sit. The etiquette of her mother's sitting room was as foreign to her as the many carved knives and forks would have been to one of her schoolmates. "Make yourself comfortable," her mother ordered cheerfully. A huge crystal chandelier hung in the vaulted recesses of the ceiling. Persian carpets covered the walls and the floor; all the furniture was deep red, and the companion pieces were covered in striped pink and white silk, each stripe bearing a design of tiny roses in all colors, so subtly woven into the fabric that much inspection was required to find them. Case after mahogany case held antique dolls. Abigail was less familiar with this room than her father's, but there was a similarity. She finally decided it had to do with her mother's antique dolls, which had the same stiff, awkward poses as the figures in the Bayeux tapestry. "Well, what shall we talk about?" her mother said cheerfully; "how is your roller skating?" Abigail, who thought her mother knew nothing of her attempts, turned darker than the walls. "Well, perhaps I should talk first," Anna said; "I feel particularly chattery today." Abigail sat still, wondering if her mother had taken leave of her senses. For some time, she had been aware that both her parents seemed to have taken leave of the century.

"Your Aunt Winnie and I are, as you know, twins," she began comfortably. Once having shaken herself like the family's old red setter, Anna rather enjoyed the new maternal role. "We were so beautiful we caused quite a problem for our mother, and worse for the governess, Butler, because she could never tell us apart. We were always together. With one exception," she carefully noted. "When Winnie had the chicken pox, we were not together. She had been engaged to your father, you know, but then she came down with the chicken pox, and poor Charles became very lonesome, especially since he was reading Milton and the joys of a family seemed very important and it was, naturally, impossible to have a family without a wife. Charles was clearer on things then. So Winnie wound up with one small scar on her knee, and I wound up with Charles. Everyone said it would never have happened if I hadn't been so beautiful, but there it was." "Didn't Aunt Winnie mind?" "Mind? For about a week she minded. Then she got involved in some Oxford group and a theory of celibacy and she swore she would never marry. When she married your dead Uncle Ian—of course, he was alive then—she thought the whole idea of marriage was a bit silly, and always seemed a little embarrassed by it. I remember she hated to show her engagement ring to anyone, but would stick it out under their noses, turning her head in the other direction. And Ian loved to travel, which is how Winnie has become such a great traveler. Your father says it is all wasted on her since she has no mind at all, and is nothing better than a camera; no, he said she was worse than a camera. He said she was like a camera without film." With a fine sense of having done her duty, Anna delicately bit into a miniature éclair.

"Do you mean," Abigail asked slowly, "that if Aunt Winnie hadn't gotten the chicken pox, she would have married Father?" "Exactly," Anna said, finishing the éclair off. "Of course, he wouldn't have married either of us if we hadn't been so beautiful." "I would be her daughter," Abigail mused. "No dear," Anna corrected, "you would not exist at all. Winnie was determined to avoid the seed-pod state, as she called pregnancy. I honestly think your father would have found it necessary to chain her to a wall for nine months to make her go through with it." "If it weren't for a case of the chicken pox, I wouldn't be here." "*And* how beautiful we were," Anna cut in, an edge of annoyance sheathing her voice. Abigail, who knew the inevitability of chicken pox, decided the blame for her existence must therefore rest entirely on her mother's beauty. At that moment, destiny came to seem a terrible thing to her. If it had not been for her mother's beauty, which Winnie merely mirrored, she would not exist. Beauty could be controlled. Her own beauty could be controlled. It was her mother's beauty which had made her the daughter of Charles Alexander

Jennings-Smith and which prevented her from understanding bagels and skate keys and had destined her to lonely years standing alone in a corner of the schoolyard like a beautiful discarded mannequin. She thought of Miss Fenwick, in whose life nothing more exciting happened than the arrival of a new button, and the possibility of a fateless life, an eventless life, presented itself to her as a crystal case for a magnificent, life-size doll.

She asked Miss Fenwick about her youth. "Please do not mention it," Miss Fenwick pleaded, genuinely disturbed, scattering buttons all over her rug; "it is something we all have to sit through, like those dreadful sermons." "But something worthwhile must have happened," Abigail insisted. "I fell in love," Miss Fenwick admitted; "it was quite the thing for a while, much like visiting the planetarium. Then it became a perpetual state of seasickness. Furthermore, it made me a governess."

"What were you before?"

"Before? An actress. But a seasick actress on the boards is a disaster in anyone's company, even the Queen's."

"You could have gone back to your family."

"In those days, daughters of good families did not go on the stage or they were disowned; not known, as they said. It was quite the thing to be disowned as a success, quite another as a failure. I would rather have my leg amputated than fall in love again."

Abigail sat at the foot of her couch, waiting for more. "I do not wish to discuss it," the governess said in her trembly voice, which had returned at the end of her last sentence; "the Lady Anna wishes me to tell you that she and your Aunt Winnie have planned several outings for you. I believe the first is to the Botanic Garden." "Why are they doing this?" Abigail wailed desperately. "Come, come, they are only broadening your horizons." "Why is she called Winnie?" Abigail asked, noticing night begin to encroach on the panorama in the window. "I believe it has something to do with a horse," the governess said.

The next day, Abigail, Lady Anna, and her Aunt Winnie started for the Botanic Garden so early that Miss Fenwick wondered aloud if it would even be open. "How could it be closed?" Lady Anna asked in astonishment; "it's a garden, you see, not a museum," whereupon Miss Fenwick pointed out that the garden was surrounded by heavy iron gates to keep out the very sort of vandals P.S. 206 had been filled with, and Lady Anna led her daughter off, shaking her head in its usual cloud of bewilderment.

The garden was in full spring bloom. The magnolias' pink flesh had thickened as if it were sated with blood; the white cherry trees were fluttering their torn wares of white lace. There were hardly any people in the garden. This puzzled Lady Anna, since it was almost nine-thirty, and, as a child, their outings had always begun at sunrise. Abigail felt uncomfortable in the garden, and had never liked visiting it, especially on field trips from the public school; now, however, the source of her discomfort was identifiable. Lady Anna had finally found a modern camera she could cope with, a fully automatic Polaroid, and she and Winnie had posed themselves in front of a giant magnolia, leaning in toward one another like two cut tulips whose stems had begun to bend. It was their resemblance to the very plants they had come to admire that struck her so forcibly. Abigail snapped the picture. "You didn't hold your hand over the lens, did you, dear?" her mother inquired solicitously. It was not often she made such enterprising attempts, and she wanted a record of it for Charles Alexander, who, perhaps, for once would not spend his day feeling so superior.

"There's quite a clot of people over there," Winnie said, pointing toward the main building. "You have an unfortunate taste for expressions," Lady Anna grimaced, but followed her sister's glance. Neither of them would point. A large group, boiling about strange, heavy pieces of mechanical equipment, had arranged itself in front of a cedar picket fence, along which the boughs of a flowering plant had been arranged in the shape of a Japanese cherry. "The Japanese garden," Abigail informed them dutifully. "Well, there is quite a fuss; I think we should look into it," Winnie announced, starting off in her simple Balenciaga frock, which she nevertheless managed to wear in a manner suggesting the additional presence of an invisible, though necessary parasol. Lady Anna started after her. Abigail followed. Lady Anna looked back over her shoulder. "The child positively *slinks*," she whispered to Winnie; "I do hope no one behind the bushes takes it into his head to rape her." "My dear sister, Abigail is completely unaware of her slinkiness. If any man whatever approached her, she would squeak like a frightened white mouse. I don't know how it happens, but men always sense such things." Winnie was genuinely an expert in such matters, and although Lady Anna had no idea of how such things were possible, she decided to take her word for it. After all, whether what Winnie said made the slightest sense or not, still it was very comforting, as was usually the case with her utterances, based as they were on some mysterious source of knowledge of the real world. "Terrible, the rash of kidnappings lately," Winnie said idly; they were proceeding along in their stately manner, Abigail, unaware of her own movements, following like a swan. She, herself, felt more of a tugboat. "Charles says it is to be expected," Lady Anna began in a rather mechanical voice of a braille reader recording for the blind; "every so many years, I forget how many, the poor experience a revulsion against the rich and some sort of protest ensues. Charles has pointed out that the kidnappings have involved only the very rich." "Spare me Charles," Winnie commanded, "and spare me those horrid details. We are not exactly poverty cases, Annie my love." "Don't call me Annie," her mother reprimanded. They were now on the fringe of the "mob."

"Whatever is going on?" Winnie asked a young man whose long hair hung to his shoulders and lapped unaesthetically over his beard and drooping mustache. "Commercial, lady," he answered, peering into the depths of his machine. "The distance is all off," he bellowed to another furry creature nearer the fence, causing the three ladies to jump backward, startled. "Commercial?" Winnie pursued him; "I believed 'commercial' was an adjective." "You're putting me on," the russet-colored man answered. "Young man, answer me," Winnie ordered in her most regal manner, "what is 'commercial'?" "We're filming a commercial for television." "Oh, one of those things you use to persuade people to buy all kinds of deadly objects," Winnie sighed, relieved of the suspense. "Something like that," the young man muttered through his mustache, peering into the tiny black aperture. "Atrocious manners," Winnie commented in an undertone to Lady Anna, who nodded her head as if a giant hat with an ostrich feather fluttered upon it. The young man smiled into his machine. Suddenly, a huge, bearish man, resembling nothing so much as an Arab marketeer, was running sweatily toward them. "Just what we need," he bellowed, grabbing Winnie by the wrist. "Detach me," Winnie replied, shaking his hand off hers like a wet leaf; "just what you need for what?" "You and your sister," he gasped, his big belly heaving under its Hawaiian print shirt; "this ad's for Tetley tea. The idea's to make it look good as English tea." "Impossible," Winnie said flatly. "Oh no," the man insisted; "not if you and your sister are drinking it." "Do you mean," Winnie said slowly, "you are asking us to appear on *television*," she gasped, realization diving into her throat like a bird, "on *television*, in a *commercial?*"

"Charles would not like it," Lady Anna said.

"Charles would not know about it," said Winnie. "Simply cut the plug to the television, and he will grumble about modern things, and switch on to his Atwater Kent."

"Are you going to do it or not?" panted the swarthy man in the red, green, and yellow shirt.

"I believe we will just do it," Lady Anna said. "Abigail, dear, stand back with the others." The swarthy man, whom others were calling Bill, began to pull Winnie toward the fence by her wrist, but catching sight of her eyes, thought better of it. "This way, ladies," he said. "*That* is better," Lady Anna said severely. "A *commercial*," Winnie smiled. Abigail, who was moving backward into the crowd, realized she had hardly ever seen either of them smile. She decided to try a smile herself. "Well, hello," a

bearded young man next to her said. Abigail promptly erased the
smile from her face, and moved farther back. Bill, whoever he
was, was arranging Winnie and her mother in front of the cedar
fence. In front of them was an old-fashioned, but newly painted,
white wicker table and two white wicker chairs. An elaborate English tea set reflected the pink blossoms in its silver surface. Bill
presented each of the ladies a tiny Imari cup. "Now," he commanded, "one of you pretend to drink while the other pretends to
talk; but don't move your lips." Both Anna and Winnie raised the
cups simultaneously. "I'll drink," Anna volunteered. "Perhaps we
should taste it first," Winnie said; "it is, after all, a *commercial*."
"Let's get going," Bill shouted, upon hearing this. "Besides," he
said, turning to Winnie, "we don't have any tea. We don't want it
spilled all over the place; you can't taste it." "It would have been
more ethical," Winnie informed him patiently. "All right, try it."
Anna raised the cup; Winnie leaned into her as if she were in the
middle of saying something. "Great, got it," Bill shouted.
"Shoot," he bellowed at someone behind him.

At that command, a thin young man with a blond crew cut and
brilliant blue eyes rushed from the crowd in blue jeans and a blue
denim jacket. It took everyone a long moment to realize that he
did indeed intend to shoot, having a gun in his left hand, on which
the sunlight glinted ominously, blue-black. Winnie and Anna, who
were absorbed in their pantomime, never looked up. Abigail was
too astonished to speak. However, the muscles in the back of her
knees stiffened, just as they always had when she realized she was
about to be thrown from a horse. "Free the poor! Free the poor!"
the young man was shouting, and there were loud explosive
sounds. Winnie sank to the lawn first, and then Anna followed her
like another leaf. The tips of Anna's fingers held on to the tip of
Winnie's long skirt. "Oh my god, my god, my god," Abigail heard
the russet-colored young man repeating over and over again; "oh
my god, my god, my god." He had his hand over his mouth and his
eyes were roundly open; he looked like an infant with false
whiskers. Abigail stared at him. "Mother!" she screamed suddenly,

"Mother!" "Find the daughter!" Bill was shouting. "Get the police! Where are the police?" People were scattering in all directions, but the man in the blue denim outfit was nowhere to be
seen. Abigail felt someone's hand on her arm; Bill was half-
dragging her to one of the white wicker chairs. "Don't sit her there,
she might be a target," someone shouted. "Target, don't be ridiculous," he said. "Where are the police? She looks too American middle-class to be a target." There was the sound of an
ambulance screaming in the background, but almost immediately,
the sound merged with the shrieks of sirens. Abigail sat still on the
chair. Her mother and her aunt lay on the ground like two flowers
among flowers. Drops of salt water fell passively out of her eyes,
watering the stretch of lawn they lay on. In her father's manner,
Abigail mentally noted that salt water was not good for plants.

Men in white were rushing up with stretchers. "Dead," one of
them said, tucking the stethoscope back in his pocket. "Both?"
Abigail asked. "For Christ's sake, didn't you see all the blood? Of
course they're both dead." It was true. Thick puddles of red had
matted the grass, caking it and gluing it down. A chauffeured limousine was driving right over the lawns and through the tulip bed
toward them. "Get that man out of there," someone began
screaming, running after the car with a rake. "It's my father,"
Abigail told the man in the Hawaiian shirt. The car braked in the
middle of a bed of daffodils. Mr. Jennings-Smith got out slowly,
leaning heavily on the silver tip of his ebony cane. "Abigail, my
dear," he said calmly, "get in the car. Doctor Stuyvesant-Dale is
there. He wants to have a look at you." "I want to go home by
subway," Abigail said, shocking herself. Her father went over to
the car, and the doctor came out. "Nothing wrong with her," he
pronounced, shaking his head. "How did you know about it?"
Abigail asked her father. "The television," said Mr. Jennings-
Smith; "I have always said," he went on slowly, as if these were the
words he wanted carved on his tombstone, "there is too much vio-
lence on television. Both of them?" he asked the swarthy man, who
was still shepherding Abigail. "Both," the man answered. "Both,"

her father repeated, as if this were the most incredible thing in the world, as if this put the royal seal on the tragedy: "Both." "Can she go home alone?" Bill asked Doctor Stuyvesant-Dale. "I don't see why not," the doctor answered, "but then I don't see why, either," he trailed off, puzzled. His main concern was Mr. Jennings-Smith, whose eyes were shedding a skinny stream of tears, tracking their way through the powdery covering of his chin like General Sherman's troops on their march to Atlanta. The two men got back in the back seat of the Rolls-Royce. Abigail saw her father lean forward and say something into the horn which communicated with the driver. She remembered that the horn had to be specially ordered. Her father, for his part, stared at her as the car backed away; there she was, almost a replica of her mother, five feet four inches tall, her Chinese black hair falling straight to the back of her beautiful knees, its blue-black glints mysteriously shining, her light green eyes catching the light like a cat's, her high cheekbones, which in his youth had always reminded him of captive Indian maidens. Abigail's color was now what it always was; her skin was deadly pale but along the line of her cheekbones she was high-colored, so that she seemed perpetually rouged. "Both," her father whispered to himself again, as the car stopped backing through the daffodils and began swinging around to drive forward through the tulips.

"I will have to let Miss Fenwick go," Abigail thought to herself, going over to the first park bench and sitting down on its gray wooden slats, "although perhaps it would be best if she first finished her button tapestry for Father." A warm breeze lifted the top layer of her hair and ruffled the frills on the bodice of her short dress. "Well, that was really terrible," a deep voice said next to her. "What was?" Abigail asked, turning to look at the voice, which belonged to a tall, spiritual-looking young man, who, in spite of his emaciated look, was exceptionally handsome. "Shelley," Abigail thought to herself, "that's what Shelley must have looked like." She looked nervously at the two rubberized containers that rested against his end of the bench, and on which he kept his right arm. "A guitar, and fencing foils," he said, following her look. "The shooting was terrible," the young man said; "I don't care how rich and stupid those two dames were, they shouldn't have shot them." "Only one person shot them," Abigail pointed out, "and, moreover, they were not stupid. They merely vegetated. In point of fact, they were extremely intelligent. Who are you?" "Rob Dillman; don't start shrieking with excitement and tearing my clothes." "Why on earth should I do that?" Abigail asked dully. "You're kidding," he said, peering into her face; "you really don't know who I am?" "You're Rob Dillman," Abigail repeated. "The famous folk singer whose picture was on the cover of *Time* magazine last week," he said pettishly. "Oh, I'm sorry," Abigail said politely, staring at the cedar fence, "we only get the *Times Literary Supplement*. And," she added, "sometimes the *London Magazine*." "Who are *you*?" Rob Dillman asked, as if he were questioning a Martian.

"I am Abigail Ida Jennings-Smith, and my family came over on the *Mayflower*; I don't know a thing about bagels and skate keys, in fact, most of the twentieth century, and since most of my family was just this minute shot, I would prefer if you skipped telling me how crazy I am or giving me the standard lecture on how cushioned my life has been and how it should have been otherwise."

"You talk like something out of a book."

"I usually do not talk at all."

"Well, that's comforting."

"Why is that comforting?"

"Because you're making an exception for me."

"It's not you I'm making an exception for," Abigail said carefully; "I'm making an exception for my mother and my Aunt Winnie. You see they were shot in a war to get me to lead a normal life; in other words, to get me to talk. They had gotten it through their heads that someone my age ought to have at least one friend."

"And don't you?" asked Rob Dillman.

"No."

"I see."

"I'm sure you do not," Abigail said in a bored voice.

"What makes you think you've cornered the market on strange situations?" the thin young man answered her. "When you're as famous as I am, you never know whether you have any friends either. I, for example, have not been sure I have a single friend since I was on the cover of *Time* magazine."

"Why on earth should that make a difference?"

"Because I'm not sure why people like me anymore."

"At least you knew they liked you before."

"I wasn't so sure then either."

Abigail was exhausted from this long conversation and couldn't think of anything else to say. She had a strong impulse to pick up a strand of her hair and begin gnawing on it, but this had been absolutely forbidden to her since early childhood. Instead, she stared straight ahead at the cedar fence. "The killing was terrible," the young man said again. "Especially since it was my mother and aunt," Abigail answered. "*Your* mother and aunt," Rob Dillman said astounded, for he had up until this minute apparently missed the point of her lethargic remarks. "God! You're going to be on the cover of all the papers." "How perfectly marvelous," Abigail said, suddenly exhausted. "You sound a little English," Rob Dillman said. "I am." "So am I," he confessed, reddening. "But you told me you were a famous American folk singer," Abigail put in; the conversation, at least, was giving her a momentary sense of continuity. Rob Dillman blushed. "I'm not; I'm English. I learned an American accent from a speech teacher when I found out where the money was; I figured there was no point competing with the Beatles. Actually," and here he blushed red as a rose, "my father is the Right Honorable Sylvester Dolittle." "I never heard of such a preposterous thing," Abigail commented, falling silent. "No one else knows I'm English," Rob said coaxingly. Abigail remained entirely indifferent. "You're the only one." She sat still as stone. Rob leaned back on the bench and studied her. "You know who you remind me of?" he asked. "You remind me of a poster of Mucha's; it's called Job. It's an advertisement for Job cigarettes," he repeated. "I look like the lady?" Abigail asked. "Just like her." "I find that hard to believe." "Nevertheless," he said. "Then the woman on the poster looks like my mother and aunt. Did you know," Abigail asked, "my mother and aunt were twins, and my father would have married my aunt if she hadn't gotten the chicken pox?" "I certainly never knew that," Rob Dillman said solemnly. "And that no one ever played with me in the playground at P.S. 206?" "Nope." "Hmmmmm." Abigail considered. "Look," he said, "why don't you come home with me?" "I don't want any children," Abigail said bluntly. "You must have heard something in that playground," he said. "Well, it's about time," Abigail agreed, and docilely followed Rob through the gardens to a shiny motorcycle chained to the cast-iron fence. "I don't have another crash helmet," he apologized. "It doesn't make any difference," she assured him.

"Let's go to my real place," he suggested, and, since Abigail didn't say anything, he directed his motorcycle onto the highway and then into the Manhattan streets, finally stopping in front of a magnificent four-story townhouse on Park Avenue and East Fifty-ninth Street. "My hippie apartment," he told Abigail sheepishly. The townhouse was furnished entirely with French provincial furniture and antiques, none of which were of later vintage than the eighteenth century; real manuscript pages (with illuminated margins) were framed on the walls; sheepskins covered the walls of the library. "This is ridiculous, you're a fraud," Abigail murmured, her sense of decorum violated; but then something happened, and she found herself amused. It was a new feeling, but not unpleasant.

"Twins run in my family," Abigail reminded Rob ominously as they crossed the threshold to his bedroom, which resembled nothing so much as a recording studio. "Well, instead of hopping into bed," Rob said in an aggrieved voice, "why don't we talk to each other?" "I told you, I don't know how to talk." "Then we'll watch television," he said. "I've never done that." He promptly turned on a huge color television and busied himself tuning in Bugs Bunny. "Who is Bugs Bunny?" Abigail asked with some semblance of curiosity. "Who is Bugs Bunny? *Who* is Bugs Bunny?" he repeated incredulously; "Bugs Bunny is . . ." and he began giving Abigail a lecture on the whole stable of Walt Disney movies, and when he found out she had not seen *Snow White*, much less *Pinocchio*, he began frantically rummaging through the *Village Voice*. "None of them is playing this week," he announced tragically, "but *The Cabinet of Doctor Caligari* is." At that moment, a beautiful love affair was born. Rob Dillman was absolutely sure that Abigail loved him for himself alone, since he had quickly discovered that her fortune was (in relation to hers) the beanstalk next to which his was a mere hill of beans, and he discovered something he had long lacked: a sense of purpose. Abigail, he soon discovered, was ignorant of the twentieth century. Without knowing it, Abigail was presenting Rob with what he most needed: a nineteenth-century woman, whose only desire was to sit at the feet of the man she had chosen, or who had chosen her. She was a childish variant of Eve before the apple, soaking up all the information denied her all her life: nothing more nor less than the entire century in which she lived. Never having heard a word about sex, Abigail had contracted no ideas about it, and hence no problems; she had a dim recollection of her father's calling this new activity "the most natural of functions." And so it seemed to her. If there was a sign of trouble in the relationship it was to be found in the fact that Abigail never left the townhouse without Rob, and seemed to have become transformed into a modern-day Rapunzel, existing on the fourth floor, letting down her hair only for the prince of the Botanic Garden. Rob himself was now more secure than he had ever been, sure that he had a real friend, which was, after all, what he had needed Abigail for. He saw to it that she called her father daily; he observed the peculiarity of her father's lack of interest in her whereabouts; he brought her food; he took care of her. Meanwhile, he continued his previous daily routine, while Abigail read steadily, and when she tired of reading, watched "Bugs Bunny," and "Star Trek," and "The Mod Squad," and "The Rookies," "All in the Family," and "Maude." She had a growing conviction of her own existence; she was learning the meaning of the heretofore theoretical word "happy." On the day when she was absolutely sure she could define happiness, or at least nod with conviction at the sound of the word, she was watching the ninth episode of "The Forsyte Saga" when Rob walked in. "You might try some of the soap operas," Rob suggested, and immediately Abigail knew something was amiss. Such instructions as to how she should spend her day were always offered in the morning. She sat up straighter on the bed. "Abby," he began. "Abby," he said slightly louder; "I'm into something else." "Into?" Abigail asked, looking at him as if he were wearing a new suit.

"I mean there's something else I want to try." "What?" she asked.

"Being gay," he said.

"I thought you were gay."

"I mean gay like in homosexual."

"Oh," Abigail said. "You mean you want a boy in this room instead of a girl. I mean a woman. I mean me. Me." "That's more or less it," Rob agreed. "Oh," Abigail said again. "Whenever you say oh," Rob said with some exasperation, "you sound just like Little Orphan Annie when Daddy Warbucks offers her something outrageous like a continent. There's this big balloon over her head, and all it says is 'Oh.'" "Who is Mister Warbucks?" "Daddy Warbucks," Rob said resignedly, and patiently began to explain. "I see," said Abigail, who had been crying throughout the entire explanation; "I had better go back to Father's." "That might not be a bad idea," Rob agreed. "No," Abigail said; "all I ever really wanted was to lead a nice, peaceful life where nothing ever happened." "Well, you might have had more luck if you weren't so damn beautiful," he said. "It runs in my family," Abigail said, still crying; "would you please call me a cab?" "I'll send you with my chauffeur; the car has bulletproof windows." "If you don't mind," Abigail said politely, "I would like to avoid limousines as long as possible. I am rather allergic to them." "I'm sorry, Abby," Rob said again. "It isn't your fault," she said. "It's a matter of destiny. You are not responsible for my face or my body. Up until now, what has happened has been the sole responsibility of my mother and father." "I don't understand what you're talking about," he sniffed. "You don't have to," Abigail sighed.

At home, Miss Fenwick and Charles Jennings-Smith were at first concerned about Abigail's state of mind; she had stopped eating entirely, and appeared to be painted on a pane of glass. She seemed to waft in and out of rooms as if doors were, for her, an unnecessary encumbrance. Gradually, however, it became evident to both of them that Abigail was intensely concentrating on something, and Mr. Jennings-Smith, who valued nothing so highly as concentration, instructed the entire household staff to leave her undisturbed. "She gives me the creeps," the gardener's son commented to his mother, whereupon he was cruelly whacked upon the bottom. "She *does* give me the creeps," he screamed, flying into the kitchen, slamming the door as loudly as possible after him.

The kitchen staff noticed the change in Miss Abigail first. Instead of sending blank menus back to the kitchen for Cook, she sent down lists that resembled miniature grocery orders for the entire mansion. Three servants were needed to carry up the heavy silver trays, and most of the trays came back down picked bare. At first Cook thought Abigail was throwing food out of the windows for the garden birds, or perhaps had a pet in hiding, but it gradually began to dawn on her that Miss Abigail was eating every morsel of the food herself. Since she refused to leave her room, however, the results of this change in her habits were not yet apparent.

On the first day of winter, one of the maids heard Miss Abigail's suite door opening. An odd-looking figure dressed in a discarded bathrobe of Mr. Jennings-Smith appeared on the landing. "Please call Miss Fenwick," she ordered. Miss Fenwick was duly summoned and set to work sewing an entirely new wardrobe for Miss Abigail, who was now almost a size twenty-six; news of this transformation soon percolated like the smell of coffee through the entire household. Everyone was consumed by curiosity. Miss Fenwick's dismay was greatly modulated by the fact that at last she had a use for her multitudinous buttons and endless hoards of fabrics. Miss Abigail wanted most of her clothes made of upholstery fabric or bold hopsacking patterns, and in the style of shirtwaists, reasoning that these would help make her as unattractive as possible. Finally, she came downstairs. Miss Abigail had been transformed from a glowing teenager on the brink of womanhood into an enormous middle-aged figure whose consistency was that of unbaked cookie dough. Her green eyes were sunk behind her chipmunk cheeks, whose high color now covered the cheek area like two blotches. "I am going to the movies," she informed Miss Fenwick, and the other astounded members of the staff; "and, on the way back," she said, looking at her watch, "I believe I will have time to find a pair of sensible shoes and a good sturdy bag. Don't worry about me if I am late; I may have to stop off for something to eat."

The eating had not begun to taper. Miss Abigail was apparently determined to reach her goal, which, she confided to Miss Fenwick, was a round four hundred pounds. When Miss Fenwick wailed that she would be a monster, monstrous, everyone would stare in horror, Miss Abigail smiled with satisfaction. Finally, even Mr. Jennings-Smith decided to take the matter up with his daughter. Her heavy tread was heard approaching his door. "My dear Abigail," he began, "about this matter of your weight . . ." "Father," Abigail cut him off, "my weight is for the greatest good. I consider it something of an iceberg which has frozen a ship or a prehistoric animal inside it. There it remains, perfectly preserved, and because of the skin of the iceberg, absolutely immovable and virtually immortal, impregnable, you might say." Mr. Jennings-

Smith decided this answer required some thought, and made no objection when his daughter excused herself for what cook noticed was her ninth mid-afternoon snack. "And, Father," she said as an afterthought, returning to the room, "I think I may soon begin to travel; it's a bit early to consider it, but I do think I would like to travel considerably. As Aunt Winnie did." At this, Mr. Jennings-Smith was so flabbergasted he put down his book and stared at the blank door for several minutes. Meanwhile, Miss Abigail continued eating, her first journey apparently up the scale to four hundred pounds. But Miss Fenwick noted, as did others, that suitcase after suitcase was arriving from the department stores for her consideration, and finally, Miss Fenwick saw her telephone a number which she had already seen listed on Miss Abigail's pad: Mr. Foote: luggage, custom-made.

It was not long after Abigail had finally seen the red needle waver and settle, like a compass needle pointing north, at the figure 400 on the special scale that she had made for her, that she began to pack Mr. Foote's custom-made luggage. Miss Fenwick, who was slowly becoming aware of Miss Abigail's intention to leave her behind, and, in fact, of traveling without a companion altogether, braved her large ex-charge in her dressing room. Abigail, as was her custom, rose to greet her. "Abigail, my dear," Miss Fenwick quavered resolutely, "I'm not quite sure how to say this, but you do decidedly ripple." Miss Abigail considered Miss Fenwick over her quadruple chins; Miss Fenwick was dressed in one of the Lady Anna's favorite garments, all of which had been turned over to her as a token of her long service to the family, and with a nip here and a bit of pruning there, they fit her trellis-like presence rather well. "A ripple?" Abigail repeated incredulously; "a *ripple?* I should be satisfied with nothing less than an earthquake." "Your stomach does rather *hang*," Miss Fenwick persevered, on whom responsibility had fallen like old leaves since the Lady Anna's death. "I consider myself a living version of the hanging gardens of Babylon," Miss Abigail said with satisfaction. "Why," she said with pride, lifting it up, "look at my arm. It waves; it absolutely waves. The skin hangs like a flag." "Flags are for countries," Miss Fenwick responded absently. "Well, this is the flag of *my* country," Miss Abigail said, undulating the sheet of flesh under her arm once more. "And have you noticed my ankles?" she continued with the air of a connoisseur; "the flesh absolutely *droops* over the tops of my shoes like melted wax." "*Miss Abigail*," the governess interrupted, "I do not want to hear another word of this. You are teasing me, and I do not like it at all." If someone had jeered at her button tapestry, now verging on completion, she could not have been more outraged. "Well, perhaps a little," Abigail conceded, "but really, I am quite proud of myself. It is no small achievement." She could not help but smile at her own unconscious wit. Miss Fenwick drew herself up straight like a brittle twig. "Miss Abigail," she said firmly, "if you will excuse me. Your mother, the Lady Anna, would have been shocked to see this." "I do not believe my mother was ever shocked in her entire life, if you could call her existence by that rather profound name." "*Miss Abigail*," the governess hissed, beyond outrage, leaving the room with a rustling sound, like that of a dry leaf blowing across a cement road.

Mr. Jennings-Smith was duly informed that his daughter had decided to take a tour of every island that was habitable off the coast of Africa. This itinerary seemed sensible to him, since it was absolutely exhaustive, and Mr. Jennings-Smith therefore assumed it must have some purpose. He assumed, he informed his daughter, that he and Miss Fenwick would see her off at the airport, but Miss Abigail said, no, she was taking the bus from the Forty-second Street terminal. Mr. Jennings-Smith now finally had his suspicions that something had gone wrong. "Miss Fenwick and I . . ." he informed his daughter, putting down his book, in a gesture so remarkable it caused Abigail to indelibly note the date: September 30, "wish to take you to the airport." "You will certainly do as you wish," she told him politely, "but my luggage and I will leave for the airport on the bus." "And what airline, may I ask, are you patronizing?" Mr. Jennings-Smith asked with an air of real concern. He knew none but BOAC was airworthy. "The Antarctican one; I cannot remember its name; however, it is very cheap." Cheap! Mr. Jennings-Smith was left staring at the empty doorway in astonishment. "I do believe she has mutated," he said seriously to Miss Fenwick. "Why, as a child she resembled her mother in all particulars; now, if it were not for her raspy voice, she would be totally a stranger to me. Perhaps she is possessed." "Possessed?" repeated Miss Fenwick, wondering in some alarm, if, at her advanced age, she might be called upon to cope with two cases of hereditary insanity. "Such things have been known, my dear Miss Fenwick, such things have been known."

Miss Abigail was seen clambering on board a bus which the footman had told her went to the terminal; the spectacle of her gigantic body, apparently constructed of sturdy air-filled canvas balloons, mounting the steps, her six extravagantly expensive pigskin cases mounting after and before her, knocking into her legs and those before and behind her left the household staff speechless. Mr. Jennings-Smith refused to look, but from her window, Miss Fenwick noted every detail, the spectacle constituting, to her mind, a far more serious tragedy than the death of Lady Anna, whose decomposition had at least been hidden from human eyes on the day of her burial.

When Mr. Jennings-Smith and the old governess arrived at the gate of Antarctica Airlines to see Miss Abigail off, she seemed already remote from them, as if she were already hacking a wide swath through jungle vegetation to some unknown destination. Reluctantly, but with a sense of duty, she presented her blotched, puffy cheek to the moth-brush of their dry lips. She gave them no indication of when she was to return, nor, for some reason explicable to them, did they attempt to question her.

Once settled on the plane, Miss Abigail began rummaging in her rope bag for magazines, of which she had bought one of every description, including a full complement of TV and movie monthlies. The man in the next seat said something to her. "I am not interested in conversing with men," Miss Abigail answered; "I am not interested, in fact, in conversing with any member of either sex." "I don't give a damn who you want to talk to, lady," the aggravated businessman said, struggling with his brown attaché case; "I just want you to move over. I can't breathe and I can't get my seat belt; you're squashing me." Abigail fished up half of his seat belt, upon which she had been sitting, and handed it to him as if she were handing over a repulsive worm. "I presume," she said severely, "you have work enough in that box to keep you busy," and she began rummaging in her rope bag again, bringing out a triple-layer, fancily decorated box of rum candied-cherries. She made no offer of one to the man alternately squirming and glaring at her in the next seat. "Crazy bitch," he muttered to himself, craning his neck to see if any seats remained empty. Miss Abigail heard and smiled serenely. She was twenty years old.

As far as Miss Abigail was concerned, her first trip, which she regarded as a trial balloon, was a thumping success. She visited each of the African islands in turn, covering every possible inch. She had been inoculated for cholera, yellow fever, bubonic plague, typhoid, scarlet fever, measles, mumps, polio, tetanus, diphtheria, and multitudinous special vaccines which the doctors administered dubiously, saying their effectiveness had not been proven, and the vaccines were merely experimental. Nevertheless, she proceeded fearlessly, observing everything with equal interest: the trees, and the plants, and the natives, taking careful pictures of each flower and nude native and leaf, each ceremony and hut, meticulously packing them and sending them back to her father, who she assumed would have some use for them. She did this for no special reason, and herself remarked to an old woman missionary that all this activity was merely the equivalent of her governess' button tapestry, whereupon, to her annoyance, she was called upon to explain.

In this manner, Miss Abigail passed the next fifteen years. She had developed a system soon in her travels. First, she would visit every island off the coast of Japan, then cover the continent city by city, then each outlying village, finally the wilder provinces, and last, the mountains and sources of streams. She arrived in Egypt before the flooding of the pyramids and covered every corridor and shaft, carefully and impassively viewing every mummy. At one point, it appeared that the monotonous Miss Abigail might present something of a problem to the Egyptian Embassy when the American State Department discovered that an heiress of her rank had been permitted access to a narrow crawlway in one of the smaller pyramids, and that only industrious delicate chipping at the ancient rock around her had prevented her from becoming another fossil in the eternal monument to man's stupidity. She was almost thirty-five, and off the coast of Guatemala, when she accidentally read of the flooding of the pyramids, and immediately chartered a plane back to the Middle East. It was the first time in Miss Abigail's later history that she had taken such drastic action. Guatemala, with its religious Easter parades, its exotic figures of Judas Iscariot hung from every tree, its gigantic crosses bearing a bleeding Christ carried by the mourners, first dressed in purple, then, after arriving at the tomb in black, all of this was left behind: missed. This left a round white blank in the logical jigsaw puzzle of Miss Abigail's life. Still, it outraged her aristocratic sense that some corrupt Arabs, or Egyptians, the distinction was not clear to her, were going to *flood* the tombs of the Pharaohs. The graves belonged to history, not to recirculated water. Miss Abigail had a grudging respect for the larger artifacts of time, and had stood under the Great Wall of China, observing the enormous length of its shadow, instinctively responding to the Chinese character: what was the wall, after all, if not a version of her own body?

The visit to Egypt was short. The pyramids had indeed been flooded. The visit was also unpleasant. Several men had attempted to pinch her four-hundred-pound body, and although their fingers could get no purchase on her enormously inflated buttocks, she felt herself violated, not because the sanctity of her four hundred pounds had been profaned but, what was worse, ignored. She immediately bought a direct-route ticket to the United States, and made plans to leave the next morning, which was only thirty-six hours after her arrival.

Miss Abigail had, however, sufficient time to express her disapproval of the Egyptian atrocities, since a grotesque photograph of her appeared in the Egyptian papers the morning she was to leave above an article quoting her as saying the Egyptians were more barbaric than Genghis Khan, and probably dirtier. The newspapers carefully noted that she had the largest single fortune in America (shared, of course, with her father, Mr. Jennings-Smith) and was often consulted on financial matters by the President himself. This was, in fact, more or less true, since the Jennings-Smiths had to give away a great deal of their money yearly, and Lady Anna had left strong instructions before her death on how it should be spent: in fact, Lady Anna did not care in the slightest how it was to be spent, but merely detested the idea that the government should dictate the spending of it to her. Miss Abigail comforted herself upon seeing the pictures, which she thought were excellent likenesses, and which gave her a glow in the pit of her stomach where the seventeen baklava she had eaten also resided, telling herself, that at her weight, her features were not really distinguishable, and no one would dare to recognize her. So concluding, she ordered another full meal from room service.

The seat belt sign had flashed on, and the hostess was demonstrating the method for using oxygen masks to the passengers, when there was a sudden commotion in the direction of the pilot's cabin. The door to the control room opened a crack; the stewardess turned her head to it, and vanished inside. When she came out, she calmly replaced the oxygen equipment in the overhead compartment, and announced to the passengers that there was nothing to worry about. Everyone looked at his neighbor in bewilderment. "There is nothing to worry about," the stewardess said again in her professionally transatlantic voice; "we are only being hijacked. It is only a matter of time before Ground Control, the pilot, and the hijackers decide what we are to do. There is no reason to panic," she recited under her completely dilated pupils, "but no one should attempt to leave his seat or make sudden movements. Of any kind," she added with a touch more nervousness. A buzzing filled the cabin. "A hijacking, how interesting," Abigail said to a mustached man sitting next to her; "I've read a great deal about them. There are usually few casualties, except," she said, "in the Arab countries. They are very volatile, and irrational, as," she could not prevent herself from adding, "their self-indulgent flooding of their national monuments proves beyond any limit of sanity." Thereupon, Abigail took out an old copy of *The New Yorker* and one of *The National Encounter*, spread the last in her lap with a good supply of pastries upon it, and proceeded to read the first in total indifference to her surroundings. The man beside her was slowly becoming hysterical, attempting to signal the stewardess, pleading with her when she came to send a message to his wife and child, or at least to call his business. Abigail observed him as if he were a hermit crab on the wrong beach and went back to reading *The National Encounter's* lead article: "I Was a Teenage Mummy for Sixteen Years."

In this way, hours must have passed. The windows outside began to darken, and the only lights visible were those lining the runway, the fluorescents shining in the terminal buildings, and a few stars. Abigail stirred slightly, not out of apprehension, of which she felt none, but from discomfort: she was becoming hungry. "It is just as I thought," she observed to the man in the seat next to hers; "hijackings are as boring as anything else in life." The mustached man, who had been sobbing violently into a sopping handkerchief, looked wildly at her and resumed his weeping. Abigail noticed that he, at least, seemed to find the event of more interest. She rummaged through her rope bag, and, coming upon a huge basket of candied fruit, candies, and pastries, forgot all thoughts of discomfort. Worry had yet to cross her mind.

In the morning, events took a slightly more interesting turn. Three Arabs holding machine guns emerged from the cockpit and threateningly waved their metal muzzles at the passengers. Silly screams filled the body of the plane. The men were thin, swarthy, and looked, in Abigail's eyes, retarded, which was, after all, exactly what she had expected. They had secured the stewardess in front of them by handcuffing her to a seat. "It is decided altogether, I mean unanimous," began the tallest Arab, who was obviously their spokesman, "that the bodies may all fall from the plane. But one body may not so fall," he continued, swelling with pride at his English. "We need a hostess," he announced. There was some whispering among the Arabs and the stewardess. "We need a *hostage*," he repeated, flushing; "a hostage; you know what that is? It is someone who stays." The passengers nodded their heads in unison. "The hostess is to be," he went on more slowly, his last mistake having made him less confident, "Miss Abigail Ida Jennings-Smith." His thick tongue wreaked havoc with Abigail's name, but it was nonetheless unmistakable. "The rest of you have left," he concluded royally. There was more whispering. "May leave," he corrected himself, flustered; "the rest *may leave*." Some muttering in his native tongue followed. The passengers, who had now begun to grasp the import of his message, began standing up in their seats, climbing and falling over one another in their attempts to reach the aisle. The door at the rear of the plane was already open.

"Now," the Arab said, coming up to Abigail, who was the only passenger still occupying a chair, "we fly you to our boss." "You fly the plane," Abigail corrected pedantically. "Of course," he snorted. There was more whispering. "They didn't say stupid she was," he mumbled, puzzled; "however, what matter it is?" They all smiled with satisfaction. The seat belt sign went on; the plane began its long taxi, and soon had lifted into the air. It never occurred to Abigail to ask the nature of her destination.

Something which resembled a 1948 Pontiac pulled up to the plane where it had landed in the middle of three sandy hills. Two men got out, babbled with the others, looked Miss Abigail up and down, and commanded her by gesture into the back seat. Three crowded in with her; the others sat in the front. The car bumped along for several hours until it came to what resembled a cross between a mud hut and a bungalow. "Headquarters," the driver said in English. Abigail peered at it dubiously. The men marched her into a room where an exceedingly thin Arab sat, legs crossed, staring at her as if he were attempting to become a living definition of the word sinister. "Since you look so menacing," Abigail began first, "I presume you are up to something. You might as well tell me what it is, since, from the time of my fifth birthday, I have never liked surprises." "Why not?" the man beside the slender one asked reflexively. "The cake was chocolate, rather than vanilla," said Abigail. "I detest chocolate cake. If it had not been a surprise party, someone would surely have thought to consult me." "Forget these cakes!" the chief roared; "we are discussing ransom."

"Ransom?" Abigail said.

"Ransom," the chief went on, narrowing his eyes, but achieving a cross-eyed effect; "you should be sorry the Israelis ever crossed the border." "I haven't the slightest idea of what you are talking about," Abigail answered; "I came to Egypt to protest the flooding of the great pyramids."

"*You* are our protest," the chief announced, waxing suddenly eloquent; "a terrible incident, a war between two countries. I see you as the spark. First, we must have money, and then we will torture you. We will send pictures; I have a Polaroid," he announced proudly. "Your Ambassador will protest; ours can do nothing. You," he paused, "may begin World War Three. Your country is behooved to protect a citizen such as you is." "Is behooved," Abigail whispered sotto voce. "So you agree!" he exclaimed triumphantly. "May I sit down?" Abigail inquired, "or is standing to be the first of the tortures?" "Sit," he answered absently, as if he were addressing a stray. "Not on that one," he said, looking up, seeing Abigail gyrate to a thin-legged wooden chair; "the big one." Abigail settled obediently amid a creaking of springs. "We are *conferring*," the chief informed her importantly. Abigail raised an eyebrow. So much she had already surmised.

After much mumbling and babbling, the chief appeared before her, his hand slid through the deep neck slit in his caftan like a dime-store Napoleon. "We have decided," he intoned, "to put you on a diet." For the first time in her life, Abigail was entirely flabbergasted. "When we release the pictures," he continued, sounding like a Paramount scout, "no one in America will feel sorry for you if you look like"—he fumbled for words—"a water blob, how water looks when it is spilled on the table." "Apt," Abigail assented, with the air of a connoisseur, "but I do not wish to be put on a diet." "You will have three grape leaves three times a day, stuffed ones, lamb stuffing, and oranges, we think," he consulted with the others, "as many as six oranges a day. But not the peel. Definitely not the peel. Six peeled oranges a day." "I will not have it!" Abigail shouted beside herself; "I wish to eat." "Although men in our country prefer their women, as their cattle, great in size, your people do not have such ideas. There are little lines with balls on them in your magazines." "What?" "Little lines, children's pictures, with heads," he clarified impatiently; "you must look like that for our plan." "I refuse," Abigail sniffed through pinched nostrils. "You might try going on a hunger strike," another man said, coming into the room. He spoke with a slight British accent, and was evidently the mastermind. "Take her to her quarters, and prepare the grape leaves," he ordered; "no mirrors in the rooms, either." "I have no objection to mirrors; I am, in fact, proud of my appearance," Abigail snapped. "I forbid the mirrors only to spare you," he said gallantly. For the first time, Abigail was aware that not only was she in the middle of a web, to which she had no objection, for she viewed a human life as equivalent to that of a tranquilized fly in silver strands, but that these ignorant men intended to change her dimensions, a change which, she began to realize with horror, would necessarily change the pull and thrust of the threads which held her, as well as their points of attachment. "I myself find you attractive as you are," the latest arrival said, "but if you will take out your compact, you will see how little you resemble a *Vogue* cover." Abigail, sitting sweatily in her hopsacking shirtdress, one of the four hundred she had made especially for her, began to feel a cold desperation.

Miss Jennings-Smith's quarters were shielded from the sun by a huge wooden board which formed a triangle with the hill and the sandy ground. The dwelling itself consisted of one bedroom, one empty room to walk about in, and a surprisingly modern bathroom. There was also a spacious closet with carved sliding doors, one eighth of which arrogantly accommodated her shirtwaists and gigantic girdles. A huge bookshelf was immediately constructed at her request, and, in a manner unknown to her, at least two hundred books, every one of which she had neatly listed in alphabetical order, were immediately procured. Wicker furniture reinforced with heavy steel filled the rooms; Abigail had taken a special liking to a wicker chaise longue which managed to mold itself to her body; when she was not sitting in it, she often stared at it. It was shaped like an undulating worm just emerged from a cocoon.

One morning, before the sun had come up, and the desert coolness still hung about in the sleeping room along with the rose strands of the coming sun, Abigail noticed a female servant sliding open the door to her closet. Lizard-like, she closed one eye, which she had opened to a slit, for she had nothing whatever of value. But when she woke up, she found all her shirtdresses had disappeared, and heavily embroidered lengths of silk, at least six feet long, were now placed on the upper shelves of the closet. After considerable rummaging, Abigail found a note, which was apparently a diagram, and a complementary list of instructions. The lengths of cloth were to be her new dresses, and under the pile was a collection of huge safety pins for fastening them, although, as the note informed her, they needed no pins when properly assembled.

Suspiciously, Abigail tugged at her shirtwaist. She slept in her dresses as if they were comfort blankets. It was worse than she had suspected; not only did the belts need to be pulled tighter, they needed to be pulled so tight there were no notches left for the spike at all. She looked down at herself. The shirtwaist was hanging from her shoulders like a curtain; the sleeve dangled from her arm like a flag. It was as if one half, the underhalf, of her arm had been amputated. Panic-stricken, Abigail lifted the skirt of her shirtwaist (she had always ordered them made floor-length, even though doctors had warned her their sweeping hems would constitute a health hazard in underdeveloped countries) and inspected the pride of her life: her ankles. The skin no longer melted and drooped over their shoes; the ankles were, in fact, as Miss Fenwick used to put it, becoming "finely turned." For the first time, Abigail felt the gravity of her situation. "I must have my grape leaves increased; also my allotment of oranges," she commanded the intelligent man when he next came to check on her health. He looked her up and down and informed her it was impossible.

Weeks passed. With indescribable horror, Abigail noted that she took more and more folds in the saris she fastened about her, and, although she refused to look down at her body, she found herself uncomfortable in bed one day and realized the source of displeasure was her left hip bone, jutting painfully into the thin mattress. Abigail cried herself to sleep.

"Excellent!" the mastermind gasped when he saw her later in the afternoon. "Although I liked you better as you were, there is no doubt you have your attractions as you are now." He promptly sent in a woman to wash her hair, brush it, and deprive her of her long iron hairpins, which, to him, resembled shish-kebab skewers. Abigail's blue-black hair now fell shining below the back of her shapely knees; her green eyes again glowed in the dark like a cat's; a high red flush lit her prominent cheekbones. Dramatic hollows marked the cheeks of her distinguished face. She looked like nothing so much as an Oriental Rapunzel with black, black hair. The Polaroid, as had been promised, now made its sinister appearance. Abigail herself had, in spite of all expectation, become considerably calmer, primarily due to a simple, if unusual, expedient: she not only pretended she still weighed four hundred pounds, but possibly five hundred. She resolutely imagined the grape leaves themselves each added a pound to her bony body, and at these times was serene as ever. But there were also times when she realized she had again been reduced to the young girl, the valedictorian of her high school, and then despair overtook her, and she became addicted to hopeless fits of weeping. To her Arab captors, this only added to her mysterious charm.

The photographs of Abigail were finally released. The result could not have been anticipated, even by her insanely optimistic captors. Although the photographs were, as Miss Abigail said, only a little better than those she had taken as a five-year-old with her Brownie Hawkeye, the effect they had on people everywhere was riveting. It is impossible to estimate how many men fell in love with the mysterious-looking creature in a sari, her long hair flowing, apparently endlessly, beyond the frame. People were seen carrying clipped-out newsprint photographs of her, and many a young man was seen to linger at a grimy newsstand to gaze once more at the inscrutable face of the American heiress which remained glued onto the front page. Women, too, were equally affected, and grocery store owners blamed a drop in their weekly gross on the sudden fad, caused, they began to realize when their own wives started to show signs of the national disease, a nationwide wave of diets whose goal was apparently to produce as many replicas of the Lady Anna's daughter as possible. Under the circumstances, it was hardly surprising that the State Department did indeed feel behooved to do something about her situation. Not even a kidnapped Jackie Kennedy could have created more of a sensation in her day.

It was soon reported that the heads of state were meeting with the Egyptian King, who had, until this point, been considering adopting the title of Egyptian President, but in his country, too, Miss Abigail was exercising her extraordinary fascination, which was, if anything, stronger there since the people felt her presence. She might be anywhere: in a basement, behind a tree, wrapped in white, selling figs in the market. The terrorists began to clarify their demands. It appeared that if the Egyptian King would permit himself to be called the Egyptian President, and if he would issue weekly bulletins threatening Israel with imminent destruction, as well as reports of imaginary Israeli assaults on their border, and the borders of other Arab countries, they might consider releasing Miss Abigail. However, the price they set for her release was fifteen million dollars, which the American government thought was rather high, if Abigail herself did not. The Egyptian King himself seemed irritated by the price, but was caught staring at a color photograph of the lady, and from his outraged expression, one of his old servants, who had attended him since boyhood, surmised the poor King felt there was something unchivalrous, if not downright vulgar, about the strange dealings he had become involved in. The bachelor King was now obviously beside himself, and in the palace there were rumors that even the CIA had become involved in what promised to become a preposterous and highly dangerous incident. If this was in fact the case, no one knew but *The National Encounter,* which daily ran bulletins on which meetings the State Department had held with the Egyptian head of state, and what information the CIA now had; they also claimed to be parties to inside information concerning the CIA's admittedly extravagant plans to rescue Abigail Ida Jennings-Smith.

In the middle of all this, Mr. Jennings-Smith himself died, thus worsening the situation, for the entire fortune, half of which had been fabulous, now settled in the folds of Abigail's gold-threaded sari. The terrorists were said to increase their demands, and the bachelor King was said to be even more aggravated with his people than before. Meanwhile, the intelligent terrorist, as Abigail called him, informed her of her father's death, reasoning that this information was only due her, and understanding that the knowledge of her new fortune might increase her feeling for the gravity of her situation. He was also interested in comforting her when she would fall weeping into his arms.

"Well, that is too bad," Abigail said thoughtfully; "I imagine he was following this incident with rather more than his usual interest. What did he die of?" "Natural causes," said the crest-fallen terrorist. "It happens to all of us," Abigail said, as if agreeing; "or it *should* happen. I myself seem to be getting perpetually younger, although you," she inspected him as if he were an insect, "are getting quite wrinkly. A bit like wet newspaper after it dries. That's it exactly," she finished with satisfaction. "We are talking about your father!" the Arab cried histrionically, forgetting who had probably been one of the main sources of the old man's undoubtedly fatal agitation. "Your father, the seed from which you sprang." "Grew," she corrected phlegmatically. "This is of no interest to me," she said, dismissing him with an almost regal wave of her hand; "he has done what all humans do, assumed his brown skin. He is now surrounded by six feet of brown skin, six feet thick. I feel no sorrow for him. I only envy him." "But he died alone!" the Arab cried piteously, reminded of a Greta Garbo movie he had seen as a child at Cambridge. "I am sure Miss Fenwick was there with him," Abigail said. "She is dead too!" "Would you mind explaining that?" Abigail asked, finally roused. "When your father, Mr. Jennings-Smith," he reminded her, "was reading, he suddenly thought a gas light might be better for thinking, and, since all the gas fixtures and pipes were still in place, he called someone in and had the fixture in his study turned on. The trouble was, a breeze must have blown out the flame, and he had fallen asleep, so when the gas spread through the house, it killed your father and the Miss Fenwick. I suppose I was wrong to say he died of natural causes." "On the contrary," said Abigail, "the gas fixture was a natural cause, a deterioration of his aging imagination. I am only surprised the two innocents failed to blow up the whole block." "They did blow up the block," the intelligent terrorist admitted sullenly. "At least, they blew up their house and four others. There were twenty-four casualties." "I think you had better give me all the details," Miss Abigail sighed. "That's all. The explosion was the last thing. But, tomorrow, you will have a visitor." "I am uninterested in visitors." "Nevertheless, the King himself is coming to see you." "I don't want to see him. The King of what?" she asked automatically. "Of Egypt." "*We* have a President," she finished irrelevantly.

In the morning, the roar of engines woke Abigail. In her languid manner, she wrapped her sari about her and waited for her servant to brush her long hair; the woman insisted on washing it every night. Then the servant fastened on an emerald necklace whose pendant hung between her breasts. Petulantly, Abigail tore it off and threw it onto the floor. The servant only sighed, putting it in her pocket. Abigail had broken its catch. Several hours later, the terrorist came to see her and to inform her that the King was waiting for her in the main bungalow. The bachelor King was in white military dress, covered with gold epaulettes. He was sitting up straight, and evidently on his best behavior. An American in a pin-striped suit came forward. "We are discussing the terms of your release," he informed Abigail; "with luck, you will come back to Cairo with us this afternoon." Abigail only nodded, as if she were listening to the sound of a shell. She sat down in a rattan peacock chair, arranging the folds of her sari. When she reached behind her head to bring the heavy black sheet of her hair over her shoulder, whose collarbone visibly quivered, the bachelor King lost all thought of negotiations. "All this has gone far enough," he informed the terrorists suddenly; "we are ready to meet your demands. We will pay the ransom from our own treasury." "What? What!" shouted the terrorist; "from our own treasury? The whole point was to put money in *your* treasury! What's the matter with you?" "Is this how you speak to your King?" asked the poor King, embarrassed dreadfully. "You are now our *President*," the terrorist reminded him, "now that you have agreed to our demands." "Is this how you speak to your President?" the King asked again. "I am sorry, Mr. President," the terrorist whined like a reprimanded child; "just don't bother us with Egyptian money; for that, we could have kidnapped a secretary." "It would have been better for you," the American Secretary of State put in. "I have only one request," the King-President muttered, his face averted from the gathering, "that the Lady Abigail stay at my palace, as my guest, of course as my guest, for at least one month." The terrorist glared at him. "I am *Miss* Abigail," the lady informed him, "and I have had quite enough of being a house guest." "Excuse me," the American Ambassador mumbled nervously, scurrying over to Abigail. He whispered to her at length.

Everyone stared at each other, but primarily at the red-faced Egyptian potentate. The American Ambassador was explaining the importance of good relations with Egypt, which apparently had something to do with oil and pipelines and borders, and Abigail, it seemed, would horribly affect the destiny of millions should she refuse this one invitation. "I have no desire to become a concubine," she said audibly to the Ambassador, who was rapidly becoming apoplectic. "My lady, what do you think I am?" the regent wailed. "*Miss*," Abigail reminded him. "Miss, what do you think I am?" he asked. "How the poor man repeats himself," Abigail observed in a strong voice; "I suppose it is something like a stutter?" The new President blushed again, fidgeting with the golden frog on his chest. "I accept," Abigail announced, "on the grounds that my body remain absolutely inviolate, and because I refuse to affect anyone's destiny." At which, the American Ambassador hurriedly shepherded Abigail into a waiting limousine, which awkwardly began its slow crawl across the rough and then sandy terrain.

Once installed in the palace, Abigail barely had time to inspect her quarters, which consisted of two rooms whose walls were made of golden mosaics, and which opened onto a courtyard, and whose floors were made of colored stones, some of which she recognized as uncut precious gems, when she began to be assailed alternately by visits from the American Ambassador and the Egyptian President. The American Ambassador dwelled at tedious length upon her importance in the current scheme of things, since the Egyptian President was apparently willing to agree to anything short of making his country the fifty-first state if he could only possess her, and visits from the President himself, whose intentions were unfortunately clear, but who became so tongue-tied in Abigail's presence that he could not utter a word of his desires.

Finally, the American Ambassador arrived. "The President," he began, "wants to marry you." "Our President is already married," she said.

"I mean the Egyptian President."

"I have no desire to marry."

"We have been over your importance before. It is not impossible that you could learn to love him."

"I regard love," Abigail said icily, "as one of the world's most serious natural catastrophes; it is a catastrophe. People merely fail to see it for what it is. I would prefer an earthquake or a tornado. Moreover, I am quite sure I could never fall in love with a King who decided to be a President. It is like a prince deciding to be a toad. But on mature thought," Abigail went on, "such a prince would be a superior prince, not to mention a superior toad."

"Miss Abigail, please let us return to the subject."

"Then the answer is no, I cannot love him, either as a toad or a prince."

"But you can marry him?"

"If a gun is held to my head, I daresay I could marry him."

"*You* are holding a gun to the head of the world!" the Ambassador exploded in desperation.

"If there is one grain of truth in that remark, then I must change my answer," Abigail said, after some thought. "I can marry him. But it will hardly be my fault if he starts a war in a fit of pique when the honeymoon is over. I myself can always guarantee proper behavior in the extreme."

"You are a *Great American*, Miss Abigail," the American Ambassador told her, fervently seizing her hand. Abigail shook it loose. "Don't bother me with such television hyperbole," she ordered, dismissing him.

"The wedding will take place before the entire world," crowed the Egyptian President; "it will be broadcast everywhere in living color, via satellite." Abigail had resigned herself to the situation, and made polite conversation as a matter of course. "Which satellite, my dear?" she asked him, without the slightest trace of warmth in her voice, throwing her future husband into a terrible state of confusion, since he had not the faintest idea.

"You will come to love me; I know you will," he assured her feverishly that night as they sat in the court. "Of course," Abigail assented placidly. "We will have children, a dynasty," he raptured, caught in his visions which poured from the folds of her sari. "Is that strictly necessary?" she asked. "Necessary? Of course it is necessary. I must have heirs. I must have daughters resembling you." "I devoutly hope that will never happen," Abigail sighed, "although of course you must have heirs. I will not object." "But you will come to love me?" he asked in a worried, fretful voice. "Of course," Abigail answered in a monotone.

Later that night, the American Ambassador came to thank her again, again to inform her she was a great American woman, perhaps the greatest, and to enumerate the changes she was wreaking in the world through her marriage, as well as those she was avoiding, in an attempt to strengthen her resolve to marry, lest it weaken minutes before the ceremony. But it did not, and it was broadcast, as are all grand affairs of state, throughout the entire world, via satellite. The bridal procession consisted of hundreds and hundreds of Egyptian citizens, the first dressed to represent the earliest rulers of Egyptian history. There was Tutankhamen as well as Cleopatra; there was Cleopatra's barge as well as Mark Antony and Julius Caesar, and in special deference to Lady Abigail, and her well-known love of the great pyramids, three enormous papier-mâché pyramids closed the procession, each forty feet high, each walking along on myriad brown legs, so that it appeared as if the pyramids were being carried off by an abnormally strong race of desert rats or ants. If Miss Abigail had any thoughts on the appropriateness of this gesture, she kept them entirely to herself. She herself was dressed in imitation of a wall painting in one of the great pyramids, and hardly seemed flesh at all, but golden skin encrusted with precious jewels.

Egypt's first lady now exercised a phenomenal grip over the people of all countries. Photographers fell into her pool with their cameras; her children often walked about in Halloween masks to avoid having their faces reproduced since their mother justifiably had an extreme fear of kidnappers. She was photographed endlessly, receiving heads of state, visiting the poor, opening hospitals. At home, she opened her room-length closet and found herself starting at two bright flashes of light and, as the flashes faded, two Chinese photographers scurrying down the corridor. Abigail had resigned herself. She worried about her children and learned to worry about her husband. She stayed up through hot nights with her thin hand on the foreheads of her feverish children. She wore cold jewels around her neck on state visits to the Eskimos. She obediently echoed her husband's views on all matters of state, but mediated efficiently, if not brilliantly, between the American Ambassador and the Egyptian parliament. The staff's orders to regulate her diet, so that she would never again become the water blob she was once rumored to be, proved thoroughly unnecessary, since Abigail had assumed her old physical state as a necessary accouterment of her new office. One night, unable to sleep and watching the late news, the American Ambassador saw Miss Abigail and her husband, the Egyptian President, admiringly touring the new Iranian skyscrapers, which were destined to collapse three days later, having been designed by a prominent builder of supermarkets, which were the newest things in the cities. She was wearing an expression of absolute radiance. He noted that the expression never flickered, never changed, never wavered. On the last night he had spoken to her, he had again told her she *might* grow to love her husband. "The only thing I have ever loved, the only thing," Miss Abigail sighed, "was a pet white rat I had named Ophelia. When she died, I prayed she would come back to me in dreams, but she never did." Gently, the American Ambassador suggested that she must have loved someone else. "No," Abigail sobbed; "I never did. I thought I did, but I never did." The interviewer was asking her something about her personal life. "You know I do not answer such questions," Abigail answered, safe in her impeccable poise, "but I can say this much: I have loved only once." The American Ambassador turned off his set, tears filling his old eyes. Abigail Ida Jennings-Smith had had an argument with life, and, though it might appear otherwise, she *had* had the last word.

II

IN THE HOUSES

His Daughter's House

By the time he reached his daughter's stop, the steps leading down from the train's platform were thickly cobbled with primitive glass. As Jacob turned down the side street, the snow, which had suddenly paused as if checking to make certain it was whitening the right place, was already beginning to show signs of age. Car tracks crisscrossed the gray ice of the streets; footprints of children and dogs formed to ice fossils on the lawns. The curbs reminded him of Sheepshead Bay, the way its shore looked when the sea washed up the huge chunks of ice choking its throat. He was already annoyed. It had taken him three hours to get this far. Why could no one in the family ever give sensible directions? The last lap into Brooklyn, the train ran outside; like a bad heart, the train had stalled constantly. Minnie and her bright ideas. *He* had heard the radio's predictable announcement: no trains leaving tonight for the Island, and had tucked that irritating bit of information somewhere in the musty folds of his suit pocket while he doggedly argued with one of his crazy suppliers. So what if there was an embargo on woolens from Hungary? If he didn't get them now, they could go ahead and throw them in the ocean. Let the whales have them. A lot of good a shipment of heavy wool would do him if it got to his place in time for spring.

The minute he hung up, the phone rang. He sighed. Forty years of this garbage with the railroad, and his wife always called the place, hysterical. The Paul Revere of Problems. Yes, he knew all about the snow. How could he not know about it? It was falling right outside his window, just the way it was falling outside everyone else's. Of course it was keeping customers away. Why should he be upset? It was a novelty, snow keeping customers out. At least now he could blame the bad business on the weather. "Business is terrible," he said. "Business is always terrible," Minnie answered. Then came silence while they listened impatiently to one another's thoughts.

"Well, where are you going to stay?" his wife asked. He paused before saying the familiar name of the hotel. "Why not stay with Jessica this time?" Minnie asked; "it's cheaper than a hotel and she's always complaining because you won't sleep at her house. Maybe if you stayed there, she'd come see us more. Are the trains running to Brooklyn?" "Jessica's always busy," he said. "She isn't," Minnie pounced, triumphant; "she just called up and said, 'Why can't Daddy stay here?' She said she couldn't understand why you couldn't stand her house more than five minutes. You always come in, sit down, turn on the television and fall asleep. That's what she said." Another silence. "And don't say you're tired out from the week," Minnie scolded; "she knows you stay awake at other people's houses. No wonder," Minnie wound up, injured, "we never see her." "She never invites us." "Well," said Minnie, "she's inviting you now. She's been heating up the guest room all afternoon and she said if for some strange reason you don't want to sleep there, you could have her bedroom and she and Robert would take the guest room." A violent gust of wind rattled his plate-glass window. Probably some on the avenue would be blown in. "All the trains to Brooklyn are running; I just heard it." Minnie's voice was getting strident. "There's no reason for you not to go."

"She'll keep me up all night with her screaming," he said. "She won't," Minnie said. "She practices down in that basement. How she doesn't break her neck on those stairs is beyond me. You can't even hear her on the second floor." "The neighbors must be happy it's winter," he said. "The room's soundproofed." She paused. "All right," he said. "Call her and tell her I'm coming. I'm leaving now." He began putting on his coat. "You call her," she said. "It's only polite. You're the one who's staying there. Make her feel like you want to come." "I don't," he said. "Well, you ought to want to. Say you're glad she asked you. Don't just growl 'I'm coming' and hang up." Jake left his coat dangling from one shoulder. What was the use? He might as well stand still in front of a moving tank.

He called his daughter. Yes, Jessica had plenty of food. No, she had nothing she had to do. Yes, she had to practice, but she'd be practicing way after he went to bed. No, it didn't keep the children up. Did he want Robert to pick him up at the station? He told her the walk would be good for him. She sounded like a child, excited and silly. The night before Christmas. She probably had a Christmas tree. He and Minnie had felt guilty enough about those Christmas trees when she was a child, but all the other children believed in Santa Claus. Her trees were fire resistant, and artificial, and she never felt guilty. Of all the children to settle down in Brooklyn. He never expected it. The three boys were out on the Coast; the youngest kept mumbling about banking in the Philippines. Let him go. Let him go and catch malaria. He was retiring any day anyway. Let them all do what they wanted. Jessica and her bare feet. Singing opera and practicing in that filthy basement. There was enough dust to start a desert. She'd ruin her voice. He didn't know why she didn't get more colds; she was forever padding around in her bare feet. She never talked sense. Last time she said bare feet were no worse for you than a bald head. He shook his. They were all the same, his children, all brains and no common sense. He supposed they came from some shoot of his wife's family; they were all crazy. You couldn't say that to Minnie. Not if you wanted your dinner. He put on his fur hat and buttoned his coat. As an afterthought, he added Jessica's scarf. Well, he answered some unknown protestor, that *was* how he thought of it. He supposed it was true he didn't accept presents gracefully.

How could he accept them gracefully from children who never had a cent in the bank? He knew Jessica earned a lot with that singing—at least she said so—but what they did with money was beyond him. Her housekeeper probably earned more than he did. And the way they all trusted everyone, he thought, turning the key in the lock, then turning the lock for the alarm system. The red light winked on. Well, at least tonight no one would have a chance to tie him up in the store; that was something. The last time they robbed him, he remembered, setting off down the stairs (they were pebbled metal; if a child walked on them, he sounded like the whole third army; they were safer than the elevator), they took two racks of suit pants and left the jackets. How stupid could you be and live? And there he was, stuck with one hundred Oscar de la Renta jackets. Who wanted jackets without the pants? Thieves, drek. They were too dumb to breathe, but not so dumb they couldn't tie him up three separate times and loot the store. He was used to it. His heart missed a beat. That frightened him. *Almost* used to it.

It was beyond him, why Jessie and the others hadn't been murdered in their beds. The train stopped in the middle of the Manhattan Bridge. He knew it, he thought, extracting his spectacles. He had one of every evening edition. Still, his eye kept wandering off to the gold and black Manhattan skyline, as familiar as the mote in his eye, except now it was magnified, enormous; he could see it in all its parts. Why not? It might as well be his own nervous system. He squirmed, taking care not to move against the ladies on both sides of him. With his luck, one would have hysterics and call the conductor. A fine time he'd have explaining that to Jessica. The things he let Minnie talk him in to. The train started again, jolting everyone. The women leaned back, pressing against *him*. Times had changed. *He* ought to scream. The subway used to cost a nickel. And now Jessie screamed away with nothing on in front of thousands of people. *He* couldn't stand there bellowing in his shorts. He wondered, opening another paper, if she'd ever forgiven him for all those years he insisted she couldn't carry a tune. He still didn't see what was so wonderful about that voice of hers. It was loud enough.

No one called her Jessie anymore. She was always sitting in his lap when she was a child, but he always made her get right down. Then she'd get mad at him and start a fight. Eating supper with her across the table was a curse. She'd keep at it until she said something rotten enough to get hit for, and then she'd run out of the kitchen, up the stairs, and lock her door. And Minnie, she was such a help. She'd throw down her fork and ask the air what she bothered cooking *for*. It was a miracle he didn't have an ulcer. Twin ulcers.

Well, tonight, he didn't want to go in to Brooklyn. He usually didn't want to go to Brooklyn. He'd been born there. He was in Brooklyn enough, anyhow, visiting his brothers or his mother or his mother-in-law. Although, sometimes, he thought, turning to Brenda Starr and the comics, going to Brooklyn was the only thing that made him feel better. It wasn't having that effect tonight. The snow was whirling against the windows as if it thought it deserved to come in and take a seat. He was short of breath. He took off his scarf and put it under his papers. God forbid he should come home without his; how would Minnie know what Mary Worth was doing now? And on the Long Island Rail Road, he needed it for a card table. Track 18, the third car, left aisle. He looked around. This car was filled with old ladies, grandmothers with shopping bags from Gimbels, just as in his childhood. They knitted or crocheted solemnly away. Even above the clack of the train he could hear the sound of knitting needles. The woman next to him had started up on an endless something. Thank God, Jessie'd stopped knitting things. Minnie always made him wear them. He was the laughingstock of the garment industry. As if his business wasn't bad enough for them to laugh about.

The wind caught him as he came out of the station. Automatically, he turned his collar up and wound the scarf around it. He never had anything to say to Jessica. Even though she never shut up. You might as well send a dove to her house as try to get her on the phone. She'd been supporting the phone company since she could talk. Minnie never should have left her fingers on her hands. She should have broken them. The first time she dialed a number.

His mother hadn't been much better, sitting and rocking in the darkest corner of the living room, although, when she opened her mouth, she always had the same thing to say—nag, nag, nag. Everything you did was wrong. The packed snow cracked under his feet. That was something like the sound that always filled his parents' house when no one was yelling. What a life he'd had. The big trees swayed and creaked before the gigantic houses. What did Jessica need with one of those old barns? Even his parents' house had been newer. It was hard to believe the old house was still there and he couldn't just walk in. Not that he wanted to walk in, but he got upset whenever he remembered he couldn't. Rock, rock, rock, he thought, picking his way along the icy sidewalk. That was all his mother had ever done—rock, rock, scold and rock, rock and scold. Probably that was where Jessica got her selfishness. The world could burn down and she wouldn't come out of the house, provided her little family was safe, and she and her dogs and cats and children and husband could go on as usual; sometimes he didn't know if she'd stop that screeching in the basement even if one of her own children fell on his head.

And that hound they had! Worse than the dog they'd had when he grew up. It took after Jessie, he thought, holding to a wire lawn fence until the wind let up. It would bark its damn head off when he rang the bell. Just as if it had never seen him before, and then follow him through the house, nipping at his fingers every time he left a room without his beloved daughter. A stupid dog. Even if it loved Jessica and the others. Jessica, of course, most of all. What did she need an attack dog for? No normal people had attack dogs. The snow started up again. One more block and then he turned the corner, then just the two long ones to her house. Of course, she had been robbed six times, each time by a person who worked there once. Raising a ceiling or lowering it, he forgot which, well, that was what his daughter was like. If she was going to get a dog, she'd get a police dog. If she was going to have an alarm system, she'd get the pattern from Fort Knox. She had a one-track mind. She always had.

The houses, as he got closer to his daughter's, made him uneasy. How many years had his own father been dead now? Probably ten. No, eleven. He died two years before Jessica got married. That was how he kept track. He wasn't in his daughter's wedding pictures. His mother was, smiling as if it killed her. Nothing special about the wedding; his mother always looked as if she'd bitten down on a lemon. She would be the one to stick around. The snow, swirling, suddenly cleared. The houses looked familiar. Probably his father had owned some of them. The steps looked familiar. The doors did too. And there he was, fourteen years old, trying to collect the rent, right in the middle of the Depression, from the old Jewishers. "Shake it out of them! Shake them!" his mother kept shouting. All right, all right, he'd say, handing her the money. Shake them! They *wanted* to pay; they gave whatever they had. One dollar, five dollars. The rent was thirty. A dollar was a dollar then. Sometimes, he must have made thirty trips for the thirty dollars. No one went on relief then; they'd rather starve in dignity. Jessie fed everyone. She had outside cats and inside cats, outside dogs and inside dogs. In the summer, kittens followed her around the garden watching her clip her rosebushes as if they were studying to be gardeners. She even had inside rosebushes. Minnie was getting to like those flea-bitten animals, and all her life, she'd been petrified at the sight of anything on four feet. Unless it was creeping and wearing a diaper. Women. There was no understanding them. Sometimes he thought they existed to annoy him. He shook his head in the snow. It was flying straight into his eyes, melting and running down his cheeks. All children helped their parents then; they had to. Or he did. The girls weren't old enough. Even if they had been, Pop wouldn't have let them go; it wasn't safe. That was all he said. It wasn't safe.

Then his mother thought up the brilliant idea of selling suits door to door, and who did it? Him. Three dollars for the rent, one for the suit. Ten trips for the rent, fifteen for a suit. The families in the buildings gave him referrals. That was the way he still ran his business. By referrals. He didn't know where most of his customers had gone. Probably moved to the Island. The city wasn't safe anymore. And Jessie always wanted to know why he worried about money so much. Well, what did she know about the old Jewishers and their cups of hot water they gave him while they searched everyone's pockets, poked in the flour cannisters, the rice bins, for nickels and dimes.

Here it came, House Beautiful. *His* father was probably still recording his sins in the silence of his coffin. He'd break his neck on his daughter's front steps. No, she'd managed to get some salt onto the ice. Surprise. She remembered there were still people outside the front door. No red light, he saw, peering through the porch blinds; the light, right next to the keyhole, was off. Well, what do you know? She'd turned off the alarm in his honor. But not that mutt. There it went, thundering the house down. "Hello," he said to Jessie, pecking her on the cheek, keeping a careful eye on the dog; "how's the mutt?" he asked. "The mutt has papers," Jessie said. He sighed. So did his daughter. They could never talk to each other without squabbling first; there was always some kind of friction. Still, she admitted, she liked him better. She ought to; she was almost forty, middle-aged. An aged child.

"How was the trip?" she asked. "Awful. Leave it alone," he

growled, tugging back his coat; "I can do it myself." Jessie's lips
narrowed. She waited until he handed over his wet clothes; why
was the front hall here always so dark? She flipped on some lights.
They always came in the back way, through the garden. Even in
winter. "Mother said to call her as soon as you got here," she told
him, taking the clothes off to the basement to dry. She hung them
expertly near the furnace. She hoped he wouldn't keep this surly
business up all night. She never knew what he expected from her.
Some father he'd been when they were growing up; they'd never
seen him. Unless he had orders to punish them, or it was Sunday,
and then he sat in his chair sulking away the week. And her
mother still had the nerve to tell her she was her father's favorite.
That woman should have written for "Stella Dallas." Probably she
was an escaped character from one of its old scripts. Probably the
show went off the air when all the characters escaped into her
family. "Be nice," Minnie was pleading. "I know how to behave,"
he said, hanging up. Poor Jessica, Minnie thought, going back to
her crewel work. What channel was that movie on? She got up
and flipped the dial impatiently.

They ate dinner in what would have been an uncomfortable silence had everyone not been making polite, strenuous efforts at
conversation. It amounted, Jessica decided, to uncomfortable silence all the same. "How's business?" Robert finally asked. "The
same." "What does that mean?" his daughter asked sharply. The
next thing she knew, he'd be talking about retirement again. Her
father chewed stolidly on. The housekeeper clattered in the
kitchen. Leave it to Jessica to find a housekeeper from Guiana to
cook pot roast and stuffed cabbage. Every time he thought of that
woman's country, he thought of a solid gold coin. A guinea. No
one said that anymore, either.

The maid had switched on the radio. Jessica shook her head at
Robert; Elsie had to know how cold it was; then she could decide
how miserable to be. Her father hadn't answered her yet. Well, he
had his own style, you had to give him that. Who else's father retired one Friday and went back to work on Monday? After they

had all worried themselves to death about how retirement would kill him (it *had* killed his father); after they got used to seeing her mother walking around with those beautiful red eyes. She'd looked just like an albino.

That morning, Jessica had awakened late for practice, turned on her side, found the bed empty, the clock glaring ten-thirty, and stared up at the ceiling. Then she picked up the phone and dialed her father's work number. She'd been dialing it since childhood. One last time. To hear it was no longer in service. Discontinued. Whatever they said when a major part of a life died, but the person was left. Instead, a recording came on. "DE 2-0123 has been changed. The new number is DE 2-7651. Please place your call again." That mechanical voice. She dialed the old number again when the shock wore off, and while the phone rang, scribbled the new number down. She dialed that. Her father answered. "Well, well," she said, kicking back the covers; "does Mother know you're there?" There was a long silence. "She thinks I'm closing up the business." "What *are* you doing?" "Working. With a partner. It's his business, not mine." "When are you getting your own? Another one?" "Not for a few months," he answered, uncomfortable. "Don't tell your mother," he said at last. "Don't worry." She hung up and got out of bed. The walls, the floor, seemed solider. She hoped he wasn't starting up that retiring nonsense again.

"Terrible. It couldn't be worse. The same as ever," her father answered. Jessica went back to her plate. She ought to be as big as a house, her father thought, watching her help herself to more meat. Instead, she was thin as a rail. Maybe that singing was hard work. Maybe she really was as busy as she said she was. Whom had he worked his fingers to the bone for? For her. For her and the others. So why couldn't he talk to her? While he was here, all he thought about was getting back to his own bed. He wasn't used to being here without Minnie. For protection. "Saved any money yet?" he asked without thinking. He was always at her, she thought, bitter; she couldn't do anything right. Not for him.

What had her old teacher once told her? Imagine herself resting on a long dragon's tail and then imagine her voice coming from the end of that tail. Probably that was why she was so successful. She was part dragon. With him for a father. Her expression softened. Everyone relaxed. Who else, she wondered, would dream of manufacturing and selling high-fashion clothing dressed the way he was—ancient, creased pants, an old flannel shirt, and usually he was unshaven. She supposed his customers felt much better about themselves after they saw themselves with him in a mirror.

Why, her father was wondering, couldn't Jessica fix herself up at home? She always looked like she'd finished cleaning the basement, not practicing in it. How they ever managed to fix her up and get her on the stage, *that* was beyond him. Well, now they would go sit in that grotesque living room; she'd probably start in about why he never went into business with *his* father. He couldn't have done it then; he couldn't talk about it now. His father, he was a Jekyll and Hyde character. Work with his father! Not after he'd seen him get mad at a man in the shop and throw him and his chair across the room. That was before unions. He didn't change after them, either. He used to be a big man, heavy. Before the pancreas trouble and all the dieting.

Five minutes in the living room, and she was already asking. "It wouldn't have worked." That was what he always said. He never wanted to talk to her, she thought; he didn't trust her. They began the usual aimless chatter about her father's business. Robert always managed to sound interested; Jessica knew she looked bored. What new lines he could try out, how to get new customers, where had the old ones gone, no one wore clothes anymore; you'd think, listening to him, they lived on a planet of nudists; where had all the old customers gone? Again. Dead. That's where they'd gone. He would never think of that, Jessica mused: some block, or some kind of loyalty. And everyone knowing he'd never do a thing differently. It was all talk.

Where *did* Minnie get these ideas? he fussed to himself again.

Why couldn't he go anywhere without Minnie? If she left for two days, he was sure to show up at his brother's the first night. They all laughed at him about it. He didn't mind being alone in exactly two places, the place, or the hospital; nobody asked him questions he didn't want to answer there. He said something in answer to a question Robert asked him. That was it, really. Minnie knew all about him. Once she knew the facts, she wasn't interested. She got busy finding out new facts. For Minnie, facts were explanations, causes. For Jessica, they were beginnings. She always wanted to lift them up like pothole covers. She'd always been like that. No wonder he always wanted Minnie around. He didn't like talking about himself. What was there to talk about? Shaking out all those nickels and dimes? It hadn't been such a wonderful life. There were some things children shouldn't hear about.

Well, he was too old to change. Jessica slumped back in her seat. He was probably counting every straw sticking out of the horsehair sofa. He was as bad as her mother. Still, she loved him, she supposed; she was too old to change herself.

Meanwhile, Elsie turned the volume of the radio up in the kitchen. More weather. "Did it say something about the Long Island Rail Road?" her father asked abruptly. "I don't think so," she answered, irritated. "I heard it." He still had ears like a fox. She never had been able to sneak into his house. "Well, go into the kitchen and ask Elsie if you're so interested." "Jessica," Robert warned. Her father went stubbornly out to the kitchen. He came back wearing his coat. "There's a train leaving in fifty minutes from Atlantic Avenue," he said; "the tracks are cleared to Baldwin." "Oh, fine!" Jessica exclaimed, throwing her napkin on the floor; "what's the point? You'll be on the train all night and then you'll just have to turn around and come right back." "Can we make it?" he asked Robert, pulling on his hat. As if she were nothing but a cloud. Robert looked at his watch; he didn't look at her. He knew better. She sat still in her chair, eyes burning. "Well, goodbye." Her father kissed her perfunctorily on the top of her head. He and Robert started out. She sat until she saw the snow swirling outside. "Drive carefully," she called after her husband, ostentatiously switching on the alarm. She saw her father look back warily at the red light. She wasn't going to say goodbye to him. Something in the hardness of Jessica's expression reminded him of his own mother, the way she had kept after his father that first time he lost his business, needling him; he was lazy, he was good for nothing, lazy, lazy, lazy, that's why he wanted to retire and open a dry cleaning store. And his father was the only man he'd ever heard of who went back into the business after the Depression and made a go of it. He'd made all his money back. They were driving around in black limousines, chauffeurs, flowers in the car vases, soon enough. "Goodbye," he said through the door. His voice sounded like sandpaper. She turned back into the hall without answering. He shrugged his shoulders, following Robert out to the car.

Jessica went into the kitchen and called her mother. "He's taking the train home." "I knew it," Minnie said; "now don't go get all upset. You know how your father is." Jessica put the receiver gently back on the hook, dug her nails into her arm. She was crying with rage. Well, she would go downstairs and practice; she should have known. What else did she expect? The minute he was on that train, he'd be in seventh heaven.

Halfway through her part in *Così fan tutte*, the intercom clicked on. "He's on the train," Robert said; he sounded exhausted. "Great; you go to bed. I'm staying up to practice. Is everyone home?" "Everyone but Mimi." "Leave her a note to buzz me when she gets in." "I'll do it now," her husband said; "good squawking." In spite of herself, she grinned. Robert went up to bed. She'd feel a lot better, he knew, when she finished with that opera. Work horses, her whole family. The intercom light went on in their bedroom. "Robert," Jessica asked, "do you know how many nights he's slept here? Exactly two. Two emergency operations, two nights. I'll be up later," she said after a pause. *He* wouldn't answer her either, she knew, not about her father. She'd bite his head off no matter what he said. That man didn't give a damn about her, she thought, going back to her music. Two nights! He'd slept at all the other children's houses often enough and *they* didn't have to tie him down. Deliberately, she began the aria in a dreadful, high-pitched shriek. Well, that was what her father thought she sounded like, wasn't it? She forced her vocal cords to relax. Soon she was lost in the music and the strange language. None of the languages but her own ever sounded familiar. She had given up wondering why.

As soon as the train jerked and bumped on its way out of the Atlantic Avenue station, on its interminable way to Jamaica, her father settled blissfully back in his seat. He stretched his legs and took off his scarf and hat. He left his coat on. At least tomorrow, when he got up, he wouldn't be greeted by that vicious mutt. His daughter's house. She'd be singing away; she was probably relieved he was gone. He might have expected someone there to get up and cook breakfast for him. He'd be happy enough to see his own bed. He made an effort to stay awake and watch the snow, but by the time the conductor reached his seat, he was asleep. The man took the ticket out of its holder in the seat next to him and punched it. At least someone else on the train was alive, he thought, trudging off to the next car.

In the basement, Jessica practiced, oblivious to everything else, until midnight. Then she refused to think about her father and fell into bed and sleep as quickly as her father had on the train. In her own house, Minnie was still up with her embroidery, waiting. She wished she could keep her plants alive through the winter as easily as everyone around her kept their grudges. She sat up in her own chair, fighting off sleep.

The Priest Next Door

In the old neighborhoods, where the houses hide as many as eighteen rooms under their peaked and turreted roofs, silence falls as sweetly on the concrete sidewalks as sunlight; cars are not heard passing under the oak leaves, and it is the sound of wind and rain that people listen to. In neighborhoods like this, it is inevitable that everyone knows the rough lines and perspective of everyone else's lives, for the children belong to the same troops of Girl Scouts, and always have cookies to sell, so that the desperate mothers band together in threes and fours, each mother buying one box of cookies from the other two or three children so that their own child will not have to sell cookies to strangers and cross too many streets. So it is inevitable that not only the rough lines of a life, but the finer details, become common knowledge as well. Yet, on streets where the great tragedies are not deaths, which everyone chronicles in the ledger next to the births of the anonymous infants whose names the neighbors all carefully learn, but the falling of the great oak boughs from the trees in an ice storm, or the sawing off of branches by the telephone company, so they will not pull down the wires, where the truly remarkable event is the late frost aborting the crocuses and forsythias, or the early frost, cracking radiators of automobiles in their garages, themselves the sizes of houses, privacy is always respected.

For the people in the old houses have learned that a yard filled with oak leaves, cinder blocks, and damp cartons may mean the man of the house has had a stroke, and his wife must stay with him, or the woman of the house has been pregnant and confined to her bed and her couch. These events remain hidden, like shoots under leaves, while members of the family stand with their neighbor under an oak tree, admiring the solid ice coating, commenting on the tree's remarkable resemblance to glass. Therefore it is often easier to build a large spiked cedar fence around one's yard than discuss the condition of a neighboring fence with its owner, so that later, it is only possible to see the yard from a few upper windows of one's home, and soon the occupants' eyes learn to avoid the offensive cinder blocks and the thick black-brown sheet of leaves covering the adjoining lawn like a failed and terrible skin.

Still, strange attachments do begin to grow up. One house, which had long been known as the most beautiful on the block, fell into such savage disrepair that its yard was surrounded on two sides by high cedar fences. The neighbors had stopped visiting altogether, claiming the ice on the steps proclaimed the family's distaste for visitors, and no one would go where they were not wanted. In the summer, when everyone else's lawn had turned emerald green, the lawn of this house still blew with dry oak leaves, which would land on the other thick green carpets like dust tongues, each one bleating contempt for the block. So it was a surprise to no one when a *For Sale* sign went up over the door, for by now it was general knowledge that Mrs. Hills had had a heart attack, her oldest son having broken down in the local Catholic school after a month of misbehavior and blurted this out to

Sister Grace. From that time on, there were rumors that considerably more of interest was taking place in the house, although no one attempted to find out what it was, since eventually, as is always the rule, the details would publish themselves in the very shingles of the house without anyone troubling to discover them.

The house was eventually sold to a young couple, who fortunately were not superstitious, for on the day they moved in, their baby's crib collapsed, and their own bed, when they sat down on it, fell to the floor in a splatter of splinters. It was a while before they had time to notice anything around them, surrounded as they were by what turned out to be seven truckloads of the Hills family's possessions: medicines abandoned in chests with the spoons beside them sticky, clothes of all sizes, dusty hangers, and, worst of all, in the basement, a trash can with an enormous decapitated doll's head, and, on an abandoned work table, a moose head, one eye torn loose, disgorging chalk powder through its socket, and above the entrance of the loft of the garage, a single leather boxing glove, cracked and peeling, hung from the rafters like a relentless old corpse.

Nevertheless, things settled. The baby who was one year old had stopped peering fuzzily around her new yellow room for the bookshelves of the study she had occupied, because the Zlotnicks' apartment had been much smaller; Mrs. Zlotnick, who was pregnant once again, began to feel the new baby kicking and was vomiting less and less frequently; it had been almost seven months since her last baby had begun growing in her left Fallopian tube, causing the blood explosion that sent her to the hospital for emergency surgery, and she would not be pregnant now if it hadn't been for God's Grace: accidents. Mrs. Zlotnick was beginning to open with the crocuses; less and less often, the emergency room climbed from its frame. Less and less often, she saw herself sitting in the receiving room; less often, she felt herself waiting for the real adults to come out of the cracks in the walls of the new house, although frequently, she did have a dream of a jagged lightning-shaped crack appearing on her stomach, a miniature doctor rising out of it as if on an elevator until he reached the level of her eyes, then menacing her with his stethoscope as if it were a hammer and shouting the names of various things that caused her to lose the baby: bananas! aspirins! antihistamines! turtles! stuffed rabbits! Edith Zlotnick often told her husband, Fred, and her closest friend, Susan, about this dream, carefully enumerating all the small changes in the doctor's list as if it were a grocery list, and always laughing, as if the dream were truly comical. Still, she had it more often than she would have liked.

"Look," Fred said one morning, as they were staring blankly out of their kitchen windows, both of them wondering whether the windows should have curtains or shades, for Fred was a champion of modesty and insisted they must have *something*. Had either of them known they had been thinking about the same thing, they would have been amazed, for, in fact, if they had begun to speak, each would have begun with a different subject. "Look," Fred said, "a fairy priest." "A fairy what?" Edith asked absently, inspecting the sludge of sugar at the bottom of her new china cup, trying to estimate the number of calories she was about to greedily consume. Fred had gone to the window and was staring with greater interest than he had shown in anything since the bathroom sink began its slow menacing leak. Edith got up, holding her stomach, and looked out the window also. In the backyard facing theirs, a priest was putting out paper plate after paper plate and cats were coming toward him through every bush and hedge. "God!" Edith thought, "our cats haven't had their booster shots." "She still hasn't had enough sympathy," Fred thought bitterly, his eyes carefully avoiding Edith, whose hands, he knew, would be supporting her mumpish stomach. "Look at that Persian cat; it's pregnant," Edith pointed, unconsciously adding, "Remember that time I was in the Emergency Room? I never thought a hospital could move so fast. I thought they just filled out forms while you wrote your will on the hospital walls." "The next obstetrician we get is going to give Green Stamps," Fred said absently; "look, he looks just like Mary Martin." "Mary Martin?" Edith echoed, studying the priest moving sideways in little dancing steps, his sharp elbow on his hip jabbing the air. "Mary Martin in *Peter Pan*; he looks like he's on a wire." "Oh." Edith considered politely. One of the cats the priest was feeding looked exactly like a kitten she had given away from her female cat's first and only litter. Zelda Cat had kept her other kitten, and still treated Ophelia as if she were a nursling. The cat Edith was intently watching was white and black patched, although even from a distance she could see he was a terrible mess. Edith assumed the cat was male. "That's a terrible mess," Edith said with more passion than she intended. "The Persian cat's beautiful!" Fred answered in a wounded voice; "it must have cost a fortune." "Anyway, the forsythias are out," Edith sighed. She had been married a long time. "A fairy priest!" Fred wondered out loud again, long after Edith had returned to the table and spooned up the rest of her sugar with her index finger. That night, Edith got into bed slowly and gingerly, not because she was pregnant, but because the shadows from the blinds fell across the floor in unaccustomed patterns, one in particular taking a shape she imagined to be that of a surgeon's knife. Fred was up very late, going over the year's forms, a habit he had developed since their move to the new house.

The next day, which was Sunday, Edith took Cara out into the backyard to rake leaves before the church bells of the neighborhood Catholic school had even begun ringing. The morning chill was beginning to leave the air, and the sky had turned from gray to slate blue and was now shimmering brilliantly at the edges. Her daughter was absorbed in a corner of her outdoor playpen, which resembled a zoo cage, pulling her doll's red wool hair, when a horrible cat voice sounded at Edith's feet just as she picked up a rake. The black and white cat she had seen from the kitchen was standing in a pile of last year's gray-brown leaves, angrily screaming up at her. It had a shocking pink mouth, a slightly coated pink tongue, and alarmingly shiny pointed teeth. "Good grief!" Edith thought, catching sight of his front paws with their long hooked claws. "I'm not supposed to touch you," she informed the cat defensively; "my husband says you'll give our cats germs." The cat screamed in outrage. "Are you hungry?" Edith asked guiltily. The cat screamed again. "If I feed you this *once*," Edith asked the cat, "will you go away?" The cat answered loudly. Oppressed, Edith went into the house. She listened carefully, but there was no sound. The cat was screaming his head off on the cement back porch. Edith decided to open his can of tuna with a hand opener, not the electric one, because she was afraid that otherwise Fred would hear, and come down and start a fuss. As she went back out, carrying the paper plate full of cat tuna, blocking her own large cat's exit with her calf, she looked through the window and thought she saw the priest's kitchen curtain pulling back, as if he were watching her.

"You are a terrible mess," she told the black and white cat's shoulders, as he hunched over the plate, gobbling his food. "I wonder how old you are?" she asked the indifferent back of his furry neck. She stopped, thinking what the neighbors might have named him. "Patches?" she whispered. The cat perked up his ears but didn't stop eating. Edith sat down on the step to watch him. The cat slid sideways, toward the edge of the porch, observing her, while chewing, from one large green eye. "Hmmm," Edith observed to the air. The cat raised his head and looked at her. "Nice cat," Edith sighed, getting up and going up to her leaves. Later, when she looked up, the priest's curtains were hanging naturally, and that night, through her kitchen windows, Edith saw him feeding the local army of cats.

The next morning, Edith woke up from a terrible nightmare in which her mother had her committed to an asylum after a violent argument over the decorating of her kitchen windows; she escaped to find her mother driving off with Cara in a purple Pontiac, and found a notice on the front door of the house saying it had been sold to her mother, Mrs. Picarillo, for sixty dollars. While she was trying to pull herself together over the baby bottle and the stove, which along with the rest of the house still belonged to her, an outrageous screaming began at the kitchen door. There was Patches, hanging onto the edge of the back door windows by his front claws. The priest's house had not yet opened for the morning, although two gray cats had taken up their stations on the railings of his porch like two cement lions. Mrs. Zlotnick flew to the back door with a full plate of tuna, then ran up the back steps with Cara's bottle, but as she was feeding her, she was preoccupied with the picture of Patches' desperate face, and her own desire, every moment more desperate, to go down and find him.

Although most of the tuna was gone, Patches was not in the backyard. Mrs. Zlotnick stood still, looking out of the back window, every minute more grimly depressed. When she heard the already-familiar grating scream from the windows of the front porch, and went into the dining room and caught sight of his infuriated face, Edith felt a hot flood of joy, utterly unlike anything she had felt in years. Upstairs, she could hear her daughter crying; she stopped, but only for a second, and went out in her bathrobe and slippers onto the glassed-in front porch. Patches took one look at her and jumped into Cara's red English carriage where, with his chin propped on its edge, he stared defiantly at her. The porch windowpanes rattled in and out in the white gale. "Cold," Edith said out loud, hugging her arms around her breasts; the nipples were cold and were standing up against the terrycloth. Edith sat down on the blue couch the old owner had left marooned against the wall. "I could get pneumonia out here because of this dumb cat," she thought without moving. She was getting colder and colder and more and more miserable, as if everyone in the world she loved had just been destroyed. "I could get pneumonia because of you," she said to Patches accusingly: "look, it's even snowing." Patches looked at her unimpressed, then stood up in the carriage, stretched, arching his back, jumped down and walked over to her. "Well?" Edith asked through chattering teeth as Patches regarded her like a miniature god from the floor. "You're very short," Edith informed him irritably. The cat regarded her without blinking. "You are a Terrible Mess," Edith said with emphasis, a fleeting cloud of guilt streaking across the gray world which held only the two of them; she would never call Cara a terrible mess, although she was, in fact, and most of the time. "A Horrible, Terrible Mess," Edith said loudly. The cat jumped up on to the couch. Joy clawed at Edith's throat. "We'll all get distemper," she warned herself; but without any genuine remorse or fear, her hand went over to him. Immediately, Patches' head twisted back on his neck and his teeth closed on her wrist. "No," she instructed, withdrawing her hand gently: "No. Hand," she said, holding it in front of his face. "Now it's here, and now," she said patiently, raising it over the tips of his ears, "it's here." Patches twisted his head back, but let her hand rest on his back. Edith repeated the lesson twenty times; by then, Patches was lying in her lap, emitting loud squeals, and kneading her swollen stomach. "My mother says cats can carry a virus that can blind a fetus twenty years later," she remembered. "Too bad," she cooed down at Patches, hugging him to her. The cat looked surprised, but did not resist. From a distance, with her head bent gently over the cat, her rapturous look shining through the March morning, Edith and the cat resembled nothing so much as Madonna and Child.

"I don't want that damn animal in the house," Fred told her; "our three cats don't have their boosters." "He doesn't have to come in the house," Edith insisted. "First he's on the porch; next he'll be in the house," Fred predicted unsympathetically. "No he won't," Edith fervently promised, although in fact that was exactly what she had in mind. "When our cats get shots, he can too," Edith sulked, her lower lip out, close to tears. "Do you know a vet who makes house calls," Fred asked sarcastically, "or should we just rent a van from the ASPCA?" "Well," Edith answered, "as a matter of fact, yesterday I was talking to Mrs. Campanella; her daughter dissects the animals? And she said her cousin was a vet who'd come to the house." "I don't want to hear about it," Fred shouted, slamming down his fork; "you'll wind up the crazy cat lady, that's just who Mrs. Campanella is going to tell the vet who makes house calls you are." "Also," Edith went on, more or less unperturbed, "that old lady next door who's always hanging out the laundry and feeding the squirrels? She said Patches used to live in this house. When the man moved, he left five cats." "That's nothing; he left seven truckloads of furniture." "The priest took the Persian," Edith finished. "I don't want to hear about it!" Fred shouted again, this time at the top of his lungs, and stomped up the back stairs to his study on the third floor. Edith tiptoed into the dining room, saw Patches asleep in her daughter's carriage, and with a lovely sense of satisfaction went back to the dishes. "Where's the cat?" Fred bellowed down to her. "Outside!" she shrieked back in an injured voice: "where you wanted him." A peaceable silence fell over the kitchen as Edith smiled to herself at the picture of Patches, stationed in Cara's precious package, and as she washed and rinsed the dishes, listening to the nipples jostle furiously in their sterilizer, she watched the priest dancing with plates of tuna among the chorus of neighborhood cats. It was obvious to her he was looking frantically about the backyard. "Too bad," Edith thought, pressing herself into a corner. The fairy priest was looking directly at her window, and she didn't want to appear either to notice or to gloat.

So the days went by, and if the high point of the day became Edith's early morning visits with Patches, who had taken up permanent residence on the couch under a huge canvasy moving cloth she had provided him with for the rest of the cold weather, she dismissed this oddity in her usual flip way, telling herself she was only meeting the neighbors, and Patches happened to be the only neighbor she liked. Meanwhile, she carried out a relentless war of wills with Fred. "Can't you at least come out and *look* at the poor thing?" she pleaded in horrendous tones. Fred came out and looked. "If your mother could see that, she'd be in the next county," Fred grumbled, watching Patches affectionately place his teeth around Edith's wrist; "God knows what he's picked up." "Do you want him to freeze?" Edith asked rhetorically. "Animal killer," she muttered. "Besides," she went on, "he chases all the other cats out of the yard, doesn't he?" Fred nodded with a bad grace.

"He wouldn't freeze to death," he said; "the priest takes care of him." "He only feeds him," Edith answered, cuddling the cat; "besides, he used to live here; the old woman said so." "She's moving, the old woman," Fred said, as if that canceled out her comment. "And stop calling me an animal killer." "We still need a door for the mail," Edith nagged him. The former owner of the house had put a lock on the porch door, but the bell itself was set into the house door so that daily mail was regularly returned to the post office. "Patches could come in the same door." "Patches can go to France," Fred exploded. "You'll scare him," Edith remonstrated; "will you do it?" "Yes, yes," Fred droned, "but he can't come into the house." Edith nodded. "I don't see what you like so much about that damn cat anyway." Edith kept quiet. "He's a toughy," Fred said with reluctant admiration. "I told you he chased away all the other cats," Edith reminded him, and then proudly began recounting Patches' heroic exploits for the fifteenth time. "And the scars on his nose are healing," she marveled, running her fingers along the long lines of caked blood on his nose, crossing each other in a tick-tack-toe pattern. "Disgusting," Fred said again, shaking his head; "the fairy priest's out in the backyard; he probably wonders where this thing is." "No, he doesn't," Edith answered; "the cat's too filthy to be a house cat. Don't worry; he stays out." "He stays on *our porch*," Fred corrected pedantically. There was the sound of a baby crying. "Who's going to feed Cara?" he asked. "You do it," Edith answered seraphically. Fred went into the kitchen, and on his third try had a warm bottle for Cara, having boiled the first so hard the plastic sack began leaking, and, having nearly melted the second bottle when he forgot to check to see if it was standing upright in its white enamel pan.

As the days went by, and Patches' visits became more regular, Edith found herself more and more preoccupied with the fairy priest. Did he live alone? Did he live with his mother? She never saw anyone else at the house. "What's he doing up there?" she asked herself from the corner of the kitchen where she often pressed herself and her swelling stomach to secretly observe him. The fairy priest was inching along on his bottom across the shingles of his roof, holding to the shingly surface with one hand and gingerly dipping the other into the metal gutter, putting whatever he fished out into a paper grocery bag. Then he slid onto the sharply inclined roof adjoining and repeated the performance. "Getting leaves out of the gutter," Edith mentally noted, filing this latest picture along with the one of the fake red felt lily she had gotten close enough to observe through the fairy priest's window by pressing her stomach so hard against the heavy diamond-shaped fence she wondered if she was doing damage to their unborn child. Edith now kept a pair of boots on the back porch solely for the purpose of walking around the muddy lawn with Patches, and although she told herself she tried to take Patches for walks when the priest was not home (he now followed her like a dog, jumping up into the air to reach the tips of her fingers) it somehow happened that she was invariably out with the cat when the priest was home, and she either saw his shadow move in the kitchen, or his curtains slowly pulling back until they were at a sharp angle to the sill. Occasionally, when she was balancing on one leg like a distended flamingo, tugging off one boot or gazing down on Patches in her bathrobe, she wondered what the fairy priest thought of her, and invariably she found herself blushing. "His Persian is pregnant," she thought to herself; "it looks like two fat skunks."

The Persian, who was evidently a friend of Patches', since she was the only cat Patches permitted in the yard, now also came to the back porch, but Edith righteously refused to feed her, reasoning she was definitely the priest's responsibility, although lately, the Persian had arrived shepherded by Patches, and Edith was weakening. Once, she arrived alone and Edith fed her in a fury, becoming even more enraged when the pregnant Persian finished the whole can, leaving nothing for Patches. The old woman had told Edith that the Persian, also, used to live in their house, but Edith was sure she was the priest's cat. "There'll be kittens all over," Fred warned her as portentously as he could, but nevertheless, he was making plans to acquire a jigsaw over the weekend and saw out a panel for both the mail and Patches. Domestic relations had become peaceful. "Look at what the fairy priest's doing now," Fred called, peering out the window, while Edith drank her Sanka, pretending not to be interested. She had noticed that lately the priest was always out in the yard wearing only his undershirt and jeans.

Then, one night, Edith, who had gone to bed early after tucking Patches in for the second time on the porch, woke up to hear the loud crying of a cat. "Oh, it's Trembler," she thought, trying to move farther onto her side, falling back asleep as the crying continued. "Edith!" Fred was shouting in the middle of their dark bedroom; "Patches is in the house!" "Patches?" Edith asked groggily. "Patches! He's in the guest room." "Guest room?" Edith echoed; "pushy cat." And she attempted to go back to sleep. "Get up!" Fred thundered; "we have to get him out. Trembler won't let him out of the room." "Oh all right," Edith said, tying Fred's bathrobe around the shifting continents of her stomach. "Trembler," Edith said, addressing her giant calico cat in a firm voice. He blinked his eyes sulkily at her and lay down on the first step of the stairway to the third floor. "See?" Fred said; "you've upset all our cats." "I didn't let him in," Edith said, peering nearsightedly into the guest room. Patches shot by Trembler, down the stairs to the first floor. "Oh fine," Edith sighed, holding the rail, trudging down after him. "He's here," she announced, seeing Trembler's nose pointing under the couch. "Come on, Patches," she said, lying down on the carpet before the couch. Patches looked desperately in her direction. "Do you want me to get a broom?" Fred inquired helpfully. "Who'll carry him out if you scare him with a broom?" Edith asked, inching forward like a worm on her side. "Nice Patches," she cooed, scratching him under the chin. "Just get him out," Fred said in an exhausted voice. "That's what I'm doing," Edith answered, observing Patches, who was beginning to purr. Fred's loud sighs rose like dirigibles, bumping heavily against the ceiling. Edith caught Patches under the front paws, dragged him out from under the couch, and, with an injured stare at Fred, marched off with him toward the three doors leading to the front porch of the house, Fred running in front of her, frantically opening one after another. "What are you doing there?" she called a few minutes later, hearing Fred in the basement. "Sealing up the gas vent to the old dryer; I think that's how he broke in." "Enterprising cat," Edith thought with satisfaction, heavily climbing the steps, taking care to breathe rhythmically, going back to bed.

Two days later Trembler began sneezing and scratching his nose until it bled. "I *told* you," Fred said; "I *told* you." "It's only a cold," Edith insisted, but Ophelia and Linda Cat were sneezing too. When Patches arrived in the afternoon, he was trembling all over; his nose was hot and caked, and his eyes were running. Edith locked him on the porch with a temporary kitty litter box made out of a grocery carton, some food and water, and went in to call Mrs. Campanella, and then the vet who made house calls. Meanwhile, Edith alternated her time between patting the three cats in the house and Patches on the porch, and staring out at the backyard of the fairy priest, which, like hers, was also empty. His shadow was moving about inside regularly and quickly. There were no plates of tuna on his porch. There were no cats in the yard.

"Distemper," Mr. Amadeo said, taking one look at the cats and writing out a prescription for chloromycetin; "the house cats will probably be all right because they've got some immunity, but that black and white cat looks pretty bad." In the days that followed, Trembler, Linda Cat, and Ophelia began to stop sneezing and to eat more and more, but Patches, who had at first been fed through a dropper, now had stopped eating altogether, and lay trembling on the porch couch, his huge head on Edith's hand, looking up at her sadly from his electric green eyes. His breathing was labored. Edith thought about an electric blanket, but then worried that he might put his claws through it and electrocute himself. Edith herself had gone into a frozen panic, and Fred had taken over the care of Cara altogether. "He's toxic," the vet said on his second visit, and from her vigil on the porch, Edith saw him whispering something to Fred. She fell asleep with Patches' head on her hand, and when she woke up, the cat was rigid, and no longer breathing. "Get up!" she screamed, starting to shake him: "Get up!" And she pressed in and out on his furry chest as she had seen all the television doctors do. The cat lay there, rigid and staring. He was cold to the touch. Finally, Fred had to carry her to their room, where she cried so long she began running a fever. She heard Fred saying "psychiatrist" to her doctor in the hall, and then, "the vet took it away." "It!" Edith began crying, silently and steadily all over again. Her mother was called in; Edith barely noticed her. On the ninth day, she suddenly stopped; her mother began packing to go home and Fred began to look more cheerful. She still had no desire to go near Cara. From the bathroom, she heard Fred telling her mother that the vet had said there was no way of telling, that one of their cats might have picked something up from their clothes or shoes and given it to Patches. "It is my fault," Edith thought to herself, washing her face, rubbing it dry with a vicious terrycloth towel.

Evidently, the doctor had told them to leave her alone, for no one followed her out into the backyard when she wandered out that evening in her robe. As if she had expected it, the priest's door opened, and he walked toward her in his clerical clothes, although by this time of night he usually wore jeans and a blue sweatshirt. "Patches died," she told him. He had a jagged, bony face, red over the cheekbones. He looked at her and snapped a twig from his well-tended hedge, then stubbed it out against the wire fence as if it were a cigarette. "All my cats died," he said, "except the Persian." "Why?" Edith asked. "She had shots from before," he said, "when she lived in your house, and my aunt took her for a booster. She said she was too valuable a cat to take chances with." His bottom lip was chewed and blood-split. "She had five kittens," he added; "do you want one?" "No," Edith answered. "Good," he sighed; "how are your cats?" "They're fine." "That's good," the priest said sadly. They both looked desolately around the empty backyard. Edith thought she heard kittenish mews. "Well," he said. "Mmmmm," Edith murmured, and, supporting her stomach with her hands, she climbed the back porch steps. Just as she was going in, she saw the priest's back door still open, and then his hand carelessly reaching out for it, as if it no longer made any difference to the lives of the creatures on the block whether it was open or shut.

Advice

Lying in his coffin, the old man was perfectly aware of the scene his wife was making. She insisted on going through his pockets and he did not like the touch of her cold hands which he felt through the cotton pockets of his suit trousers. "Here," she shouted at the Director of the shabby funeral home, "money! You want to bury the money and leave me to starve?" The Director tried to reassure her; the funeral would be quiet and calming, not the sort of thing to try a widow's nerves; besides, he would have checked the deceased's pockets and given her the money whether she came down or not; that was all routine. The money, he droned on, was part of the dead man's estate and not to be dealt with capriciously. Thus he exhausted his small change of words for the occasion.

She suddenly sank down onto a metal folding chair next to the casket. "A piece of paper," she said in disgust, handing it to the

Funeral Director. He took it, automatically stuffing it into his pocket. "Six dollars," she said; "six dollars and two quarters. Six fifty. Two weeks' food," she mumbled, "the way I eat." She didn't like the look of the money or its feel; she wanted to spend it as quickly as possible, and was annoyed with her husband for having died in such a way as to make her wait until morning, when the stores opened, to spend the little fortune she had found upon him. She looked uneasily at the worn quarters; they stared up at her. She wondered, fleetingly, if the coins were old enough to be worth anything; someone in the butcher shop said something about some coins being worth hundreds of dollars. She looked down at them again, shuddering.

In his coffin, the old man was happy for the first time since leaving Russia. He knew the coins were his dead father's eyes and now they were staring accusingly at his wife. Even if they stared at her for only one night, the rest of her life, he knew, would be blighted. Now he could rest in peace, at least until his father found him, but he doubted they would both be going to the same place, if there was any place to go to. For the first time since he arrived in the new land he felt sorrow: sorrow for his poor, mumbling wife, his thwarted children, himself, the much-put-upon rabbi, even for the Director of the Funeral Parlor in which he now so comfortably rested. He regretted the vicious gleam he knew was stealing into his eye as his wife, whom he would not miss for an instant, got up to leave, hugging her treasure to her, her hand clenched over it like a claw. When the lid came down, reverberating, he welcomed the dark. He was becoming more and more sleepy, and his sleep, he began to hope, would be dreamless and sightless. It is doubtful he ever saw or heard anything after that moment.

* * *

"Let the dead bury the dead, and come and follow me." It is unlikely if the dead man had ever read these lines during his lifetime, occurring as they did in the New Testament, but if he had, it is almost certain he would have launched a small, personal crusade against the speaker of such a huge untruth; he knew the dead could not be buried. After all, he had lived a life which seemed, at times, only a few lines in a huge moral tale in which he was a minor character, although, to himself, he usually was not. When he thought at all, he thought bitterly, his meditations always circled the same carcass, and no matter how high he soared (and now that he was so old, it seemed, paradoxically, easier and not more difficult to reach the higher, thinner blues), there was never anything like forgetfulness, never any distance great enough to obscure the one event of his life which stood perpetually against the horizon like an immense sepulcher under which he had long since been laid to rest.

It was true that nobody loved him. His son and his daughters did not speak to him. His wife tolerated him as she would a crack in the wall, cooked for him, lowered her eyes to her crocheting as he passed. He spent his mornings, afternoons, and evenings in the synagogue. Silently, the rabbi often commented on his diligence, and wondered, every day after dinner, why, should he be asked by some sage who among his congregation was the blackest scoundrel, he would unhesitatingly pick out the old man, so faithful in his attendance.

The old women in the park always nodded to him when he walked his dog, but never moved aside on the bench, never so much as moved their net shopping bags, never tugged their woolen skirts down where they rose up over their loose-fleshed thighs, exposing the ancient silk stockings rolled at the top. When anyone else passed, they would adjust their clothes, one bench after another, as the man walked by. Thus they showed their respect.

And even when he picked up his little dog and carried it—it had short legs, and he always observed the moment it tired—the women would avoid his eyes, looking down until he passed, the sound of their whispers reaching him in hisses after he passed. When he returned to his apartment, the dog still in his arms, his wife would raise her head briefly, automatically observing the dog, its breathing, checking it for alertness, cheerfulness; she never raised her bespectacled eyes as high as her husband's face. She was familiar with the glazed, sainted look she would see there, the radiant expression of the unwrinkled face which shone slightly, as if varnished, that sainted look of a man no longer of this earth. Yet, if anyone had asked her, had moved the stopped machinery of her mind to thought, she would have said whatever element she lived in was neither good nor happy, but some extension of the slum which had crept up on their once reputable apartment building; she would have said there was something malevolent in his safe passage through dangerous corridors and alleyways; she would have said he was one of the damned. Now she said nothing to him or to anyone in the neighborhood, although she did speak to her one living sister at length whenever she called, which was not frequently; they would exchange information on deaths among their old acquaintances and what particular ailment had removed them.

At one time, everyone knew his wife blamed him for her miserable life, although she had never been capable of precisely isolating what made her so miserable; now, the only witness to the long years which had reduced her to a prisoner in her apartment, fearful of the streets, the muggers, spoiled food, was her sister, who agreed (and with as great a vehemence) that it, whatever it was, was all his fault. All the two women could agree on verbally was this: it had something to do with a newspaper. At one time, there had been almost eight witnesses to the onslaught of his strange behavior, although at the time, everyone thought he had been merely overworked and had exploded at the sight of the first inanimate object to jump at him when he entered the door. The inanimate object was *The Jewish Forward,* a paper he usually brought home directly from the press itself; he would devour it as if it were food, ignoring everything his harassed wife had put on his plate. Their marriage was still young then. It was still young enough to hatch hopes when he came into their first apartment, saw his brother-in-law reading the aforementioned paper, snatched it from his hands, ripped it up, screaming incomprehensibly in Russian, trampled upon it, and began stumbling around the room as if drunk.

Those present remembered the way he attempted to make his way across the room. As if sightless, he tripped over folding chairs, over feet, groped along the wall until he found the doorknob, entered the room amid a crashing of bottles and mirrors he dragged from the vanity by the doily, finally collapsing on his bed as if he had been dropped upon it from the ceiling. When his choking sobs grew louder, his oldest brother went into the room to talk to him, to comfort him, to ask questions: perhaps he had the worker's disease, perhaps he had a brain tumor. He had been to the doctor and was mortally ill; anything was possible. But he flew quickly back to the others, followed by a stream of curses and a flurry of several books which followed him out of the doorway like demented, awkward birds. The brother's demure wife suggested, without looking up from her swollen lap, that for a dying man he was unusually strong, while her husband could use a little more sleep himself and his color wasn't any too good either.

After that, the apartment emptied quickly. Blood was blood, but trouble was trouble, and if no one wanted to take sanctuary in one of their apartments, they had nothing more to do here. They had troubles enough of their own, and no one, husband or wife, wanted to stay long enough for the scene to make a deep impression on *his* spouse, lest they find the same scene repeated in the depths of their better-carpeted living rooms. As yet, the couple in question had no children; the troubled husband and his wife were no babies either; whatever the trouble, they would work it out on their own.

Once everyone had gone his wife stole into his room, whispered something comforting about sleep and something warm to drink, and for her efforts was rewarded much as her brother-in-law had been; she, however, lingered in the doorway, watching her husband, her brow furrowing, eyebrows lowering, when, to her surprise, a beatified look spread over her husband's face, his head on the pillow bearing an uncanny resemblance to an aged angel's. She felt fright then, but soon forgot the nervous clench of her stomach, the feeling that she could no longer breathe, for the look soon faded; it was to be years before she saw it again, but when it did reappear it would not disappear. At unpredictable intervals, it would happen: her husband's distinctly angry, bitter expression erased by that angelic mask behind which she was afraid to look. And by then she had a mask of her own, one which she was unaware she had assumed: the mask, not of indifference, but of nonexistence. Neither of them ever attempted to look for their early, real faces. In her dreams, she was haunted by a fear of having turned evil, as if somehow his nature was a contagion, which, through some fault of her own, had possessed her.

Probably it had. Her children would have nothing to do with her; occasionally, they would remember a vague gesture of hers, made indecisively toward them, hinting at the odor of affection, loyalty, worry; they remembered her then as gesturing toward them from her perpetual seat overlooking the street, as if already half-dead, a fish in water too deep and thick. What stuck was the bitterness, her ineffectuality against their father's unpredictable rages. As they passed exam after exam for entrance into special schools, special programs, he would refuse to sign the necessary forms. Their mother would sit in her familiar chair, looking at the blackened street as if she could no longer distinguish between day and night, moaning, almost inaudibly, "Oh my God, oh my God," while he would turn from them, momentarily distracted, thundering at her: she was a rotten mother, a rotten wife, a despicable human being. She ought to be helping him out, not sitting there mumbling, "Oh my God."

Probably he believed she had no right to invoke the deity; that was his privilege, haunter of the synagogue. There were rumors which reached the children of sudden separations which had occurred during their younger years—one of them had been put to bed in a drawer, not, as they originally thought, out of some crazy Jewish superstition their detestable father insisted upon observing, but because no other receptacle was available; rumors that their father had beaten their mother after she dropped the little boy down a full flight of apartment steps after following him to the synagogue and back to the apartment of "the religious woman" with whom he took tea. Neither of the children knew who had told them what, or when they had been told their father had broken their mother's nose. As the years passed, such things grew harder for them to believe. In his thirties, their father already appeared aged, sexless, priest-like, his appearance that of the extraordinarily elderly. Echoes of the hatred remained, shreds of loyalty to their vague mother who seemed a perpetually fading photograph of her pallid self; neither of them seemed believable or alive.

Their mother continued to sit by the window, watching the street. She developed difficulties involving the inner ear and frequently fell onto the sidewalk in front of the butcher shop; the young boy inside would help her to a chair in the bloody depths where for hours she would watch blood running down the butcher block, transfusing herself with conversations of other women. She would go home, strengthened, but not strong. The years had passed like speeding cars with no brakes, occasionally shrieking to a halt in front of her building, throwing out a screaming bundle of blankets which somehow she knew she had to tend. She would have liked, she mused cloudily, to think of years passing as they did in the movies she once frequented in theaters, pages from a calendar, flipping by, creating a gentle wind which would ruffle her hair, appear to stroke her cheek, a breeze she could call time, not passing as these outdated but elegant cars, which passed and passed, reminding her of what she never had.

At times, she wondered why she was incapable of earning a living; she had been once. She knew the longer she was married, the less she could do. Once she had cooked meals; now she and her husband ate peanut butter sandwiches or sardines, straight from the tin. Then she would reproach herself, saying she ought to have tried harder. She ought not to have returned after the last flight down the stairs, the last taxicab ride to her sister's. She ought to have stopped— But what? She did not know what she ought to have stopped. So she would resume gazing out the window, fingers automatically tracing the worn design on the oilcloth covering the card table next to her. Waking in the middle of the night, smothered with a heavy sense of guilt, she would slowly push the pillows to the edge of her bed, and off, stealthily, as if someone was watching in the ceiling, someone who would divine her fear the pillows had tried to strangle her. She was no longer completely rational. Worse, she knew it, as, possibly, a deep sleeper retains a latent image of a fire she slept through. At times she would wake suddenly, convinced she had almost slept through an automobile accident. It was important she wake up, even though she was not the driver; she had slept through a heart attack, an ambulance with red light flashing. At other times, she knew these as shorthand pictures of her life. Once she held a position as a secretary. Once, she had kept her seams straight, her stockings smooth. Once she had been able to do such things.

One remarkable night, she woke from a dream feeling cool and happy, as if a dangerous fever had unaccountably broken. She knew she had been dreaming and that this dream was not to leave her; this time it would not abandon her, that vision of her husband, dead, on his back in his shiny black casket (they had wisely paid for their plots and caskets in advance, in installments; they even attended the yearly meeting of their Burial Club at Rattner's, where they discussed new improvements in caskets, the most elegant set about between the small tables; there were fewer tables every year), arms folded on his chest, a tiny stuffed dog resting on his breastbone. Although she was awake, she felt herself lowering the heavy lid; she heard the click of the hasps. She was aware of the casket's weight, slightly disturbed she could not move it, yet she did not mind its presence. She hated him. A gentle breeze blew in the curtain, which danced languidly, as if pleased.

The rabbi, too, dreamed of him often. The rabbi wondered who else dreamed of him, how many others. He had long nursed a theory he hoped the next world would confirm; he believed both the good and the bad had access to other people's dreams, entering them as characters, coming and going at will. The old man was strange. He would insist upon grabbing the rabbi's dark coat, hanging onto him along the long blocks to the rabbi's house, confessing this sin and that sin: he was having an affair with Mrs. Plotkin of the rabbi's own congregation; he had torn pages from his prayer book; he had beaten his wife. Yet if the rabbi attempted to say a word, either of advice or admonishment, the old man would begin talking faster and faster until comment was no longer possible. At times the rabbi suspected him of attempting to commit as many sins as possible, but if the truth were told, as the rabbi said to his wife, he was no better at that than at anything else. There were plenty more in his congregation far more despicable in their actions, if not in their characters.

He fascinated many. This made the rabbi nervous; over the years he had grown into his conviction the man's nature was evil, he was human drek; then he would suffer tremendous stabs of guilt. His convictions were baseless. Perhaps it was true the old man was not all there. One afternoon, in the middle of his repetitious confessions, the old man had seized the rabbi's copy of *The Forward*, tearing it into shreds, dropping the strips into the gutter, smiling strangely, as if from a far place, while the rabbi, shocked, holding back a desire to giggle as he had not giggled since Yeshiva days, also felt his skin begin to crawl, as if in the presence of something unholy. At least that day, he consoled himself, the old man was not following him home, but floated off like a piece of paper picked up by an ill wind.

The day his wife finally heard the news of his long-awaited death had been a good one. She had spent it watching the butcher, listening to the women. She came home to the cheering news that her husband was dead. Now her only concern was his life insurance and what money he might have had with him when he was taken. Over the years, she had carefully paid the premiums on his policy. She never questioned the amounts, paying instantly, although her children had been driven frantic by her other financial dealings. If she paid their medical insurance fees, she was likely to decide on what amount *she* considered reasonable, paying only that. Once, the children had hoped for her arrest after the government agent came to the house and served papers forcing her into court for accepting social security while her husband earned a good salary.

But her elaborate explanations to the judge! Her insistence she had read somewhere, in the papers maybe, that the government gave a few people allowances free and she knew she deserved one after all she had been through; she was doing nothing wrong. After all, by cashing the checks, the government was saved a lot of trouble; there were no outstanding checks to worry about at the end of the year. And that was only the beginning of her explanations. In the end, she was sent home with a warning, the judge having imposed no penalty, contenting himself with muttering the city was lucky the two of them weren't public charges, then snarling at his court clerk. Of *course* he did not want that remark entered into the official transcript. How stupid could people be? The judge went home with a violent headache. Every so often, he would awaken from a nap, starting in his chair. He had been dreaming she was back, explaining a murder, an abortion, a stillbirth, a felony, an accident caused by a flowerpot fallen from her high ledge. In her dreams, she was always dressed in black; in dreams, her hair was white, while, really, her hair was dyed a brilliant red and she wore the splashy floral prints, popular and fading, even in the forties. Everyone, he thought, who met her probably dreamed about her. He was not greatly mistaken.

The judge wondered how such a person could come to exist, but soon gave the riddle up. The rabbi, however, afflicted with the old man's presence for so many years, had found it expedient to assume him the victim of some terrible tragedy, an unimaginable catastrophe, but when, during one of the old man's remarkable perorations, it developed *he* had been the object of his family's sacrifice, the rabbi's detestation became almost uncontrollable. Instead of the refugee from the concentration camp the rabbi had imagined him, he was, instead, the favored youngest son of a poor Russian family! When trouble came to the Ghetto, his father, who was entirely blind, decided that his last son, whom he had never even seen, was to be saved and sent to America; what money they had was scraped together for him. They greased the palm of a ship's crew master, and amid a waterfall of tears, he left. He left, promising his blind father he would send him the first money he made in America, and so distraught was he at the prospect of never seeing his father again, or his mother, or his other brothers and sisters, he too marched sightless from the parting, up the gangplank to the looming ship. Once he was on board, his seasickness was compounded by his fear of losing his only remaining pictures of his family, those he kept safe behind his lids. He began to live in dread of waking, turning his eyes inward, and finding their frames empty.

Yet, even in America, they remained distinct, perhaps the more so because the New World disappointed him. He had come at the end of the season; tailoring jobs were unavailable. After several weeks, he hired himself out unloading bags of salt from a Russian ship, and at last he had five dollars in his pocket. Even after he paid for two weeks at his boardinghouse and bought himself a suit of clothes he still had "several" dollars left over, and his next week's pay due the next day. The several dollars lay, folded and refolded, in his pocket, next to the folded and refolded envelope already stamped and addressed to his parents in Russia. Every night he would take out the envelope, shed many tears over it, spread it out, imagining it as the oceans separating him from his beloved family, but he did not put the first money he had earned in the new country within it. Gradually, that money began to obsess his waking moments, then his sleeping ones. A kind, immensely fat woman down the hall received the confession of his plight and earnestly advised him to write to *The Bintel Brief*. It was good advice, good advice, she intoned solemnly, nodding her head so emphatically all her chins rippled. That night, he unfolded the envelope, crossed out the name and address in Russia, and readdressed the envelope to the sage of the newspaper. "Esteemed Editor," he wrote, "I hope you will advise me in my present difficulty. I am a 'greenhorn,' only five weeks in the country and a tailor by trade. I come from Russia, where I left a blind father and a mother. Before I left, my father asked me not to forget him. I promised that I would send him the first money I earned in America. When I arrived in New York I walked around for two weeks looking for a job, and the bosses told me it was after the season. In the third week, I was lucky, and found a job at which I earn eight dollars a week. I worked, I paid my landlady board, I bought a few things to wear, and I have a few dollars in my pocket. Now I want you to advise me what to do. Shall I send my father a few dollars for Passover, or should I keep the little money for myself? In this place, the work will soon end and I may be left without a job. The question is how to deal with the situation. I will do as you tell me. Your Thankful Reader."

The Thankful Reader reread his letter, ears burning. Why had he called the money "the little money"? To his father, it would be a fortune. Besides, he knew the answer to his question; hadn't he carried the envelope, ready to receive the little money and take it all the way to Russia all this time? But if the man at the great newspaper told him he was permitted to keep his first money, and if he was as wise a man as everyone said he was, why then, perhaps he was wrong in his convictions. Times changed; promises were canceled. Every day after work he rushed home to inspect the table top on which the landlady dropped the mail for all the boarders. He was not long in suspense.

The editor wrote back telling him, in no uncertain terms, he was a young man and should send his father the little money for Passover, because his father was blind and would certainly not be able to earn a living in Russia, and even if he did, it would be easier for the young man to earn a living in America than the old, blind man who had given him breath. So that was that. He would send his father the money in the morning. But one day bled into the next and still, the little money remained in his left pocket, untouched, while the new, more considerable money went in and out of his right pocket. The "greenhorn" gradually became wary of strangers, then frightened of them, for the editor of the paper had printed both his letter and the answer given to it. He was sure people could identify him as the ungrateful son who had held back the little money from the poor blind father. He began nerving himself to send the money. Each day he addressed an envelope and each night he tore it up. Each night he took the money out of his pocket and laid it on the table (he would mail it in the morning, on his way to work), and each morning he put it back, where it rubbed nastily against his thigh. Perhaps he ought to write to the editor again, confessing his disgusting obsession with the few dollars, but the editor would only write back, as he did to other writers he vilified, calling them repulsive specimens, degenerates, black scoundrels, that he could free himself if he really wanted to and had enough strength of character to achieve his aims. He would write and say his best move would be to free himself at once. Imagining the answer, the young man would sigh helplessly, avoiding the eyes around him (by now, he did this automatically), and feel a deep despair, immediately relieved by a hope he would send the money that very night, or, at the latest, the very next morning.

The very next morning brought news of his father's death and his mother's. They had died, wrote his older brother, after a brutal beating at the hands of the police; it was some kind of pogrom. The brother apologized for not sending him an address to write back to, but all who had been spared were fleeing across Russia and naturally did not know where they would be from one day to the next. His letter overflowed with sympathy for his poor, innocent brother who was evidently jobless and alone in a huge, unknown country with no one to whom he could turn. The young man at first sighed with relief; his dilemma was over, he was absolved from his promise. There was no longer anyone to whom he could send money, much less an address to put on an envelope.

His relief was short-lived. He began to have dreams in which he was blind and his father could see. His father would never accuse him, but merely repeated, tirelessly, as if reciting a newspaper account, how his son had earned his little money, how he had promised to send it to him for Passover, and how his son had not kept his promise, but had kept the money in his pocket like a miser, not even spending it. Finally, his father was with him everywhere. The young man told the kind, fat woman a garbled version of his story (with his father listening behind him), and she suggested he get married and get his mind off things. He married the first reasonable woman he met; she worked as a secretary and made a good living. That impressed him, that and her independent air, although, as soon as they were married, he insisted she give up her job and make herself entirely dependent on him, as any good wife should do. He quoted imaginary letters from *The Forward* at her; she finally gave in.

Marriage did not distract him; nothing distracted him. His children did not distract him. His children were the worst part of his marriage, for, as they grew, they reminded him of his own youth and how it had led, inevitably, to the many envelopes which were never mailed. He began to dislike his wife for having brought them into the world, although of course he knew he had done his share, and even managed to praise her many times a day for having given him children, and thus, immortality.

* * *

Meanwhile, the Funeral Director was adding up the costs of the old man's burial. His office was shabby, the walls painted mustard yellow, the white ceiling streaked with dust. It was randomly stained with yellow splotches where the rain came through. He had long ago given up calling the roofer. Perhaps the roofer had died and that was why he had stopped calling. He no longer remembered. Something began to make his thigh itch. He shifted in his seat and heard the weak crackle of paper. He recognized it at once. It was the paper that repulsive woman had given him. He wouldn't have been surprised if she'd opened her poor, dead husband's mouth to look for gold fillings. He was tired and wondered how long it would be before he was gift-wrapped in one of his own shiny, overpriced boxes.

To distract himself, he began unfolding the yellow paper. It was a newspaper clipping: a greenhorn wondering what to do about sending his father some money. The mountains some people could make out of molehills, the Director thought. He hoped there were more people dying that month, because that month he had many bills and few bodies. He knew other people thought he was cold when he spoke that way, but after all, business was business.

And indeed, across town, another old man was dying. His relatives, surrounding his bed in Flower Fifth, were valiantly trying to keep him quiet, but he kept repeating the same thing over and over: "Keep the money. Keep the money." Then he began saying something else: "I never told you anything." Initially, the man's wife thought the first meant for her; his sons thought the second meant for them. But his name sounded familiar to his private nurse, and when she asked, the old man's son said yes, his father used to write answers for *The Bintel Brief*, but he hadn't lasted long at it, and it was *his* job now. The nurse nodded and said that all her life she had heard her family reading the letters to *The Bintel Brief* over dinner, arguing over whether the answers given were the right ones. They never, at least not in her house, she told him, ever agreed all at the same time, so finally, she said, shyly smiling, she had come to the conclusion that the person who wrote the answers was never wrong and he was never right. Of course, she said, blushing, she was only a child when she had decided that.

Antiques

From the beginning, they held fascination for me. For one thing, theirs was the only store I knew of in the city where the owner would rush out, as if playing the witch in *Hansel and Gretel* (but jarringly blond), and scream into your face, peering into her darkness like a bat, "What do you want?" Desperately, I tried to think of something to say. There were little dark images of her all over the walls. "A mirror," I said, "I want a mirror." Grudgingly, I was let in. It had been hard to see the merchandise from the street, covered as the window was with a thick iron grate in a pattern of diamonds, the color of dried blood. Often, I had pressed my face up so hard and so close I left the print of my nose in the center of one of them like a misted-over eye. The shop was open at odd hours.

Inside, the store was like a peddler's cart come to rest. I began to poke about, my blond shadow saying blackly, "Be careful!

Don't open that! If you break that, you pay for it!" I had never felt less welcome, but for some reason I didn't care enough to be insulted, or annoyed. It was as if, even then, I sensed she and the man she shouted to in an adjoining room had chosen to live as if under a rock, but theirs was more like an oyster shell, gray and gritty, even hairy, but when you turned it over, there was the iridescence of pearl. And the aura of money hung in the air more palpable than the stew she was cooking on the old hot plate in the forbidden back.

Occasionally, shouts of "Evgenia" would filter out through the other half of the store adjoining hers by one small door, and she would shout back, "Not now, Yuri," but finally, she would give in, disappearing, and reappearing, as twitchily as a mouse. Finally, I decided to buy a silver brush and comb. This was my passport; without them, I could never come back. "Fifteen dollars," Evgenia said to me, making out the bill on an old yellow pad, now browning around the edges with age as if burnt.

"Can I pay you by check?" I asked. "No checks," she said, tearing the bill in half, her accent invading her throat. Desperate, I told her my bank was right down the street, and I would be back with the money in half an hour. The brush and comb went into a crumpled paper bag. "Thank you," I said, leaving, and her face softened slightly, as if coming unglued. Behind me, I could hear one lock after another slipping neatly into place as if managed by the hands of an accomplished thief.

After I began to know Evgenia and the voice better (he had a name: Yuri), I saw another source of my fascination with them was their Jewishness. This took me a long time to see. At my home, Jewishness was like a third arm, an amulet to ward off members of the same race, the same blood. There were frequent outbursts on the part of my mother, usually accompanied by a migraine, about how any minute we were due for a pogrom right here in America, and then we would be sorry, and later, when we were all in high school reading about the student sniping at the others on the campus from the bell tower: "At least he wasn't a

Jew." That sent us all scurrying to our respective caves, the sound of the banging doors echoing in the perfectly carpeted living room.

But Evgenia and Yuri each had blue numbers running down the inside of their forearms, like poultry, permanent social security classifications, and though occasionally they would be playing Yiddish music, or a Yiddish program when I came in, they would turn the radio off after they opened the door.

After a while, we seemed to adopt each other. It was one place where I could go to listen. No one expected me to talk; it seemed to be the last thing they wanted. We drank tea out of Yahrzeit glasses for so long I got over my sense of doing something morally hypocritical, and I began eating the lemon slice at the bottom of the cup, which they both thought was very funny. Bits of their story began to emerge like the beautiful veins you find in an ugly rock, split, and split right. They had been very wealthy in Russia. They both remembered the big Moscow houses and the wide Moscow streets I had only seen pictures of. Once, Evgenia got out a Russian children's book and listened to me read my Russian to her, getting every word wrong, or, if right, mispronounced, sounding for all the world like a retarded second-grader. As for Evgenia, it was as if she had suddenly acquired the patience of a true saint. I had never been so happy.

Yet the real source of my happiness there continued to elude me. Yuri was a shadow, running into Evgenia's part of the store with a hammer, a shears, upholsterer's tacks, a bit of sandpaper, instructions about what I could do to my old file cabinets with linseed oil ("boiled, forget the *Minwax*," he would shout dramatically, like Oedipus' messenger), but on all other occasions, only to hear Evgenia finish a story about a vacation where they had driven eighteen hundred miles to find the only typhoon in the country, a bombing in Israel, the time they lived on tree bark in the labor camp in Siberia, the nuns who had taken Evgenia in when she had been separated from her husband and child, the eighty-four-year-old Russian woman who had just been pushed down the steps of the local library by a gang of local hoods (she was trying to find a book on the philosophy of old age she had just read about in the paper) and had broken her hip. At appropriate points, Yuri would nod emphatically yes, or shake himself, emphatically no. Then he would disappear, and the hammering would begin.

By now, I sat on my accustomed seat, a red wooden chair next to the locked glass jewelry case which rested on an old painted table, its surface used for the breakfast dishes, lunch, and supper. As I sat there, I leaned my cheek against the cool pane of the glass, and, as it began to seem that the old earrings and rings and bracelets and pins and stickpins were beginning to grow in, barnacling my skin, attaching themselves to me like so many umbilici, Evgenia would begin to lower us both deeper and deeper into the past, but the odd thing was, the deeper we went, the closer her married daughter with three children seemed to come, a stranger never before glimpsed, who now seemed to stand, looming in the corner of every painting, her blond hair and all her features hidden by a loose, blue-gray wool shroud.

"My daughter never eats," Evgenia would begin ritually, and this would lead to a description of how they had been fed at the Siberian labor camps. There, they were not allowed to have stockings, or even gloves. Each had his own pot, and when it was filled with the boiling hot soup, the top layer, looking like cream, but only yesterday's scum from the huge, unwashed pot, his frozen hands would drop the pot, or spill the soup on his frozen clothes and belly, scalding himself. At this time, the men and women were in different camps. "For dinner," Yuri called from between hammer blows, "we had only some bread and a little bit of margarine." "That was on your side," Evgenia called back in her bitter voice; "in ours we had no margarine." The hammering got louder.

The telephone rang. "*Slushai*, Vavara," Evgenia began in her hard, angry voice, "I have company, I will call you back." Unceremoniously, she hung up. "You think it's any better here?" she asked me suddenly; "here the people starve themselves. You should see my Olga, such a beautiful girl! And what is she now, skin and bones!" Then this would somehow bring up the robbery which caused Evgenia to be beaten and Yuri to be shot, and the "bullet is *still* in his head, it sits on the skull," Evgenia would announce triumphantly, and out Yuri would come, pointing to his head to show his was indeed the one with the silver bullet. "They make so much heat going through the air," Evgenia said, "they sterilize themselves." It was as if life was to her a series of operations, some sterile, some not. "Thank God for that," she would sigh, stirring her tea, inspecting her slice of lemon as if it were a shark. "Eat it," I suggested, sleepy as a preoperative patient myself. "Ai, what nonsense," Evgenia sighed, peering at it again, then fishing it out and chomping it down. "Not too bad," she said with a mischievous grin. "Yuri," she called to the hammering, "you should try some lemon like Anita here, it would sweeten you up." "It's not *me* who needs the sweetening," he called back through the upholsterer's pins lining up neatly in his French provincial chair like so many well-drilled soldiers. "Ai," Evgenia sighed again, then lapsed into silence. It was one of our silent treaties, and possibly our best, that we would always assume that my life was an unruffled water, that I had no problems to speak of. And indeed, while I was there, I half-believed it myself.

"Maybe you could talk to my Olga," Evgenia said, waking up. "About what?" (Neither one of us intended I should do anything of the kind.) "She never eats," Evgenia said, lapsing into silence again. "More lemon?" she asked, suddenly joking, jolly. "Not for you," Yuri called out; "you look like a wrinkled lemon yourself." "She doesn't sleep lately," he called out to me as if reporting the doings of a particularly incorrigible child. "You should have seen my skin when I was young," Evgenia said, "people used to come up to me and say, 'Evgenia, your skin is so beautiful, what is your secret?' It was for true! And then, do you know what, the next day, they'd come up and pinch me. 'How wonderful you look, my dear!' They wanted to see if some of the makeup would come off

on their hands. But there was none! None at all!" Even now, she
felt the pure triumph, the unspoilt vanity. "You still have beautiful skin," I said. It was true; it was as if some miracle of preser-
vation had taken place in the Siberian cold. I had often been
tempted to ask Evgenia about the secret of her perfect complex-
ion. "Ah, now," she said, "I'm an old frog. You should have
seen me before the camps. I had the most beautiful teeth, so
white, like snow." "Like ivory," Yuri called out to annoy her.
"Like snow!" Evgenia shouted, pounding on the table until the
glasses jumped into the air, "not these yellow stumps. Old vampire, that's all I am now." "That's from the car accident," Yuri
called in his annoyed voice; "get some caps." "At those prices?"
Evgenia demanded, astonished. "No," she went on, "it was the
camps, thirty below zero, and they gave us boiling coffee to drink.
With the same old scum on the top. Made with one bean. The
same bean all week. All these cracks, I look like an old china cup."
And, she would go on upbraiding herself, and I contradicting her,
and Yuri's comments floating out more and more parodic and
ironic, sadder and sadder, confirming every word as the absolute
truth.

Gradually, I began to meet the eighty-four-year-old ladies who
came to speak Russian to Evgenia, and depending on the state of
their finances, about their children's failure to find a good home
for their brass samovars and Oriental rugs. She was as careful with
them as she was with her most fragile and valuable glass. Some of
them had lived for years in Argentina after fleeing from Germany,
and we would all drink tea with lemon, while the others politely
tolerated me for Evgenia's sake. As one outspoken porcelain-
hipped lady had made clear, removing her black net gloves, I was
little better than a gentile myself. But they all had the same
remarkably preserved skin as Evgenia's, though at their age, it had
more the texture of fine crepe de chine than unflawed silk. I
began to think the air in the store had magical properties, and
then would scold myself for thinking so.

But gradually, I began to acquire the notion that Evgenia had contact with the dead. Every now and then, I would be told that this or that old woman had died, and invariably, Evgenia would begin her own version of her epitaph: "Such a house! Such *gorgeous* things! You have never seen such things! Marble cleopatras (I have one in the front, you can look later), brass samovars, three sets of slip covers, it was a different place in the summer and winter and spring, and the chandeliers, the most magnificent chandeliers, tiers of light, a choir of angels!" And then, with an imperious wave of her hand, "Yuri makes all these chandeliers." "But I don't have time to clean them," he called back tragically, and then came running out, a hammer in his hand; "a little ammonia, they shine like the ceilings of heaven!" For the first time, I noticed that the dark, grubby ceiling was entirely hung with chandeliers of brass and crystal, some of which had evidently not been dusted in years. But toward the back of the store, in its brownish depths, one of them glittered like an opal sea struck by the sun. Usually I sat with my back to it. It was impossible not to admire it. "Is it very expensive?" I asked. "Very," Evgenia said, not even bothering to quote a price. "It comes from Katerina's home, you met her, the old lady who broke her hip." "How is she now?" I asked. "Dead," Evgenia said, shrugging her shoulders, "but when she was eighty-three, she could still stand on her head." "Probably on a Persian rug," I said, moth-eyes still glued to the chandelier, brilliant, but in the depths, casting a dull light. "It's rolled up in the back," Evgenia said, humorless; "you want to see it?" "No," I said, "I couldn't afford it." "No," she said, completely without inflection.

So this is how I got my things, my antique Chinese robes ("You should have seen the lady who wore them; they don't even need cleaning"), my Greta Garbo scarf, black chiffon with an enormous border of sequins that flashed in the inside night like moonlight, my silver comb and brush where it all began, my chocolate set with roses so beautiful I kept expecting them to wilt.

Evgenia was selling my Danish modern desk for me; it was the last new thing I had. It stood outside her store on the sidewalk like a huge Dalmatian puppy, immensely healthy, ready to lick people's hands and put its paws up on their shoulders. Soon someone would be taking it home. Clean, clean lines. I wanted things that were more frail, that needed gluing and oiling, and sanding; sometimes, I thought I wanted to move right out of this century and into another, surrounded by objects which had histories, and family trees, and the slow, thready pulse of a strong heart wearing down.

So perhaps that was it: Evgenia's store was the door to that dark, mysterious world. And so I visited, and things went on. I became confirmed as a tea drinker. Old ladies named Olga and Varenka and Mitzu came and went, and crystal lamps and silver trays and old sets of Czechoslovakian plates appeared silently in their wake. Occasionally, I would find a Russian newspaper, and Evgenia and I would stumble through a few paragraphs before she would spread it out as the tablecloth for our lunch. My cheek continued to press against the jewelry case, and after a while, she did not bother wiping off the mark it left, which looked, in some lights, like a ravenous mouth.

Then, one morning, I came in still groggy with sleep. There was a terrible commotion. An old Jewish man wearing a prayer shawl over his shiny black suit and holding a coffee tin with a slit in its cover for coins was trembling in a corner, waiting for the donation they would give him for his cause; what it was, I never guessed since I could not read the Hebrew in blue and white on the label he had pasted on the can. "Stop screaming!" Yuri was screaming at Evgenia; "you're always screaming, always screaming! Scream, scream, scream! Why do you have to get so excited?" "You're not screaming?" she screamed back, and then, smiting her chest, screamed to me, "See what I have to put up with? His own grandchildren murdered, he stands by, like in that book I read, Beetleberg!" "Bettelheim," I corrected, talking to the tornado. "His own grandchildren murdered, he wants me to be quiet, well, I'll *be* quiet!" she bellowed at the top of her lungs. "You don't know *how* to be quiet!" Yuri threw back at her, running into the upholstery section of the store: sanctuary. Then a complete silence fell on the store like a bomb. The old man waited a minute, then anxiously rattled the coins in his can. "Ai!" she shrieked, diving into the bottom drawer of her Dickensian desk and coming up with an old cigar box from Muriel cigars. "*Again ai?*" shrieked Yuri from inside, enraged. "What do you know about it?" she screamed back; "nothing, that's what you know!" Then she upended the cigar box on the same sheet of paper we would be using for our lunch. The old man grabbed up the coins, his hands eager as claws, and fled from the store.

"How much?" Yuri called out. "I don't count," Genya screamed back, defiant. "Write down six." It was the first time I'd ever heard him give an order. Evgenia scrabbled around on her desk and found a sheet that had an old business heading crossed off, and in pencil, in big letters, the word *CHARITIES.* She wrote down "six" at the bottom of a sloppy column. I was flabbergasted. What on earth was going on here?

"What's going on here?" I asked, afraid to sit down. "My Olga," she said, bursting into tears. "Go ahead, scare her to death," Yuri shouted, smashing something with a hammer; "Genya, I ask you again, have you lost your mind?" "Is she sick?" I asked, frightened. "She's going away," she said, making it sound as if she meant passing away. "Where?" I asked feebly. "Yes, where, tell her where," Yuri shouted from the other room, beside himself. "To Europe," she said, strangling, "with her husband." Now I looked even more bewildered. Yuri's head popped out of the connecting door like a papier-mâché puppet. "Go ahead, Evgenyushka, explain, this I want to hear," he said, his voice dripping sarcasm, "before she runs out into the street to buy a paper and see if there's a third world war she should know about."

By now she was sobbing hysterically, and the only word I could make out at all was "babies." "Babies?" I asked, as if we were busy translating again. She nodded her head violently, then plunged it into her damp white handkerchief. Sounds like "the monstro" or "the monster" began to emerge from its moist depths. I sat down on the red chair, leaned my cheek against the glass case, and waited. From the amount of noise Yuri was producing in the section of the store adjoining, it sounded as if he were adding a tunnel to the underground subway.

After many false starts, it appeared that Olga (who was all skin and bones, only worse now than before, but had been once such a beauty that people used to stop her and ask if she were Joan Fontaine, and now what did she look like, a ragpicker) was going with her husband (whom neither Evgenia nor Yuri called by name, as if his were of no importance) on a business trip to Eastern Europe for three weeks. Again she disappeared into her handkerchief like a demented fish. "Have a tissue," I said sympathetically, extracting one from my pocketbook. "No, no, you keep it, you may need it later." The sobbing resumed. "But she's coming back, isn't she?" I asked. A huge snort came from Yuri's territory. "In time to bury them all," she sobbed dramatically, starting to sniff; obviously, she was getting ready to talk.

"Bury who?" I asked, feeling like a broken record. "Bury who?" Yuri boomed, mocking like an echo. "Bury who?" I had no idea he could make so much noise.

It turned out that the disgraceful Olga ("Sometimes I am sorry to know she exists," Evgenia said; this followed by an incomprehensible explosion in Russian from Yuri) was leaving her three children with the full-time maid who lived with them for the entire three weeks.

"Maybe she needs a vacation," I suggested hopefully. "From what?" she demanded. "What does she do? She stays up all night; she writes things." "*I* write things," I reminded her. "*You*," she said, refusing to see any similarity, "you write for a paper; they pay you for it. It comes to something." "What things?" I persisted. "Who knows?" she sighed; "you think she would show me anything?"

"She's going to have a vacation whether she needs it or not," I began. "I still don't see what's so terrible." "She'll come back more tired than ever," she predicted gloomily. Now *I* looked closely at

Evgenia; her face was haggard and thin, her bleached hair un-combed. She looked like she had survived the electric chair. "Is *that* what's so terrible?" I asked, incredulous.

No, it was the maid Olga was leaving the children with; there was something wrong with her. What? She had a bad heart or epilepsy. "Well, *which?*" I demanded. "Not either," Yuri shrieked. "Diabetes." Evgenia mumbled something about the maid sleeping with Tab cans, but when I exclaimed helplessly, she refused to repeat a word, pointing in Yuri's direction. Suddenly he had become the secret police. Evgenia was sure the maid would fall into a coma while ironing ("not that she ever irons") and burn up the house and the babies. "Has she ever done anything like that before?" I asked. "Once is enough," she said, as if talking to an idiot.

Apparently, over Yuri's objections, Evgenia had set up a schedule with her "lyuba," or mother-in-law. They had arranged that the children not be left with "that maid," not even for a minute. The mother-in-law's shift began right after breakfast, and Evgenia's and Yuri's right after supper. They began closing the store earlier and earlier. At lunchtime, Evgenia was at Olga's supervising both her "lyuba" and the maid. They slept at Olga's house ("on a waterbed") and Evgenia appeared to spend most of her time checking to see what the maid, Evadne, a farm girl, had not done—or worse, what she had. She had not vacuumed the living room floor, but she had started to wash the kitchen floor, and then forgotten about it, and the baby had slid on the slippery floor, and banged his head on the stove. Also, Evgenia was sure Evadne did not give the children their vitamins. "You can't see what she *doesn't* do, Evgenia, only what she does do," Yuri said with the voice of a downtrodden serf. "Idiot!" she muttered to herself, stalking off to find the vitamin bottle.

Day after day, the hysteria went on until I was convinced that she was right; Evadne was an angel of death holding the three grandchildren over the fire, with only Evgenia's magic net there to save them. And through it all, I would hear Yuri, repetitively and futilely telling her not to exaggerate, not to tell people about all this, while by now, both of them shrieked at the frightened customers who suddenly could not find the right password that opened their door.

The subject of Evadne, the maid, and the endangered children was a black cloud eclipsing everything else. It was impossible to talk about anything else. In desperation, I found myself buying the marble head of a woman, which I had long admired but could certainly not afford; she had a beautiful face, skin as smooth as Evgenia's, and wore a lace mantilla (the marble so delicately carved it looked like fabric) shadowing her fragile, perfect features. She did not say a word, and she did not reproduce.

Eventually, I even found myself embroiled in an abortive attempt to find a substitute for "the monstro," but at the last minute, all efforts failed, and from Yuri's peculiar reluctance to discuss the subject, I understood Evgenia had somehow managed to undermine these efforts. Was she afraid of her daughter? ("Do you know what she asked?" she asked me; Olga had called the night before; "she asked me if Evadne was still there!" And she burst into laughter. It was the first time I had seen her laugh in almost three weeks.) It was hard to tell.

She bought Olga's oldest child a large calendar so he could cross off the squares of days and see how many squares were left. That way he could tell for himself how many more days it would be until his parents came back. Mentally, I began crossing off the squares myself. Evgenia was now existing without sleep; she could no longer swallow food. Yuri seemed to live on a combined diet of Tums and Rolaids. Otherwise, he ate only hard rolls dipped in milk, or sometimes tea. People on the street avoided the store like the plague. Everyone but me: I was waiting for something: a revelation.

Wednesday, the promised day of arrival, came and went. The parents did not arrive. Evgenia found Olga's older child asleep in his parents' bed. He told them he could not sleep in his own and thought he would fall asleep there. But Thursday, Evgenia, who by now looked like a ravaged mop, appeared, peering at me through the iron grate of her door. Even through the dust on the pane, it was clear she was jubilant. They were back. Yuri was smiling, ear to ear: lemon slices reappeared, like smiles, in the tea. Evadne, it appeared, was staying on. Things went back to normal. The earrings, rings, and pins embedded themselves in my cheek; peacefully, I slid down into the soft brown mud of time.

Then, one morning, while I was listening to the story of the new apartment, whose ancient contents were slowly filling Evgenia's store, and the genealogy of the old woman who had taken them in and cared for them like children, the front door gave its familiar tinkle through the impregnable grate.

"My daughter," she said, as if she had caught a glimpse of her worst enemy. Immediately tension thickened the air like gelatin. There were endless questions about the child who accompanied its mother: how was his stomach? was he getting enough to eat? what about his vitamins? Evadne just spilled them on the front of his shirt. Was Evadne still starving him? ("She drinks a gallon a day," Evgenia said, and Olga told her to shut up, the scream in her voice held in place by the restraining jacket of long-trained vocal cords.)

But I could not stop looking at Olga! She was a beauty! She was not what I expected at all! She had sun-streaked hair, and it radiated light like one of Yuri's chandeliers. Small suns seemed to glow under her son's cheeks. The child looked healthy as a horse, a small angel. Meanwhile, Yuri had yet to emerge; he could be heard puttering in the other room. Olga's son squirmed on her lap like a wriggly puppy and he kept raising his arms to the chandeliers on the ceiling as if he expected they would be able to lift him right up out of his mother's narrow lap.

Finally Yuri came out. Promptly, the little child stretched out his arms as if he were the plant and Yuri the trellis. Evgenia was completely ignored. "I know what he wants," Yuri said; "he wants the lights," and he carried the little boy over to where I was sitting. In front of me was a pull chain that turned all the chandeliers in the shop either on or off at once.

Yuri stood so close to me his body pressed against my leg; through his pants, I could feel the entire outline of his penis, and it was firm. Yet he appeared completely absorbed in the little child in his one-piece terrycloth suit. Experimentally, I moved my knees, swiveling. Yuri moved, subtly, adjusting his body: our positions remained the same.

Meanwhile, the child kept pulling the grimy cord with its ivory plastic pull, turning the magnificent chandeliers on and off. What could I do? Yuri had come to seem like a father to me, but like all émigré fathers, I thought, ineffectual. And here he was, his penis pressed against my knee.

The old misted eye still left on the window of their store began clearing, and opening, the ravenous mouth print left by my cheek on the locked jewelry case to swallow, and close. It had been Yuri's cord all along. He wired the magnificent lamps that allowed me to see into the case, to inspect the ancient silk of the antique robes. It was his cord through which the necessary current ran. He was teaching me a lesson; he was teaching Evgenia a lesson her capillaries would absorb through mine. The child turned the lamp on and off. It was this, the song of the toad he heard so well, that kept his wife alive in a labor camp in Siberia, eating tree bark until her stomach was bloated and swollen like a sick cow's, that kept her alive loading huge sacks onto trains in the snow when she herself weighed only eighty pounds, that kept her alive behind her metal grating the color of caked blood on one of the worst streets in the city, that kept her nerves under her skin, and her veins, not rising against her like snakes, that let her rave about Olga, who was starving, sure she would not. It was this that kept her vain, picking out her lipsticks and blouses, "the newest style," blushing like a teenager at compliments, that gave Olga the strength to pull free of the orbit of her mother, and her own three sons to rise in the sky like three new constellations.

The penis pressed against my leg. I tried to feel insult, disgust. The next morning, I came back at the accustomed time and took up my spot at the accustomed place. Then I bought a beautiful crystal lamp Yuri had built himself (it would take me two years to pay for it); it resembled a Persian mosque and caught whatever light there was and transformed it to sequins and iridescence and unicorn horns. Now, everything I read and write is done by its light.

III

PARABLES

The Exact Nature of Plot

I remember exactly how it began. It was November 16 in our small town, a cold, brilliant night, the clear, glassy wind hurrying strangers home. My husband was at college, teaching. I had just woken up from a nap. A friend called, and I told her as soon as the program I always watched was over at seven-thirty, I was going to begin the novel. At seven-thirty, I turned off the television and sat on the couch contemplating the number of patterns in the living room. There was one for the pillows, one for the curtains; the living room rug was Persian, another pattern, the couch's upholstery fabric; then halfway through, I could not remember if I had counted the tapestry on the wall, the pattern of the crocheted afghan, the crocheted pillows. It was like adding up a long column of figures and losing your place somewhere in the middle; some streak of stubbornness prevented me from making a list, marking down the subtotal, then standing securely on the plateau of the straight horizontal black line. Suddenly, the room twisted slightly, as if seen by an insect's mosaic eye. This was the reward of avoiding work, I told myself, and sat down at the typewriter, and as I had promised, began work on the novel.

The novel went unusually well, flourishing like a weed in a hothouse, then, as the process became more advanced, sprouting thick, fat leaves, fleshy, like the leaves of African violets. There seemed to be no stopping it. Every night, at eight o'clock, I would read the last line I had written, and by eleven o'clock, another twenty pages would have joined the others, lying loosely, like leaves, in the manila folder. When it was all done, I would take the marble statue of the Chinese dog and place it carefully in the center of the pile, weighing down the pages; for some reason I could not quite understand, I had been reluctant to number them, and did not relish the idea of the cat spattering them erratically over the rug in the study, a patterned Spanish rug, of blue and black. At this time, I began to have a sense of when the novel would be finished; I knew, too, that it would be exactly four hundred and twenty-five pages. When asked about its progress, I would invariably answer that it would be complete by December 27, and, when anyone looked surprised, would mutter that it was just a matter of typing. No one asked further questions.

But it was about this time that I began to notice that my memory was not as good as it used to be. In the past, friends had resented my ability to recite, verbatim, conversations we had had over twenty years ago; they seemed to consider this tenacity of the brain cells a fault in my character, and indeed, I had often wished for a less accurate version of the past. But near the beginning of December, I would find myself forgetting perfectly routine things: had I made my husband's dinner? I would go into the kitchen and look at the sink; yes, there were two dirty supper plates, one still streaked with ketchup, and hot sauce, two glasses, two cups and saucers, a thick black sludge at the bottom of each cup like Egyptian silt. But still I was not sure. Were these dishes from last night, or had they just been placed in the sink, carefully placed in the sink, for they were my grandmother's dishes, a few hours before? I would find myself leaving the typewriter and traveling back and forth to the sink, eager for clues. There were the peelings from the carrots. Had they begun to wither and brown? They appeared fresh. Then it was almost certain I had made dinner. It was certain I had. I would go back to the typewriter, but as I wrote, it occurred to me I could not remember *what* I had made— if indeed I had made anything at all. I told myself this confusion came because I was new as a writer; I was simply suffering from the celebrated abstraction of artists; it proved I was the genuine thing. At the end of each session, the twenty pages had completed themselves, adding themselves to the fattening pile. Then for days, I could remember everything about every meal I had cooked: every detail; how many times I had ground the pepper mill over the chicken livers, and the sound of typing, like sly teeth in the cabinets, an incessant clicking, somewhere inside the walls, was something I could easily ignore: so it was a passing thing after all.

It bothered me more, when, in the middle of a chapter, the baby began to cry; it wasn't that I had any doubts about whether or not she had been fed; I simply couldn't remember her name. But this was the sort of lapse I was accustomed to; at parties I would forget the name of someone I had known for thirty years, and I would try to pretend it was a joke while the old friend completed the introduction himself. Still, it was embarrassing. From previous experience, I knew the thing to do was stop thinking about the blank space; suddenly, the name would swim into focus, a fish into the net. Perhaps, I thought as I went to get the baby, it had something to do with my age. I couldn't remember when my birthday was, or how old I was. I would have to look at my wrist, I thought, when I tested the milk to make sure it wasn't too hot; perhaps this wasn't my baby at all, but my daughter's. I would have to look at my wrist and see if it were flecked with little age spots, the brown spots, the toad flesh. But I had a premonition I would not do this; I did not know whether it was a fat wrist, or a thin wrist, whether it was arthritic, or supple and strong. After I fed the baby, I wondered where I had gotten the bottle, and when someone was coming to take her back; it seemed more and more of these details remained unaccounted for, and it seemed that this sketchiness, this erasing of my mental blackboard, this chalk dust fogging my eyes, had something to do with the typewriter, the endless clicking of keys. It would stop when I stopped.

My husband, now: his was a name I could remember. Adam, the first. Of course, he had not been the first, but it was something about the courses he taught that had interested me first. Later that night, he came home. I always made a point of being finished when he came back to the house from his night class. "How did it go, dear?" That was the question I would always ask, invariably. Tonight, he made a face to signify that it had not gone well. I wanted to ask him what had not gone well; I could always tell him it was the nature of the subject, and not his fault at all, but then it occurred to me I didn't know what subject it was he was teaching. "Have you eaten?" I asked him instead. "Not since dinner," he said, thus making it unnecessary for me to ask him about dinner. But December 27 was getting closer. I was getting closer to the day of my liberation; this would soon be over. "I'm going back to school now," my husband said, putting something in his briefcase, and when I started to protest that he had just gotten back, I stopped myself, because I was not really sure. Instead, I went into the kitchen, and, as was becoming my custom, looked at the plates in the sink and the squares on the calendar, each day looking more and more like unfurnished rooms, never more than two objects apiece.

I really did not have very far to go. It was almost nine. "So that's how you see it?" he said, his voice threatening. "Will you stop reading over my shoulder?" I demanded; "you know how nervous it makes me." "I never was very polite," he said grumpily, taking a seat across the room from me. "Don't stare at me while I write!" I insisted nervously. "Besides, I didn't know you were coming tonight," I complained, in a voice unusually querulous. "I decided it was necessary," he said crossing his legs, staring at me. "I asked you to stop!" I burst out at him. "You're thinner than ever, you know," I went on crossly, "I can practically see the wood grain of that chair through your arm." "You always had a sharp eye," he said, staring at me. That remark made me terribly nervous. "Can't you do something else until I'm finished?" I asked; he seemed amused by my discomfort. "Disgusting, to be so thin!" I muttered under my breath. "Not until I show you something," he said. "For God's sake, what is it, get it over with," I shrieked, beside myself with impatience. "It's not important," he said, as if that explained the constant nature of his interruptions. I was silent with rage. "Well, here it is," he said, beginning to take something out of his pocket; in spite of myself, my eyes were riveted on his hand. "No," he said, changing his mind, and putting it back, "there's something else I want to show you first," and he got up, coming toward me. "Look at my arm," he said; "when I get up, a layer of wood grain sticks to it; that's why you think you can see through me," he explained. "Do you mind?" I demanded, getting out a clean sheet of paper; "leave that chair alone, it took me long enough to get it repaired." He was sitting down again, smiling. "So? What is it?" I couldn't concentrate on anything at all. "Just this," he said, reaching into his pocket, and taking it out again; it crackled like crepe paper, and I noted he kept his hand over most of it. "Get on with it!" I insisted, shrill. He opened his hand, and the paper unfolded; it was a crepe-paper dog, like a Halloween ornament, but a dog instead of a cat. "Very good," I said, indignant; "I don't know what's the matter with you." "I thought you wanted to see it," he said, wounded, and then I heard its snarl.

It was the largest dog I had ever seen. It had two gigantic fang teeth in its lower jaw, and its lower jaw was misformed so the lower bone jutted out past the upper one, the lower teeth pushing in front of the upper ones; I had never seen such an ugly dog. "He's very smart, too," he went on, "attack-trained." I sat still, saying nothing. "Get her!" he commanded in a low voice. The dog sprang at me, slavering; he was going to rip out my throat. His fur was mottled and patched, like the worn skin of an old coat. When I tried to get up, I found I was rooted to the seat, a page in a book no one would open or turn. "Well, that's the way it is," he said, folding the paper dog up and putting him back in his pocket. "I just thought you'd like to see it," he said, getting up and leaving. Later, I could not remember whether he had put on his coat, or had gone out the front door or the back. "Pest!" I thought to myself viciously. When was my husband coming home? I didn't for a minute believe the rumors he had died, the hints, the implications that came out of the margins of thin air.

The next night, he was back in the same chair. "Don't start with that dog," I warned him; "I won't stand for it." "Dog?" he asked absently, falling asleep, his cheek propped on his fist. He shook himself awake, just like a dog himself. God, he was thin! "I knew I had something to tell you," he said groggily, gesturing vaguely with his transparent hand; "she wanted to talk to you about something," he mumbled, dropping off. He seemed to have aged greatly overnight. "I can't talk to anyone right now," I said. "This is the only time I ever get to work; it's simple enough, eight to eleven, people ought to be able to remember."

"Well, you can't always have your own way," she said in that puritanical voice, irritating beyond belief. "It doesn't seem like I'm asking for much," I answered automatically. "You said we always used to fight on Mondays," she said, "over the grocery money. You know, that wasn't true. I got my allowance on Fridays, and none of you were even up when your father left." "I don't see why you're always rehashing ancient history," I said, trying to ignore her. "But it wasn't that way at all; I had complete control over the money. Actually, little fish"—"Don't call me that," I shouted, "you know I can't stand it!"—"it had nothing to do with money," she said, getting up and starting toward me. He was asleep in his chair. "I don't want to see it!" I said, terrified; I could see she had something in her hand. "Actually, little fish," she went on, "it had to do with this." She came and stood in back

of me, and held her hand over my shoulder; in her palm was one
perfectly formed breast. "And you said I was very young. Actually,
I was quite a bit older; you can see that from the veins. See the
way they stand out? And the nipple? Look at it carefully, now,
you can see it's been nursed at." "What on earth are you talking
about?" I demanded, trying to look to the right, but all I could see
was where he was, his thin legs crossed in his chair, the grain
showing through the skin. "You said we met at school," she went
on, "but really, we met at a dance. I was wearing a black dress;
you know, in those days, no one wore bras, the dresses were tight
and slippery. We were doing the Charleston, and out flopped this
breast; there it was, white as marble, with its blue veins, and its
nipple standing up like a flower. Your father practically dropped
dead of embarrassment." "What did you do?" I asked in a hoarse
whisper. "Put it back, of course," she said, putting the breast back
in her pocketbook where it turned into a lace-trimmed handkerchief. "And the next thing," she said, "was when we went to the
movies, and my girdle was too tight and I took out one of the
stays and started playing with it, and it flew out of my hand and
hit a man way up front. I still remember," she went on medita-
tively, but beginning to grin, "he had such a bald head, the picture on the screen was reflected in it, the burning of Atlanta.
Your father didn't mind at all when he found out about my two
little children." "Two little children!" I repeated incredulously;
"you don't know what you're talking about!" "You said you
wanted the truth," she said, pouting. "Look," I said, "before you
turn into the lace coverlet, or whatever it is you do, would you
mind asking Bessie to iron my linen napkins? I don't have the
time; I have to get this finished." "I don't understand," she said,
shaking her head, "you were always so neat." "I was a slob," I
shouted at the top of my lungs; "all writers are slobs." "And we
always thought you'd get married; your father couldn't wait to be a
grandfather." "Mother, for God's sake"—was she senile, or what?—
"you know all about the grandchildren." But she wouldn't answer
me, just sat in the other chair, staring at me, occasionally dab-

bing at her eyes with the lace-trimmed handkerchief. "It serves her right," a third voice said, male and deep, and hard, like a hard novel. Now, who, in God's name, was that? "What is this, Grand Central Station?" I demanded out loud. "How am I going to get anything done?" "We'll take care of it all," the new voice said, but by now, it was ten-thirty, and I had only written fifteen pages, and I was in a great hurry, and ignored them all.

The next night was the twenty-sixth. Usually, by this time, the bills for the next month would have begun to come in, but I could not remember having been to the mailbox, or, if I had been there, finding any bills. "These details must be attended to," I told myself, didactic, getting out a new sheaf of paper. But it was safe to put things off, because in the morning I would be free of restrictions. Thinking about that made me wonder what the weather would be like in the morning. I turned the radio on, hoping for a report. There was nothing but static. "I should have changed the batteries," I mumbled to myself, turning on the Zenith on the desk. I was surprised at the vividness of the dial, its exact markings, the fluorescent green of the needle indicating the station, while the desk itself seemed awkward, ungainly, as if it had been drawn on construction paper by a child with a broken crayon. The radio's dial glowed in the dark like a cat's eye, but there was no sound, just an occasional crackle, like a sheet of crumpled paper, unfolding.

I sat down at the typewriter; freedom was hanging over it like a great, hanging lamp. The typewriter switched on immediately, its electric purr soothing as a cat. There they were, three of them now; he was sitting in a chair, the wood showing through his arm, but more wide awake, and my mother, sitting straight up, as if at a graduation, her handkerchief tucked into the throat of her dress. "You said she had black hair," a deep voice to the left of her protested, "but it was blond, the most beautiful blond I ever saw. No wonder I was afraid to let her out of my sight." To mark his words, he reached into his pocket and took out a long braid of blond hair. "Here," he said, pointing to the end where it tapered into silver, "this is what happened when she got older; it turned silvery white, like that song she was always singing, 'Shine on, Silvery Moon.'" "Harvest Moon," my mother corrected him. "But he's right," she said to me, "she was blond; the other children were so jealous, they used to pull her hair." "What nonsense!" I exclaimed, feeling like pulling out clumps of my own. "And she never really got to know her father; you thought she was her father's favorite child, but her father took her sailing, and a storm came up, and he was struck by lightning right in front of her." "I can't stand any more of this," I said, pressing my fingers against the keys so hard their ten tips turned white as moons. I had the sensation their print lines were disappearing, beginning to erase. "*You are all insane.*" I said it as slowly and as positively as I could. "You're the one who can see through people," the thin legs said, uncrossing themselves. "You just don't want to believe it," my mother went on, "it doesn't fit in with your idea of what she was like, but he's right. That's how it happened, in a boat, whether you like it or not." "Right out of 'The Perils of Pearl Pureheart,'" I sneered; "how can you expect me to be such an idiot?" "Well, we never expected it, exactly," my mother said; "we've just learned to live with it," he said, fingering the braid. "Please, will you put that thing away? I'm almost finished, I have to get done." I was startled at the sound of my voice, thin and reedy, pleading, the muted soprano of fear. "And how do you think we liked it, when you said all those things?" he demanded. My mother nodded, miserably. "What difference did it make to you?" I demanded; "you just went on as usual. I didn't change anything." "You didn't know what you were doing," he said in his deep voice; "you should have thought about it more." "All right, I'll think about it later," I said, typing a few more words. "You'll think about it now," my mother said, advancing on me menacingly; behind the curtain, I could hear a snarl. All three were starting to move toward me at once. Suddenly, one of them started to giggle, as if he had been poked in the side, ticklish. "You see, the thing is," my mother said, laughing, "there just weren't enough chairs." She suddenly seemed to have gotten very young. "Not enough chairs at all," he said. But he was thin! "You don't have to worry about the dog," he said; "it's only the chair we want." "Well, you can't have it," I said, definite; "you have to learn how to behave when you're a guest." "Well," my mother said gently, "that's not exactly right, I mean about our being the guests." Then they started scrambling about the chairs; there were three of them and only two chairs. Musical chairs! "Mother, cut it out!" I ordered her, annoyed to distraction; "your bad hip, you'll be in a wheelchair in the morning!" "Her chair!" he shrieked, taking out the braid and running over to me; he began tickling me with it on the cheek, on the arm. "Musical tables, turning the tables!" My mother giggled like a girl. "Get away from me!" I insisted; "you know I'm ticklish; I've got to get done." "Ticklish, she was always ticklish," the first one said, triumphant. Finally, I jumped out of my chair. I was going to throw them all out. But *he* was sitting in my chair with his wood-grained arms, and he was starting to type! "Now this *is* too much," I exploded, tilting the chair forward, so he fell out, sliding down onto the floor. But immediately, my mother had slid in, and she was typing, line after line after line. "Out, out!" I shrieked, tipping the chair again, but she just laughed and pointed at one of the empty chairs on the other side of the room. Suddenly I was desperate to get to it. I ran across the room, but he got there first. "This braid is a pretty good pendulum!" he said happily, swinging it back and forth in front of me. I saw the chair next to him was empty, and scrambled for it, but he got into it first. Then I ran to the one by the typewriter, but the dog was in it, snarling his snarl. "Musical chairs!" My mother laughed happily.

Suddenly they were all running faster and faster, and there was always one chair empty, and that was the one I had to sit in, always. That is all I remember, all I have ever remembered, where I sit in my room, its four walls like four book jackets, shut in between hard covers, that mechanical voice, mechanical laughter, the mechanical tapping of keys. Days, I argue silently to myself about the probable color of my hair, nights about the names of my children, but they are on the last page, or the page before the last page, and they say I am the crepe-paper dog, or hinged like the crepe-paper dog, or bound like the crepe-paper dog, I can't get it right, it has all been taken care of, the last line has been written, this is the right shelf, and nothing at all can be done.

The Taxi

There was a taxi driver who had one story he liked to tell over again, and over again. "One day in December, it was unusually warm and unusually beautiful; there were no clouds in the sky, and patches of blue sky were fallen to the curbs in small puddles left from the old melted snow. Everyone was walking and the cabs were empty as coffins. It wasn't until two o'clock in the morning that it began to rain, and even then it was a light rain, so there would be no fares for that day. I am a late riser and a late sleeper, and so is my wife, so I went out to get some cigarettes. Most of the stores were closed; I got into my cab and began driving around.

"I had not gone more than two blocks when a man flagged me. Even from a distance, I could see he was elegantly dressed. The street lights glinted from his brown leather coat and his attaché case, and when he got in, I could see his coat had a heavy beaver collar. He had on some very thin leather gloves made of an even lighter shade, and the stitches in them were lighter still. The man wanted to go into Manhattan; we drove to 165th Street, and I waited. Then he wanted to go to the Island, and I waited; he went into a house that was huge, half the size of our block and with a porch supported by great white columns. He came back; he got in; he smiled. Then he gave me his address in the city; he said he had to pick up his suitcase; he was going to the airport. When we got to Eighty-sixth Street and Central Park West, I was to wait again. By this time the meter read almost sixty dollars, and I thought, what makes me think he will ever come back? But when I opened the door to look out, the doorman came over and told me not to worry about him, he was always good for his money.

"We drove out to the airport. He had nothing to say; he stared ahead, his perfect marble face diminished in the mirror, seeming not to breathe, nostrils of marble. Some seagulls cast dim shadows over the silvery marshes as we drove in the gray light; there were some shrieks; it was five in the morning. When we got to the terminal, my eyes, used to the dark, kept closing and closing in uncontrollable blinks. He got out, handed me some money, took his case, said keep the change, and left. Then I counted my money. One hundred and eighty dollars! A one-hundred-dollar tip! It was a miracle I didn't get killed driving home to tell my wife. Naturally she wanted to know where I'd been. Naturally she didn't believe me. I showed her the money; she still didn't believe me.

"I got angry. Who knew, it was possible two such things could happen, twice in one night. I got back in my cab. From its window, I could see my wife, in her blue terrycloth robe, watching through the dust-streaked windows of her apartment. She was a good housekeeper, but the snows, when they melted, were too much, even for her. I remember pulling away from the curb as if I were leaving a dock. The streets were empty. No elegant man at all. But on the front seat was a black attaché case. I didn't stop driving, but opened it with one hand, and guided the steering wheel with the other. There was a gleam even before the lid lifted. Inside, was a solid gold head, like the man's, but eyeless, and with real hair growing out of its metal scalp. By now, it seemed to be shoulder length.

"I pulled over against the curb to get a closer look at it, but the curb vanished to mist. It was obvious the head wanted to keep going. I began to drive and it began to look pleased. The more we drove, the less scenery there was, and the more pleased it was. I kept thinking, it would tell me something soon, tell me where we were going. Its gold lips never moved, its hair kept growing, and I kept one hand on a cheek, steadying it, as if it were a sick cat, or a child, frightened. But when there was no scenery at all, only the pull of the road, its lips seemed to turn up at the corners, or so it seemed to me then. There was never a problem with engines, or tires, or gas.

"It was the radio that spoke to me first. My daughter had gotten a scholarship to college, my wife her insurance. It was thought she would marry again. Naturally, she would buy a new robe. I didn't have to hear this, and I knew it would be smooth, like silk, or else fuzzy, like velvet. My son was growing up to look more and more like his father, and fighting in the playgrounds. The gold hair spilled over the seat and onto the floor near the accelerator pedal. The meter has long ago lost its ability to register the fare for the miles that we cover, but still it keeps on, like an electrified heart. It clicks. It clicks. I keep waiting for the gold head to speak to me, for the gold lips to part, but so far it has said nothing, although it seems that now, when I drive, I have to place my hand on the cheek differently, which may mean it has changed its position and is now staring at me."

The Yglesias of Ignatius Livingstone Island

Somewhere, right off the coast of Guatemala, is a small island known as Ignatius Livingstone Island. The people who live there are Guatemalan Indians, and the wealthy Americans who have come to live on the island have not taken root in the soil even as strongly as mushrooms. The people there live simple lives. They have no electricity or appliances. They find their medicines in the herbs or roots of the rain forests. Recently, the Palatine Sisters have come to the island and many of the children in Castenango now go daily to the flat red building made of brick which serves as a school. The sisters have taught the children to read and write and do arithmetic and more and more of the children are leaving the island in hopes of making more money, leading a better life, and eventually bringing the rest of the family after them. The people of the village of Castenango are proud of the peace in their village, which is very quiet (not like the streets of New York, which seem to them like long newsprint photographs filled with wind, noise, and snakes), though the people always look away when the dead body of a troublemaker is washed up headless on the shore, for the waves wash the body up silently, and, in the village, the mornings are quiet and peaceful once more.

Altogether, the village is entirely unremarkable except, perhaps, for three things, one of them being its physical beauty. There are real tigers in the woods, haystacks to play in, and it very often happens that a child deliberately hiding from school and the eyes of the Palatine Sisters, and who has spent the day picking cashew nuts, which the children call seeds, rests in the haystack, stretches out his dark arm on the gold hay, attracting a large black scorpion, and the worried family, applying poultices to the swelling, forgets about the truancy until the following morning. It is a fertile green place, and it seems to the inhabitants, as it seems to the observer, that anything can grow there.

The village is remarkable for two other things. One is a legend surrounding the Yglesias family which has lived in the same extravagant mansion covering the top of one of a pair of twin hills overlooking the bay. The mansion has been there longer than human memory, presumably as long as the island itself. The Yglesias family now has over two hundred members, most of them teachers and lawyers. The women marry wealthy plantation owners, or make their husbands wealthy when they marry. On every holiday the family collects in the mansion atop one of the twin hills; for days in advance, the ferry brings members of the family who have traveled out further on the spokes of the family wheel, bringing them into the hub, the mansion on the hill.

On the other hill, which is the twin to the Yglesias', lives a family named Vera. They are a poor and ordinary Indian family but they too are remarkable in the village because every daughter of their family always produces at least two sets of identical twins, and, sometimes, two additional sets of fraternal ones. The Vera twins are a great trial to the villagers, who can never tell them apart, and when a villager comes to the family to complain, the

father of the family, who is the principal teacher in the local
school, takes the twins into a room and asks them: who committed the offense? Solemnly the two twins turn to face each other,
and, like people in a mirror, one real, one image, point expres-
sionlessly at each other. Then their father takes them into his
room, one at a time, and makes each kneel down and asks for the
truth. On their knees, none of the children ever lies.

The latest offense requiring investigation involved a walking
basket of bread. One of the twins was walking home from school
when she caught sight of a huge reed basket walking down the
dirt road. María caught up with it and asked it where it was going.
It seemed odd to her that a huge basket of bread was walking
down the road kicking up clouds of red dust, and even odder
when she saw its feet were just like the feet of any grownup, only
much shorter and smaller, and the sandals on the feet just like
anyone's rope sandals. "Where are you going?" María asked the
basket, which did not answer, but just marched along, the round
loaves of bread bumping together and sending out a smell like pol-
len. All the Vera children were very curious, and María was no exception. She was sure there was a head somewhere between the
loaves and so she threw them down on the ground one at a time.
"What are you doing?" the loaf of bread asked in an infuriated
voice, whereupon María threw herself down on the ground in
front of the astonished basket and peered underneath. An enraged
midget was standing underneath the basket looking very much as
if he wanted to wave a fist, but couldn't because it was holding up
the basket. "A little person!" María exclaimed, astonished. "Don't
make fun of a dwarf!" the dwarf shouted, enraged, stamping his
foot. "I'll tell your father!" he yelled after her. María ran off and
when she looked over her shoulder, the little man was running
around in an eccentric circle, picking up loaves of bread and
smacking them against his poncho and pant leg in a futile attempt to clean them off.

That night María and Flora pointed solemnly at each other
when their father asked which of them had thrown down the

dwarf's bread. But on her knees, María confessed. "Why didn't you call me to come look?" Flora hissed. María reminded Flora that she had been in school, where she was supposed to be, and Flora made a terrible face.

That night the whole family sat upright at the long mahogany table which was really like a bench fastened high on the wall. "And another thing," their father was telling them, looking down the table since the youngest children were at the end, "you stay away from the Yglesias hill this year." Preparations for the party were now going on; the whole village could see carts winding up the dirt road like big black ants, but the Vera children could see more. They could see the carts arriving at the gates of the mansion and going in. Señor Vera, who never scolded without a reason, knew that the children of both families often met at the river at the foot of the hills. Señor Vera feared his children would learn envy from the Yglesias; even more, he feared they would learn of the legend of the Yglesias and instead of avoiding them, as they should, would become even more fascinated. But that year his fears seemed groundless. All the children were busy at something: the two oldest sets of twins busy with tailoring and cutting dresses, the two youngest sets picking cashew nuts to sell to the tourists. As usual, they sneaked into the neighbors' yards first, picking as many of their nuts as they could before touching their own. Their mother, a tiny dark woman, named by her children as the Little Smiling Indian, stood in the doorway when she wasn't cooking, smiling.

The third set of twins, Nacho and Juanita, went down to the river one afternoon. Nacho, whose full name was Ignatius, pushed away the vine leaves and saw the rippling water before Juanita, who could still hear only the splash of its green and silver tongues. Sitting on the opposite bank with her back toward them, wearing the customary full skirts of the village, and a thin embroidered white blouse, was the youngest daughter of the Yglesias: Cristina Estrella. Nacho was in the water splashing madly, shouting to Juanita, but Cristina did not turn to them. "Look," Nacho began screaming to Juanita, and he pointed to a shiny black log that had not been in the river the day before. Nacho and Juanita began diving from it, screaming with laughter, but Cristina Estrella would not turn to them, instead staring like stone into the forest, and after several hours of watching Cristina Estrella out of one eye, Nacho and Juanita seemed to forget about her. Finally, Juanita and Nacho got tired of splashing in the water and stirring up the mud near the bank, looking for the huge frogs, and lay on their backs on top of the shiny black log. It seemed to Juanita that the log moved, not with the current, but in and out, like a lung. After a while it seemed like that to Nacho too. The two of them scrambled off the log, splashed through the water, and onto the shore, running up the path and through a field as fast as they could to the hut of Señora Sánchez, who was always interested in anything unusual or strange.

Señora Sánchez floundered off the bank like a tarantula and in her strange way crept over to the shiny black log which she climbed up on like an insect. Juanita and Nacho watched from behind the bushes. For a long time, Señora Sánchez sat quietly on the log; then she seemed to rear up in the air. Señora Sánchez, who went everywhere with the knife she used to split cashews and cut loose avocados, gave the log a good stab and blood spurted up into the air. Juanita and Nacho began screaming, the log began moving, and Señora Sánchez was wriggling up the bank like a fat tree root, and still Cristina Estrella did not move, while the shiny black log undulated in the water like an immense snake. The twins flew through the village to the little mud building of the police, and the police chief called someone on the mainland. The next day some men came with huge nets and pulled the log, which turned out to be a monstrous snake with red eyes, out of the water. The man operating the net machine promised the children who were lining the banks that they would be able to visit the snake in the zoo on the mainland, and Nacho and Juanita were sure they saw Cristina Estrella, wearing an odd kind of white garment, watching from the top branches of a tall thick tree half-covered with vines.

The next morning the tale of the snake was more or less forgotten in the fuss over Flora's dresses. Señora Vera had begun to notice that although Flora wore a different dress every day, she rarely could be seen washing them, so she began to ask questions. María, her twin sister, naturally would say nothing, but the younger twins, especially Nacho and Juanita, were only too happy. "Oh, Mamma," Nacho said, "she takes off her dresses while María holds up the sheet." "And then she hangs them up in her part of the closet." "Unwashed?" their mother asked. "Sí, Mamma," Nacho said solemnly. In a household with fourteen children, even the very youngest twins, Paco and Perdita, agreed that everyone had to do his job, and in the morning, at breakfast, each child would take his wooden bowl to the head of the mahogany table, or shelf, and dish out his own portion with the iron ladle, take his fork or spoon and napkin, sit down and eat, wash everything and replace it just as it was. Two children were responsible for cleaning the huge pot and ladle each day, and the big ones dressed the smaller ones. By six, everyone was out of the house picking cashew nuts or avocados, studying under trees, sneaking into farms to steal milk from a cow, and at night, the same thing went on, except that each child had to wash the clothes he had worn that day, and since many of them worked in the jute fields, with machetes after school, everyone agreed this was a good idea.

But this had been a bad week for Señora Vera. Earlier in the week, before the appearance of the snake, her third set of twins, Juanita and Nacho, had gone down to the river and seen a shining silver canoe half-hidden in the reeds fringing the water, and, seeing a beautiful fishing rod protruding from it and hanging over the water, which was also flashing silver, they could not resist the opportunity of going fishing and swimming, since the canoe was so very silver and the day was so very hot. They had pushed off into the middle of the lake, leaving the two paddles on the bank. It never occurred to any of the Vera twins to worry about paddles since they all swam like fish, and when a canoe stopped moving, one would slide overboard into the water and kick the boat along on its course like a motor. So that day, Juanita and Nacho climbed expertly into the canoe, only looking once for the American they presumed was somewhere about digging for worms, and slid out into the middle of the lake, Juanita giving instructions, and Nacho kicking. Juanita was to kick on the way back, but at the last minute, both of them decided it was too hot to live in the air, and they left the canoe in the middle of the lake and swam back to shore, where they dressed, picked some avocados and apricots, and returned home well pleased with themselves. But by then, Señora Vera had already heard the story six times from other Castenango parents, all of whose children swam in the very same river. So Juanita and Nacho had been forbidden the river for one week, and sent to clean the American's house when they were not in school, and Señora Vera privately wondered if the snake had been sent as a sign or a punishment.

Clearly the river and everything its waters touched was causing trouble. Now it was Flora's clothes. Señora Vera had spent several days deciding how to solve this new problem. She took it very seriously, as would anyone in the village of Castenango, where everyone believed that only perfect manners and perfect appearance kept the town as peaceful as it was. Oddly enough, this commonly held belief, stronger than any army, had been undermined by the arrival of the Palatine Sisters, who came with new and dangerous words, and who taught the children in their convent school that there were such things as sins (they already knew this, but they had called evil doings "bad behavior") and that these sins could be washed from them like mud, without a trace, by doing *penance* and praying to Saint Francis, the patron saint of the island, and seeking *redemption*. This doctrine appealed strongly to the Vera children, but its influence was most obvious on the youngest twins, Perdita and Paco, and Carmela and Carlos. Señora Vera, however, was a small woman, but a determined one. She did not intend to have her daughter Flora repent of her clothes and continue to disgrace the family in Castenango, where her husband was the principal teacher, and perhaps even have her set a bad example for the other children, and it made not the slightest difference to her whether or not Flora's smelly clothes were excused by Saint Francis.

So that morning she waited until all the children had left for school, and hung all of Flora's clothes from the top railing on the porch, and when the children came back, there they were, waving in the wind, sending an acrid odor out onto the air. "Oh, Mamma!" Flora cried, her whole body flushing scarlet, rushing up to the porch and seizing her dresses by whatever part of them was handy, an arm or a hem, and all the time watching the youngest girl, Carmela, standing crying in a corner of the porch, a wet diaper over her head. Shame worked well for the Veras, and their children were always toilet-trained earliest in the village.

Nacho, who had been watching, but really only seeing Cristina Estrella in a strange white dress perched high in a tree covered with vines, knew this drama with dresses would occupy his sisters, all of whom would seem to be sympathetic, but would accidentally manage to find bits of Flora's clothes that Señora Vera had missed. Having done nothing wrong for at least twenty-four hours himself, he decided to sneak down to the river alone. He was sure Cristina Estrella Yglesia would be there, and since he had never spoken to her, but knew from the midwife who scuttled back and forth between the families on their twin hilltops that she was exactly one day younger than he was, he was determined to speak to her. As the eldest, he felt he had the right, and, having been born so close together, one might consider them twins themselves. "Pappa always looks so proper," Nacho thought rebelliously, "but somehow he always does what he wants, and I will too."

Since the snake had been taken off in a net, the river was deserted. Finally, Nacho saw a bit of white, looking like a spider web, in one of the trees. "Señorita Cristina Estrella Yglesia," he called in a quavering voice. "I am she," she answered, as if it were an ordinary thing for her to receive visits while sitting in a tree. "I want to talk to you," Nacho went on bravely, heartened by the knowledge that Juanita was back in their house on the hill watching Flora scrub her clothes. Cristina Estrella Yglesia parted the vines and looked down. To Nacho, seeing her heart-shaped face with its white skin, green eyes and blond hair framed in vine leaves, she seemed a creature not of this earth. "Yes?" she said again, as if answering a knock at the back door. "I wondered," Nacho stumbled, "if you knew whether they took the snake to the mainland or the big zoo in Honduras." "Honduras," she answered, letting the vines close over her face as if the audience had come to an end. "I wonder," Nacho went on desperately, "what kind of party they're having at your house. We can see the wagons going into it from mine."

"A wedding," Cristina Estrella answered, without bothering to part the vines again. "My older sister, Lucía Amparito, is marrying the owner of a coffee plantation in Honduras. But it's a safe wedding," she said in a small voice; "Lucía Amparito doesn't look like the picture." "Do all the women in your family have two names?" Nacho asked. "They did," Cristina Estrella whispered. "What picture?" Nacho asked suddenly; "what picture doesn't Lucía Amparito look like?" There was a slight rustling of the vines overhead; it seemed Cristina Estrella was climbing into an adjoining tree. "Do you look like the picture?" Nacho asked, his fear of the rustling leaves making him bold, but Cristina Estrella was gone.

"Nacho," Juanita called from the bushes, "what did she say? Did she tell you if she looked like the picture?" "Where's Flora?" he asked, trying to change the subject. "Washing her clothes in a tub in the front yard. She's crying." "Juanita," Nacho said, suddenly excited, "suppose we went to see Señora Sánchez and asked her about the legend of the Yglesias." "You know what Pappa said," Juanita warned him, but she was already pushing aside the fleshy green leaves that hid the little path Señora Sánchez's sandals had made between her grass hut and the river. As they got closer to the hut, Juanita and Nacho found themselves closer to each other; by the time they were in sight of the dwelling, they were holding hands without realizing it. Señora Sánchez was standing in front of her little door, nodding at them as if they were two criminals who had come to give themselves up.

"We thought," Juanita quavered, "since we told you the secret of the snake first, you might tell us something back." "And what might that be?" Señora Sánchez smiled coldly; "your own father knows everything there is to know about Castenango." Juanita and Nacho looked at each other, surprised. Señora Sánchez had spoken bitterly of their father. "There goes the fancy fish, that's what we used to call him," the old woman said; "the long green fish in the river with the yellow stripe, always dressed up." "She's jealous," Juanita and Nacho thought together, and both of them remembered at the same time that their parents had taught them jealousy was a terrible thing. "We want to know about the legend of the Yglesias family," Juanita recited. "Because you saw Cristina Estrella at the river," Señora Sánchez prompted. The twins were silent. "There's a curse on the whole family," she announced, sitting down on the little bench in front of her hut and, folding her arms over her breasts, stared at them as woodenly as a tree. The twins waited but it was hot in the sun and Juanita began squirming irritably, kicking up little red dust clouds with her rope sandal. "Why?" Juanita demanded, putting her hand on top of her head to keep the sun from giving her a headache; "they're a good family. And they have lots of money." "No one knows where it came from," Señora Sánchez commented, without bothering to explain herself further. "They always help the poor in the village," Nacho pointed out, seeing Cristina Estrella's face before him like a golden cloud. "No one knows where they got their money," Señora Sánchez said flatly; "there's always been a heavy gate in front of those brick walls."

"What kind of curse?" Juanita interrupted; "there are no such things as curses. They taught us that in school." "The Palatine Sisters," Señora Sánchez sneered; "the Palatine Sisters and their

Saint Francis are new here." "We used to put curses on each
other in school," Nacho reminded Juanita. "They never worked,"
she answered, "except for the time we gave Carlotta warts."
Señora Sánchez stood with her arms folded over her breasts observing them narrowly. "If you are going to talk about curses in
school, I have to get some herbs," she said, pretending to turn her
back. One of the remarkable things about Señora Sánchez, aside
from her love of everything horrible or terrible in the village of
Castenango, was her habit of talking, apparently without moving
her lips. Nacho and Juanita ran around in front of her. "So," she
said, "the children of the fancy fish want to hear about the legend, even though there is no legend?" Nacho and Juanita stood
quietly in the full sun, watching Señora Sánchez in the shade of
the thick green tree at the edge of her clearing. Suddenly, she settled slowly down onto her full skirt, melting onto the rough green
grass like a candle. The leaves cast strange shadows over her face,
so that each second, she seemed another person, one very young,
one very old, one very cruel, one very kind. To Nacho, she looked
like a poisonous mushroom; to Juanita she looked like a heap of
crumpled clothes.

Señora Sánchez began speaking, again without moving her lips,
and it seemed to both of them that they were not hearing her
voice at all, but the voice of the black snake with the red eyes
Cristina Estrella had said was taken to the big zoo in Honduras.
Her voice came from somewhere deep and dark, as if the black
earth were speaking, and they both remembered how many times
their parents had told them never to go near her. "Every twenty
years," Señora Sánchez began, "a girl is born to the Yglesias. She is
always a special child, not because she is very intelligent, or very interesting, but because she looks exactly like the great portrait in
the entrance hall of the Yglesias' mansion. Whenever that child
looks at the picture, everyone who sees her stands without moving,
because they look so much alike it seems as if the girl is looking
into a mirror. And it always happens that when that girl is sixteen,
she meets the man she is going to marry, and on the day she meets

him, something very strange always happens in the village of Castenango." "Or in the river," Juanita whispered to Nacho, who felt a chill at the back of his knees like cold spiders. Nacho and Juanita had just turned sixteen last month. "Then, when the girl reaches her twentieth birthday, she marries, and the family always dresses her in the ancient wedding gown they keep stored in the mahogany chest right under the picture, and then they comb the bride's hair exactly as it is combed in the picture, and the minute they do that, the two girls are exactly alike, and by the morning after the wedding, the bride is dead, and they bury her with the same dress on. They say Cristina Estrella looks like the girl in the picture."

"I don't believe it," Nacho argued. He was insulted. "If they bury the dress every twenty years, how can they bury someone in it all over again?" he asked, sounding a great deal more sarcastic and confident than he really felt. "They lay the dress on the corpse," Señora Sánchez corrected herself, "and then when they get ready to bury the body, they lift the dress from the corpse and put it back into the trunk and carry it back and put it back under the picture in the entrance hall where it sits and waits for another twenty years. It's been waiting in the trunk," Señora Sánchez calculated quickly, "for sixteen years now." "What was the name of the last one?" Juanita asked. "Soledad Cara," Señora Sánchez answered without moving her lips. "And the name of the one before?" "Caridad Gabriella. When they named Caridad, they used up the list of the virtues; now they're giving ordinary names." "Cristina Estrella?" Juanita wondered aloud. "The trouble with the Yglesias is that they think *that's* ordinary," Señora Sánchez said with bitterness.

"How did they get their money?" Juanita asked. Nacho was still in a trance, seeing Cristina Estrella's pale face and green eyes staring down at him through vines in a high tree. "By being good," Señora Sánchez said solemnly. The two children stared at her. She broke off a piece of grass and chewed its root like a goat. "My grandfather remembers the great plague, almost eighty years ago.

No one was supposed to go near the river, or even out of the houses. The Yglesias were very good; they never went out. Others in Castenango weren't so good; they died like the grass here." "Why did the Yglesias stay when the others went out?" "Because they were so good," Señora Sánchez said bitterly; "ask your father. He's the principal teacher. He knows all about goodness." Juanita and Nacho stared at each other. "He taught you good manners; why, some people say you have the best manners in the village, and he and your mother always smile at everyone. Your sister María sings 'Good Morning to You' when she goes to work. Your father, the fancy fish, smiled his way all the way to school the day your great-grandmother died. Goodness is a wonderful thing, isn't it?" Señora Sánchez asked sociably. "Oh yes," Nacho and Juanita nodded together, for, as Señora Sánchez had said, they had been excellently trained by their parents and did, in fact, have perfect manners, especially when speaking to elderly people. "Let's go," Juanita whispered, tugging on Nacho's sleeve. "Good afternoon, Señora Sánchez," she said politely. "Good afternoon, Juanita and Nacho Vera," she answered the twins. They trudged home through the fields, silently thinking. "It can't be true," Juanita said in a small voice, but Nacho didn't answer and when they began the climb up the hill to their house, he was following the golden face of Cristina Estrella floating in the air before him like a magnificent piñata.

Over three years passed. The older children went to America, where they became nurses and carpenters and sent back enormous amounts of money to the family. They came home to their house on the hill to gather roots for cures for the patients of the doctors in America, doctors they secretly thought of as stupid, and who could do nothing for the people they treated. Often their ministrations seemed to bring relief to the sufferer, so that the women of the Vera family, especially María, were greatly appreciated, yet the agencies employing them were constantly plagued by complaints from their clients that the Vera girls were "too cheerful," and thus had to be let go. There was also a disturbing rumor that

Lorraine, the only child with a foreign name, had adapted so well to her new country that she now belonged to a gang of young women who drove by the glass and brick houses they worked in, smashing windows and setting fire to the cars of families they believed had offended them. It had all begun, María reported, when Lorraine was working as a housekeeper in a wealthy place called Croton-on-Hudson. The little child Lorraine called "Little Sister" knocked the phone off the hook and Lorraine heard the lady of the house saying, "Oh, these stupid Indians, they're not worth much." Still, shocked though everyone was, no one really could find it in their hearts to disapprove.

Otherwise, things continued much the same. Juanita had married at eighteen and her year-and-a-half-old daughter, Inés, was now standing on a corner of the porch, a wet diaper over her head, sobbing. Already, other little children were coming to take her picking cashew nuts and avocados. Not only had Nacho never married, but he had never shown the slightest interest in any girl of Castenango. His family was seriously beginning to wonder if he might not be the first priest of the island, since before the arrival of the Palatine Sisters, there had been no priests at all.

Nacho began to wonder if there was something to the idea of his becoming a priest, since all the other young men his age who did not have families to support had long since married, or at the very least, were planning on marrying any day. Nacho had become a very skilled carpenter and spent most of his time making elaborately carved wedding trunks, although he and Paco also worked in the village tailoring and altering. Of all the twins, Nacho alone had developed the habit of solitude and spent a great deal of time lying on his back on top of a mahogany raft he had made himself, looking up through the vines to the filtering sun.

"Did you ever see the snake in Honduras?" a light voice asked one day from the upper branches of a tree. "No, did you?" Nacho asked, stiffening all over, but answering as if it were the most natural thing in the world to renew his conversation with Cristina Estrella after so many years. "No," said Cristina Estrella, and to

Nacho's astonishment, there was a rustling of leaves, a lowering and snapping up of branches, and Cristina Estrella stood before him on the wet, hard-packed mudbank, her dress immaculate in spite of her habit of climbing trees and in spite of her surroundings. Nacho had an irresistible impulse to splash her, and he scooped up some water with his two hands, dashing it at her. Cristina Estrella began to laugh even before the water hit her. She had an odd laugh, half cackle, half giggle, and to Nacho, Cristina Estrella seemed suddenly human. "There will be a big party at my house next week," Cristina Estrella volunteered. "I know; I saw the wagons. Cristina Estrella," Nacho went on, reddening, "would you ever come swimming in the river with me?" Cristina Estrella only smiled. Her eyes stared so hard at Nacho there seemed a ribbon between them; then she began walking into the water. Nacho stared in astonishment as the water went over her white shoes and stockings, then over her ankles, began sucking in the hem of her dress, then floating it up, and the next thing he knew, Cristina Estrella was climbing onto the raft, the white dress clinging to her body like a second skin, her blond hair plastered to her skull like copper, her sharp cheekbones slashing the cloudy gold dust that seemed always to surround her.

They sat on the bank for some time, talking. The sun began to fade, turning the scene from bright green to grayish blue. Nacho went to the party at the big house, and Inés and José, the youngest set of twins, duly reported this to the family, but no one believed them, any more than Nacho himself believed what he had seen when Cristina Estrella, sitting on the bank, began to dry almost magically, and, when she stood up, stood up without a stain on her dress or the slightest disorder in her cloud of golden hair. Nacho's father, the principal teacher, found the whole story so incredible he took Inés and José into his room one at a time, and made them kneel down, asking them who had thought up this dreadful lie, but to his astonishment, neither of the twins would admit to it. After that, Señor Vera was often to be seen walking about the house, slashing at the grass with his walking stick. He was also seen in conference with Juanita, but his talk with her only increased his slashings at the thick grass and weeds.

Several weeks later Nacho came home after missing dinner, which he had only done once before, when he broke his leg in the forest, and asked his mother and father to come into the study with him. "I am going to marry Cristina Estrella," he said irritably, conscious of the disturbance his words were causing. Señor Vera moved a hand, as if to brush off a fly. "Don't say a word," Nacho warned. Señor Vera's face purpled. "What did Cristina Estrella's father say?" Señora Vera, the Smiling Indian, asked. "Señor Yglesia said that in life, we were all like Master Willy, the pig who dressed himself up so fancily, he held his nose so high up that he walked off a cliff." "They are all deranged," Señor Vera whispered. "It is all settled, Pappa," Nacho said, as if he understood the meaning of Señor Yglesia's comment, although in fact he had not the slightest idea of what he meant. "When is the event to take place?" Señor Vera asked stonily. "The day before my birthday," Nacho answered. Señora Vera lifted and dropped the fringes of her woolen shawl. "They will make all the arrangements," Nacho said finally. "I cannot understand why they bother," Señor Vera said; "Nacho, the curse." "I refuse to discuss it," Nacho cut him off, in a voice none of them recognized.

The day of the wedding arrived. The whole Vera family was dressed in their fanciest, newest clothes; all the children but Inés and José had new clothes, since Señor and Señora Vera had decided that, no matter what it was they wore, they would only ruin it. Two bands had been brought from Honduras; the entire top of the Yglesias' hill was decorated as if for a magnificent fiesta. As for Cristina Estrella, she would certainly have been considered the most beautiful bride in the village, if not the world, had she been standing among the other women with her cloud of gold hair, her green almond eyes, her slender figure in the ancient magnificent dress of the Yglesias family. But she was forced to greet all guests, as was the custom of the Yglesias at marriages, by standing at the foot of the great portrait in the entrance hall. And there was not an eye among the throng that did not move from the image of Cristina Estrella to the image of the woman in the picture, whose name had long since been forgotten. Both of them stood there in the same dress, weighed down by countless seed pearls, their hair, parted in the middle, escaping from under their white lace mantillas, and curling in tendrils about their perfectly heart-shaped faces. So it was not surprising that the guests, so noisy and merry in the courtyard, fell silent as they entered the house on their way to the garden, which was enclosed by the four sections of the mansion.

Nacho himself, standing next to Cristina Estrella, looked extraordinarily handsome, but his happiness could not help but be marred by the sympathetic looks cast at him by guests, known and unknown, which seemed to imply they knew of his doom, and sympathized, although most of the guests also could not help regarding him without a slightly puzzled expression. Nacho became more and more annoyed since he had privately decided, without consulting Cristina Estrella, that there was no such thing as a legend about the Yglesias family, much less a curse visited upon it which returned every twenty years. So it was that Ignatius Joaquín Vera and Cristina Estrella Yglesia were married on August 1, and that night, after the last guest had left and before retreating to their private room, they signed their names on the blank pages in the old leather record book resting on top of the Bible, which had arrived much later. Both Nacho and Cristina Estrella signed their names with as many flourishes as was possible, and as they were kissing over the record book under the approving eyes of Señor and Señora Yglesia, Nacho was seized with a sudden desire to take the record book with them to their chambers.

As soon as they entered, Nacho had an irresistible impulse to read through the leather record book, which was cracked and peeling, cream-colored patches showing under the cracked chocolate surface, and, watching him, Cristina Estrella, who had removed her ancient wedding dress and laid it carefully on the carved chest at the foot of the canopied bed, was similarly seized by a desire to examine the book. The two of them sat cross-legged on the embroidered bedspread, one half of the book resting on each of their laps. A wind had come up and the leaves outside were lashing the windows, but as soon as they had turned the first page with its illuminated margins, the wind died down and the rain streamed silently over the windows like a seamless silver veil.

"Look," Cristina Estrella said, pointing, turning with her angelic smile to Nacho, who followed her finger and read the first entry aloud. "Today, August first, Diego Felipe Vera took to wife Caridad Rosa Yglesia, in this year of our Lord, 1723." "1723," he marveled out loud; "but Vera, it's a common name." Together they read the entries, Nacho reading one, Cristina Estrella the next, as if the entries formed a kind of catechism, Nacho asking, Cristina Estrella answering. In the great hall, the grandfather clock struck one, the round brass sound echoing through the house. "Here!" Cristina Estrella gasped excitedly: "Today, August first, Domingo Miguel Vera took to wife Caridad Lucía Yglesia, in the year of our Lord, 1933."

"That's your father's name," she said excitedly, but at the same time turning very pale. "Vera is a common name," Nacho repeated, but this time he definitely sounded defensive: "half of the village of Castenango is named Vera." "But Domingo Miguel Vera," Cristina Estrella pressed in her tiny voice; "there can't be too many Veras with just that name." "But my father is not married to a Caridad Lucía," Nacho protested. Cristina Estrella stared at him sadly, her eyes open wide. "What happened to Caridad Lucía?" he finally asked. "She died," she answered, her eyes sliding sideways, almost back into her skull. "When?" Nacho asked. "Young," said Cristina Estrella, who never answered in monosyllables. "When?" he repeated. "On her wedding night," Cristina Estrella answered, her face turned half from him.

The rain streamed over the window for fifteen minutes before Nacho spoke again. "What happens to the husbands of the women who die every twenty years?" Nacho asked at last. His bride had turned whiter than stone. "They did whatever they pleased," she answered, her voice coming to him from the ceiling where it seemed to be hanging like a bat in the corner of the room. "The family always gives them whatever they want"—she hesitated—"to make up for the fact that no one ever believes in the legend. Although they say there was once someone who believed in advance," she went on thoughtfully. "The family let the husbands choose, you see," Cristina Estrella said in her faint voice; "sometimes it was money, sometimes property on the mainland, sometimes just to stay in the mansion, and there was one"— Cristina Estrella turned back several pages—"here: Roberto Miguel, who wanted to be buried with his wife, but the family naturally had to refuse the granting of that request. So the man took poison instead and they buried them in the same grave." "The fancy fish," Nacho muttered to himself, not realizing what he was saying, for he was really most concerned with Cristina Estrella's intimate knowledge of all the details of the legend. Then he felt her hand close the book, his hand snuffed out the gasoline lamp, and after the golden ritual of the wedding night was completed, Nacho lay still in the darkened room, the pale round moon lighting Cristina Estrella's gold hair as she lay curled in his arms like a schoolchild. The clock struck four as Nacho lay awake listening to the soft moth-wing sound of Cristina Estrella's breathing, then five, and some early light was beginning to challenge the moon with its spears, when Nacho, finally reassured, fell into a restless sleep.

At ten o'clock, one of the servants knocked at the door with the silver breakfast tray. Cristina Estrella was still asleep. "Put it down on the chair," Nacho instructed the maid; then he began to wake Cristina Estrella. She did not stir. Nacho pulled her toward him by her shoulder; it was cold as stone to the touch.

At the funeral, Cristina Estrella was covered in the same ancient wedding dress she had worn the day she and Nacho were married. It was a very hot day, and two black flies kept circling her face as if they were attempting to land on her eyes and coax them open. Señora Yglesia, who could not be moved from the corpse, or kept from crying, kept trying to brush them away. The whole Yglesia family was there, as was the Vera family, so it seemed as if the whole island of Castenango had come to witness the event. As for Nacho, he could see nothing but the heart-shaped face of Cristina Estrella and her green eyes, appearing to look at him through their closed lids. Señor Vera pressed his hand stiffly, the rest of the family attempted to embrace him, but he noticed nothing but his bride of less than twenty-four hours unaccountably sleeping in the full sun under her wedding dress, failing to raise her delicate hand to brush away the two fat flies.

When all the guests had gone home, Nacho went into the study with the eldest Yglesias. Señor Yglesia cleared his throat loudly: Señora Yglesia sat in a triangular leather chair, crying. "Ignatius," Señor Yglesia began, "as a member of our family, we are responsible for you. After this tragedy," he said stiffly, his hands gripping the arms of his chair, his knuckles showing white, "we would like to inform you that anything our advantages can provide you with you are certainly to have, without any question." "I only want to stay here," Nacho answered; "in the room of our wedding night." Señor Yglesia nodded solemnly.

Years passed. The village of Castenango began to notice that the Yglesias hid Nacho Vera from sight, certainly from social gatherings. The Yglesias themselves were now even more disturbed by Nacho's behavior than they had been by their daughter's death, which had been, after all, something they had expected for almost twenty years. Nacho had begun to speak in a voice exactly like that of Señora Sánchez, who had died the very day after Cristina Estrella. The Yglesias now dreaded the sound of his voice, which made only the most terrible pronouncements concerning the motives of the people of Castenango. And one subject on which he never exhausted himself was that of his father, Señor Vera, the fancy fish, and the Yglesias, listening to him, had long ago gotten the distinct impression that he held his father responsible for the death of Cristina Estrella. Long ago they had tried to persuade him otherwise, but his strange voice, which was the voice of Señora Sánchez, always answered with a question: "Where did they get their money? You got your money by being so good." And today, a visitor to Castenango will find that there are two legends, one concerning the Yglesias, and a darker one beginning to grow up around the Vera family, that every generation of Veras produces a dangerous person, even a murderer, although no one on the island can understand where this legend came from, or even how the first rumor of it began. Meanwhile, the child born to Cristina Estrella's younger sister, Felicia Lluvia, on the day of Cristina Estrella's death, is already showing a distinct resemblance to the portrait, and beginning to grow up.

Why the Castle

By now, it is not the fact of the castle at all, of the impossibility or possibility of getting there, of the many routes tried, difficult or easy. What draws the attention back again, as a suspended sword will when swinging, is the absolute certainty of its appearance and the absolute uncertainty as to where it will appear. And, since it is now known that the castle can, and will, appear to several people at once, it is no longer possible to say that, at any given moment, it was there and not here. The question of the viewer's responsibility for his vision has been much discussed of late, especially since the appearance of the castle generally heralds the disappearance of its beholder, this disappearance most frequently caused by death. Viewers of the castle regularly drown in the gray waters which line the silvery edges of the island, the chosen home of the castle, and their bodies are found stretched out among the silvery fish washed up on the shore, fish and men staring upward into the gray sky with apparently blind eyes.

When, according to local newspaper reports, the castle appeared to a man in the scummy waters of his galvanized tub, the visionary jumped from his bath shedding a wake of white lather, and returned with a mirror and a slightly damp towel. The naked man, breathless with anticipation, held the mirror up to the castle, and then covered the mirror with the towel, hoping to capture its image. The man's wife rushed in shouting, "Fool! Idiot! Estúpido!" but because of the castle's reaction, it is now believed that the castle weighs intention more heavily than achievement, since, in this incident, the man (who has yet to dress himself, preferring to remain in a corner of his kitchen) insists that the castle rattled its turrets at him, swayed them like speckled snakes, and even drew back its towers and hissed when it saw him cover the mirror with his damp blue towel. Because of this encounter, experts have concluded that although the castle clearly wishes to be seen, since it will appear, like it or not, in tubs, water glasses, windows, on the faces of coins, even inside shoes, it will only be seen by whom it chooses.

Which is why the castle's last, and some believe final, appearance has captured the wandering attention of so many. Heretofore, it was believed that when the castle appeared, it always did so in the same form: that is, a fully dimensional object, whose actual size varied, but which nevertheless always exhibited the three dimensions of any island dwelling, even the most humble. This kinship with other island structures has given rise to the widely held belief that the castle, regardless of its caprices and tyrannical whims, was fundamentally benevolent in all its intentions, a belief exemplified in the island superstition which holds that viewers struck down after their encounter with the mysterious edifice merrily inhabit one of the castle's many luxurious suites and wander, with faces silvered like the moon, through the endless, fragrant courtyards.

Therefore it was with great shock that the public learned of José Tulipán's encounter with the castle, and day and night, the population of the island trembles with fear that the castle will revenge itself upon them all, and all because of José Tulipán's journal, discovered by his wife on the eve of his death. José Tulipán had hidden the journal, which contained an account of his meeting with the castle, and which he illustrated profusely from his remarkable memory, between his scalp and his toupee. The cleverness of the hiding place, as well as the industry which permitted José Tulipán to complete his account, unquestionably explains the remarkable and unprecedented fact of the journal's survival. (At this time, it is perhaps best to note that the Tulipán residence, or hovel, is now taboo to the rest of the islanders, who have surrounded it with a thick carpet of gray ash which stretches from the Tulipán fence to the edge of the woods surrounding.)

The castle appeared to José Tulipán (other writers are hereby warned against any dealings with the journal in question, since this writer's fingernails have wrinkled and his hair has fallen out since attempting this task) as a small wall-covering, or tapestry, tacked to the peeling, painted wood of his children's bedroom door. The two children did not see the castle, since it appeared at night, and, like all children who work all day in the sugar fields, they slept soundly.

At first, their father did not recognize what he saw, but instead mistook the castle as evidence of further extravagances on his wife's part. He rushed into the kitchen, and, seizing the clay duck in which he knew she hid some of each week's household money, he threw it to the floor. He was surprised, as he did so, at how heavy it was, for he had assumed coins extracted from the duck had been used to purchase the wall hanging. When he saw coins covering the floor, indeed covering all the kitchen's surfaces, he was ashamed and began to pick them up, placing them all in the huge pottery vase in the corner of the room. He swept up the remains of the shattered duck and returned to take a second look at the tapestry. His wife, whose sleep had been troubled by a crash and the clicking of coins, thrashed about in her bed, but did not wake up.

When José returned to examine the castle, the first thing he no-

ticcd was the moon, which had been cut into four crescents. Two
adorned each corner of the canopy which surmounted the entire
castle, and two floated beneath its foundations. José shook his
head, for he now knew that there was another sky above the para-
pet, and could see, as if in a dream, one sky stacked upon another,
each with its necessary moons and suns. He also knew why the
night outside was impenetrably black. He could see that the
castle floated without moorings, which explained another
difficulty of his miserable life as an island fisherman. On dark
nights, his small boat was perpetually running into something
small and hard, hard enough to put one or two cracks in the prow
of his small boat. So it was not with the customary reverence that
he continued his inspection of the castle.

What he saw told him very little. Suffice it to say, his vision
persuaded him there were virtually no safe places within the castle, since, in most places it was entirely devoid of depth, and only
a few walkways or ceilings seemed safe enough for the human
foot. He had no interest in entering the edifice, nor could he
imagine how he would enter it should he so desire, for the entrance halls were filled with walls of gold light which he immediately knew to be impenetrable. Because the castle adorned the
door of his children's room, and because the castle had appro-
priated the moon, so that he knew his friends were at that moment running into rocks and sailing over fat schools of silver fish,
and would have to live with the grumblings of their hungry families, his one intention was to drive the castle off. He assumed this
could be done by sketching the castle right in front of its eyes. He
took a small book his mother had evidently meant to fill, for it
had spaces for his birth date, first words, and so on, but she had
not gotten beyond the doings of his sixth month since that was
when she had died. At the time of her death, she was distracted
by something which she believed was diving at her, and his father's final words went unheard by her, since she was absorbed in
swatting at whatever that was. As he opened his book, José, who
had heard the story of his mother's death many times, knew she

had been fending off the castle, considerably smaller, of course, than it appeared to him now.

José began sketching the castle, which he did with remarkable accuracy, drawing precisely to scale. At fairs, he was in demand for wedding portraits, funeral portraits, portraits of prize-winning horses and chickens, even portraits of prize radishes and rutabagas. He was widely respected for his ability to seize the life of a thing and transfer it somehow, without harm to the original, onto the brown paper he stored up for that purpose during the year. He was the closest thing the island had to a photographer, and they venerated him accordingly, pressing steaming rubber leaves to his hands whenever he twisted them or caught one of them between his oar and the boat.

As he sketched, José watched the castle cannily. He wondered how long it would be able to remain quiet—without taking steps. He had never heard of the castle enduring such an insult. But, perhaps because he kept his sketches away from the castle, or because the castle was feeling more smug than usual, his work proceeded without interruption. True, he heard the slam of small doors deep within the castle; true, warm breezes wafted out of the courtyards and swirled around him. He thought little of it. He was absorbed in his drawing and could not have said when an awareness of his imminent demise began to pervade him. This awareness did cause him to hasten the execution of his work, and the disposal of it, for as soon as he noticed the castle begin to shimmer and seem to float upon the old wooden door, he ran into his bedroom, threw himself behind the flowered curtain which formed his closet door, removed his toupee and secured the small notebook beneath it.

When he returned to the hall, the castle was hovering in midair, waving slightly as if tacked to an invisible wall. When it sailed off like a flag fastened to a bodiless ship he had already lost consciousness. His wife found the journal before the other women came to help wash the body. She noticed the strange shape of his head. In death it seemed to have grown square, as if, at the moment of dying, someone had slipped a book beneath her husband's scalp and his skull. Unquestionably, she was hoping for a miracle as she removed the toupee, expecting to find a copy of the good book between her husband's ears. As soon as she saw the first picture of the castle, she knew how it was. Her own father had died after he attempted to walk on the air immediately beyond the railing of his balcony. People down below were sure he had been trying to catch something. She would doubtless have made good her threat to destroy every trace of the pictures had not the women around her been afraid, and, unsure of what the castle intended the drawings' fate to be, they held her arms behind her back until the priest had the journal safely conveyed out of the house and to the parish church.

The parish church was actually the only church on the island, all the other churches which had been far grander and more costly having been destroyed when the tidal wave hit the island. They were the outermost buildings since the priests had decided that anyone approaching the island should see and be impressed by the godliness of the people beyond its shores. The one church remaining, popularly thought saved by miraculous intervention, had become the home of doubting priests from surrounding islands who came to stay until the breaches in their belief had been mortared up, as well as small children and old ladies who believed themselves possessed by the divine spirit. The first stayed until their spiritual beliefs returned; the second, until the spirit within either made itself known or returned whence it had come. José Tulipán's journal was handed to a young disbeliever who happened to come to the door and he promptly took it to his whitewashed cell, and began writing out his commentary and interpretation.

Undoubtedly, the parish priest would have retrieved it and examined it himself, but a beetle blight had afflicted the mango crop, which meant, as it always did, that a blight of disbelief had hit his crop of worshipers and he was unusually busy with house calls. In this way, the doubting priest came into sole possession of the journal. He promptly disregarded the commentary, which

seemed to be a repetitive indictment of the castle, which, according to José Tulipán, had taken the form of a tapestry the better to
strangle his two precious children, and concentrated on the pictures.

It was the strangeness, the shifting, of the perspective which
fascinated him. At some points, the castle had been represented as
three-dimensional, while immediately above or below, there were
no dimensions indicated at all. Lines merely indicated the beginning or end of a terrace so that the castle had the appearance of a
sheer mountain face, elaborately decorated, but providing no foot-
hold for human life. He did not immediately notice the moon. Instead, the torches, which seemed an integral part of the castle, fascinated him. One huge torch bisected the castle, which was all of
a piece at the ground level, but seemed divided into two castles
above the railing. The great front arches, Oriental in design, suspended enormous Persian oil lanterns which shed an intense gold
light. The whole castle was preoccupied with light. Either it shone
from the walls or it shone from the countless torches and chandeliers. The arches were welcoming, seeming to promise access to a
world infinitely warm and welcoming, infinitely rich and deep.
But something made him hesitate, even though by now he was
sure he could, if he wanted to, enter the castle through José
Tulipán's drawings.

What alarmed him most was the profusion of moons. One of
the two towers sported moons atop each of its many turrets.
Moons were woven into every decorative frieze. The lanterns, upon
closer inspection, were two half-moons joined together into a
globe. Moons patterned the floor of the courtyard. Moons surmounted the arched windows. Yet there was no moon in the sky
immediately above the castle: that sky was black. Instead, the
priest saw, as had José Tulipán, that the castle had divided one
moon into four quarters and each shone in one corner of the tapestry whose shape the castle had assumed. Yet the moon shed no
light, or perhaps could not make its light known. The only light
came from the enormous torch which formed the central pillar of

the castle, rising high above its towers, and sending its red and green flames into the night.

The priest did not like the moons, which seemed to him pagan and somehow savage. At the same time, he began to suspect that, in the castle, he had found the home of the moon. At about this time, he became preoccupied with the structure of the castle above its doorways. There, rising into the upper distance, were what appeared to be two huge square towers separated from one another by the enormous yet delicate torch.

The two towers were distinctly different from one another. For instance, in the center of the courtyard on the left, the central design of the floor was circular, black paths radiating outward like spokes of a wheel. The patio on the right, however, had no central floor but was divided into three levels. The first level was fronted by a railing; the other three walls were composed of arches which led deeper into the castle. The only adornment here was an enormous palm of some alien variety. Its second level was dominated by curious statuary, which, upon closer inspection, were seen to be specimens of various types of turrets. The third level seemed to consist of many small houses.

But it was the patio on the left which insisted upon his attention. The circular design and the paths radiating from it constantly returned his glance to the strange edifice in the central circle: an unadorned black cube. Its only entrance was a door, as ornate in design as the castle itself. Yet the door seemed strangely separate from the cube, as if it were floating before the black wall and did not really belong there but had been captured by the artist in the midst of its flight from one place to another.

The smooth lines and the symmetry of the cube gave it a foreign air, as if, by contrast to the splendors of the curlicued castle, the cube had become rare, and hence more precious. And although each of this tower's spires were adorned with stone carvings of men and women, all of whom looked curiously modern, it was the suggestion of life in the many apartments of the tower on the right which temporarily succeeded in fixing the young priest's gaze.

About this time, he began to sense that the two towers were in competition for his attention, although he did not understand how this could be the case. He had, while examining the drawings of the two towers, come to the unshakable conclusion that the drawings presented two radically different views of the same tower and that the artist had represented the one tower as two because he was unable to capture its various elements in one picture. Although the priest knew there was only one tower, he felt forced to choose between them, enduring an agony of indecision without once considering whether the portals of the castle's lower level would ever grant him admittance.

It now seemed to the priest that, when his attention was drawn to one tower, the other seemed to fade until its lack of definition caused it to seem tremulous and even sad. He could not understand why it seemed impossible to contemplate both of the towers at once. But the priest believed this a trick of his eye and compared the effect of looking at the castle to the result of staring into the sun and then attempting to look at something less bright, obliterated by the after image. It was as if, having come to one definite conclusion about the castle, the priest realized how few were the conclusions he had been able to reach. He was possessed by a desire to turn up a corner of the tapestry (although clearly, this was impossible) and look at its rough knotted side. At this point, the priest became violently agitated by a premonition, or hallucination, in which he did see the tapestry's other side and found it infinitely more beautiful, more harmonious, and more complete than anything which partook of the earthly life.

When he looked at the castle again, he was surprised to see how many knotted threads were disfiguring its surface. There were also many clumsy long stitches stretching carelessly across parts of the main design. The knots in the threads of the tapestry did not appear to be stationary, but would disappear and reappear at random. The priest found this phenomenon inexplicable, since the picture of the castle remained constant, yet the position of its constituent threads did not. It did not occur to the priest that the castle might indeed be stationary and that he, its viewer, was in constant motion.

At the same time, he began to suffer from the sensation of being roughly thrown about, as if he was once more a child in his father's donkey cart riding over one of the island's uneven mountain roads. His vision, too, was affected, and, as it did to the now unfamiliar child lying in the bottom of the cart, the sky seemed a floor he floated beneath, while the mountains themselves floated and sometimes violently bumped each other in and out of view. The priest, resting on a rough wool blanket, fell asleep in the bottom of the cart. When he awoke, he was not in the parish church. He was not immediately sure where he was, but, when he fell to his hands and knees, his fingers closed on what was unmistakably the wet, silvery sand of the island's ribbon of beach. The priest sat up and looked about. It was too dark to see anything. It was, in fact, absolutely dark. The priest began to suspect that this was not the darkness of his own sky, but the darkness he had glimpsed on the wrong side of the tapestry. At that instant, he became aware of the unusually rough texture of his robe. He became obsessed with his attempts to follow one thread as it wove its way through the nubby cassock, but each thread seemed to twist and return upon itself and to emerge as the beginning of what he had believed to be a separate thread. In his strange despair, caused by his attempts to isolate the course of one thread, he walked toward the murmuring sea. The sea was absolutely still and it was only through the most careful observation that the priest discovered traces of the almost imperceptible waves which reached the beach in silence and without force.

The priest sat down at the edge of the sea with the intention of making himself as small as possible. He tucked his head under an arm and contorted his limbs. He did not cease his efforts until he was sure he resembled a slight imperfection, a dust mote, caught in an otherwise perfect painting of the sea and its beach. As he wrapped himself around himself, he became more and more certain he had indeed entered the castle, not by the side portrayed in José Tulipán's drawings, but through the other side, or perhaps he had reached the other side by traversing the long, narrow corridor within the cube of the left tower. Why this feeling caused him to drown himself, which he did expeditiously and with a great sense of purpose, nobody knew. However, it is not known if any of the circumstances regarding the priest's death were or were not understood by any of the islanders. Suffice it to say, they found his bloated body washing in and out with the tide. The elder priest found the journal of José Tulipán, or what was left of it, since the sea had licked off its inks and it is believed that the father had his suspicions concerning the role of the castle in this tragic event, and that the people of the island, for no reason whatsoever, also blamed the castle for the young priest's death.

People who live on the island know that the castle continues to appear and disappear, although no one will speak of its existence to strangers, nor will they, among themselves, refer directly to it. A stranger from the mainland became attached to one of the island children and gave her a book about a princess locked in a tower who found it necessary to let down her hair so that her beloved could use her tresses as a rope which permitted him to climb the sheer wall to keep her company.

The child read the story to her mother. She always read her stories since her mother was unable to read a word herself. But when the child read out the sentence, "The castle was lonely and dismal," the mother terrified her daughter by abruptly jumping up, slamming a hand over each ear, and shouting an ancient refrain—"Bury my ears, oh God of mud!" Shouts like this are heard ever more frequently on the island, and at night, a stranger might wonder why this same cry moves from house to house until, with the rising of the stars, it sinks, exhausted, to its undiscovered nest.